# Jack Stedfast;

## OR,

## *WRECK and RESCUE.*

### BY

### JAMES GREENWOOD (THE AMATEUR CASUAL).

EDWIN J. BRETT, 173, FLEET STREET, LONDON, E.C.

*AND ALL BOOKSELLERS.*

# JACK STEDFAST;

## Or, Wreck and Rescue.

### By JAMES GREENWOOD.

JACK STEDFAST.

No. 1.

# JACK STEDFAST; OR, WRECK AND RESCUE.

## BY JAMES GREENWOOD.

———◆———

## CHAPTER I.

### WHICH TELLS OF MY PARENTAGE; THE LOSS OF MY PARENTS, AND HOW I BECAME FRIENDLESS.

I WAS born——

And there I halt; and mighty ridiculous it must appear that an individual ambitious enough to attempt the narrative of his life as far as it has progressed should stumble and stop ere he has written half a dozen words of it.

The difficulty is one I did not dream of. Since the words are written, there they may stand, for undoubtedly I *was* born, though, when it becomes a question of when and where, I am as ignorant as the most perfect stranger.

Nor is this so singular as the polite reader at first may imagine. I will venture to say that even at the present day there are thousands of youthful gutter-prowlers —of which disreputable fraternity I was once upon a time a member—who have no more idea of when their next birthday will fall or how old it will find them, than they have of the date of the flood.

How should they know?

Their birth, nine times out of ten, is regarded as a calamity rather than a blessing, and by no means an event to be annually celebrated by festivity and rejoicing.

Birthdays, Sundays, Christmas days, they are all as one to the little savage of the city. That each succeeding day brings its light, and every night its darkness, and that summer time is hot and winter time cold, is all he knows, and all he requires to know.

Robinson Crusoe himself, alone on his desert island, and with no better almanack than a log with notches cut in it, was better off in this respect than the poor little wretch in question, for at least he knew, by a more lengthy notch than the rest, when Sunday was, and refrained from all manner of work that he might honour it.

But Crusoe had riches in store, and all the while he was reclining at ease his goats were fattening in the fold, and his corn ripening in the field.

The little gutter-prowler's is a harder case. He has to pick up his food as stray dogs do, and he must be out and about picking it up Sunday as well as Saturday —rain, blow, or shine—or go hungry.

But we will have no more of that ugly theme just at present; enough of it will appear in its place, I am sorry to say.

Let me, then, make another start on ground that I am more sure of, since out of my personal recollections and experiences I am able to vouch for them. Let me go back to the day when I first awoke to the awful responsibilities of existence, when my eyes were open to the stern fact that now I was face to face with the world, with no one to help me, and no one to care for me; free to swim if I were able, or to sink if my strength failed me, and no one troubling himself at all about it.

Well do I remember that birth-day (for so I may call it). A bleak, drizzling day in the chilly month of February. Time, the dusk of afternoon. Situation, the grim shadow of a prison wall, of all places in the world.

How old I was at the time is with me a mere guess word and conjecture. Perhaps I was seven years old; perhaps eight, maybe a little older; though that could scarcely be, I was such a small chap I well remember, when mother, talking in a mad way that frightened me, leant against the black wall for support, hiding my face in her apron so that the people passing by might not see that I was crying. That was outside the Central Criminal Court in the Old Bailey.

This was the picture.—Father within the prison, awaiting his trial;

Mother with her poor shabby old clothes saturated with rain and clinging to her bony shoulders, and with her eyes hollow and feverishly bright, and her thin cheeks awfully white, with poor little ragamuffin me by her side, cowering in the shelter of the prison wall,

Waiting for the verdict.

And now, as well as I am able, I will explain the growth of the said picture until it arrived at the stage of perfection described.

There was no other child beside myself at home with father and mother, and our place of abode was Rickett's Rents in the parish of Shadwell. Since it is unlikely that the reader knows Rickett's Rents, or will be moved by curiosity to go and find it out, it will be unnecessary for me further to describe its locality than to state that it was in the east part of Shadwell, the worst part, in fact, and where the unfashionable inhabitants of that dusky end of the metropolis congregate thickest.

Our neighbours were chiefly coarse, rough men who obtained a living on the ballast vessels lying in the river, or did portering work about the docks and wharves.

My father, however, was not one of these; I wish to heaven he had been, for then he might have kept out of goal, and my mother's life been prolonged.

Then I might never have known the sort of life an outcast boy lives.

No, my father was not a heavy, clumsy fellow with a canvas smock, and a hairy cap, and a great pair of "ancle jacks" on his feet. My father was quite a genteel person—in appearance, that is.

Mother was meanly clad enough (one of my earliest recollections is seeing her in her grey stays washing out her old cotton gown, which was her only one) and had scarcely ever a decent pair of shoes to wear.

As for me, I was as perfect a specimen of the genus Flibbertigibbet as even Rickett's Rents could produce; but my father was quite a swell in his way. He wore black clothes, a tall hat, and a spotless, well-ironed shirt, and not unfrequently a ring on his finger.

Mother had a jagged red scar just over her upper lip, where the ring on my father's fist one day struck her because she resented his kicking me down the stairs as a punishment for peeping through the keyhole of the back room (of which affair the reader will presently hear something further).

He was a terribly fierce fellow, and used to serve poor mother very cruelly at times; especially when she indulged overmuch in her grievous habit of drinking.

My mother made friends enough amongst the women of the Rents (the majority of whom were possessed of the same shocking weakness for gin drinking as possessed her), but my father was of a more reserved disposition, and seldom spoke to any one.

The rough, ramshackle men of the Rents nick-named him Don Harry, on account, I suppose, of his highly gentlemanly appearance; but I don't think that he was much liked amongst them. He never seemed to be at work. His hands were always white and clean, and he had no regular hour either for leaving home or returning.

The house we lived in accommodated many other lodgers, and we occupied the two topmost rooms, one at the back the other at the front. It was only the front room, however, that was available for domestic purposes; the back room was made quite private by my father, and when he retired there he locked the door and bolted it top and bottom.

It was, from my earliest remembrance, a matter of speculation to me, what could induce him to take so much pains to make the door secure. That induced me to peep through the keyhole as before mentioned. I made a discovery. I no longer wondered that my father was so particular about the door; he had money hoarded in the room; I saw it, all new and shining, half-crowns and shillings, piled in a tea tray.

One of my young acquaintances used to relate to me and his other young friends marvellous stories concerning his grandmother, whom he described as a miser, and who, while pretending to be so miserably poor that she could get no more bread than the workhouse folks allowed her, had unheard-of wealth hoarded in the leg of a pair of velveteen breeches, the property of her husband, many years since dead.

I never believed that boy's story of his grandmother; none of us believed it, though it was very nice and exciting to hear him relate the particulars of his discovery of the concealed wealth, and we would frequently beg of him to repeat it.

But now I believed every word of it. Was not my father, too, a miser? Had he not that very morning growled and swore because he was, as he declared, too poor to afford more than half a pound of rump steak at his breakfast (we had dry toast), and here he was with quite a heap of money!

Mother was away from home at the time, or possibly I should have gone and told her of my strange discovery, and no harm would have come of it; but I was so full of it, and so anxious to confide the amazing intelligence to somebody, and going down stairs who should I chance to run against but my acquaintance who was always bragging about the wealth of his old grandmother.

It was an opportunity not to be lost.

Beckoning him to a retired corner of the passage, I proudly informed him that my father, too, was a miser, and possessed of more money than not only one but both legs of his grandfather's velveteen breeches would hold, even were they stuffed ever so hard; and, when he laughed and shook his head incredulously, I asked him what he thought of a tea-tray piled with money —new half-crowns and shillings.

He seemed to think a great deal of it, as, worse luck for my father, very shortly afterwards appeared.

When I got upstairs again, I needs must have another peep through the keyhole of the back room door, and there was my father still busy at the tea-tray, though his back being towards me I could not make out what he was doing.

I tiptoed to get a better view, and the toes of my boots scraped against the door, and, looking round with a sudden start, my father instantly detected the eye at the keyhole. He had a file in his hand, and his arms and his face were spangled with glistening metal dust.

For an instant he seemed dumb-stricken, and his face turned ashy pale; the next he hastily asked—

"Who's there?"

"Only me, father," I answered, in a fright, and then with a savage oath he sprang at the door, and unbolted it, and, seizing me by the neck, kicked me down to the next landing, at which my mother, returned from her outing, had just arrived.

Then there was a row between my father and mother, and she got her mouth cut with the ring he wore on his fore finger.

But that was neither the last nor the worst of it. It was just after Christmas time, and the days were very short, and father, who seemed to be very busy, had, after the row, returned to the back room, threatening to burn my eyes out if he ever caught me prying through a key-hole again.

It was candle light, and mother and me were sitting at tea, and she suffering from her recent thrashing, and me from my kicking, we were both sad and quiet.

When all of a sudden there fell on our ears such a terrible noise of smashing and crashing that caused us to spring to our feet in an instant.

It was as though some enormous weight had fallen on and crushed through the ceiling of the next room, and we rushed out to see.

I never shall forget the sight. The place seemed full of policemen. They were crowded on the stairs and on the landing, and all of them had their lanterns flashing in the darkness, and one of them a great hammer in his hands. And there was the door of my father's private room all broken, and splintered, and open; and there was my father white with rage and terror, and there was the new, shining money still piled in the tea-tray.

"It's no use, Jack," cried the burly policeman, with the sledge hammer. "The game's up. We've wanted you a long time; you'd better go quietly."

There was a pot on the hob, and in it an iron ladle.

Just as the policeman spoke, my father caught sight of me, trembling with fright and clinging to my mother's apron.

"You little villain!" he exclaimed, with a horrid oath, "this comes of your key-hole listening!" and with that he seized the iron ladle out of the pot, and would have dashed its contents at me had not the foremost policeman struck up his arm, when a shower of molten lead splashed the ceiling and the hats and coats of the officers.

Next moment my father's hands were fastened together with a pair of handcuffs, and, still cursing and swearing at mother and me, he was carried off.

Whether I was in any way instrumental in bringing about my parent's arrest, the

JACK STEDFAST; OR, WRECK AND RESCUE.

reader is now as well able to judge as I am. I am afraid that it is not improbable that such was the case, and if so I am very sorry. I think it is the more likely to be so, from the fact of the father of the boy in whom I had that morning confided, being a sort of sub-constable at the London Docks, and, moreover, never at any time on good terms with my father. At the same time I must repeat that I never knew for certain that such was the case.

Had he been a good man and all that could be desired as a husband and a father, my mother could not have exhibited more affection for him, while, strangely enough, as it seemed to me at the time, from the hour of his arrest, instead of finding comfort in me and treating me with extra kindness, she turned against me for all the world as though it was my fault he was taken away.

She would scarcely look on me or suffer me to be where she was, which was no great loss, perhaps, for where she was, poor creature, so long as she had a penny to spend, was at the bar of one of the low public-houses in which Shadwell at that time, as now, abounded.

While I, poor little ragged outcast, prowled about the streets picking up a crust from the kennel.

" Don Harry " had been some time remanded, and at length arrived the day when he was to take his trial.

A day of days for me, and ever memorable.

In the morning my mother took more than ordinary pains in arranging her shabby clothes on her back, and, to my great astonishment, bade me come with her; she in her old thin shawl and battered bonnet, and I in a little ragged jacket and trousers to match, and a cap, for which

mother, only that morning, had given three-halfpence at a marine store shop, and a pair of slip-shod boots much too large for me, and which audibly admitted the mud and ooze every step I took.

So we set out through the cold and sleet to learn the fate of the prisoner, my father, at the Old Bailey.

It was about ten o'clock when we reached the place, and there we loitered about the wet and chilly stones hour after hour. I had never known my mother in so strange a humour.

As we walked about, she holding my hand in hers (an unusual mark of kindness contrasted with her late harsh treatment), I could feel that she was shivering with cold, and I wondered why she did not step into a public-house and buy some gin.

But, as though dreading the temptation and resolved to avoid it, she kept on the prison side of the way, where there was no public houses, and when she came opposite to one turned her head to the wall, as though she dare not even trust herself to set eyes on it.

In the afternoon she gave me twopence to buy some cake that was displayed for sale in a shop window, but she would not eat a bit of it, though I pressed her very hard to do so, but with her thin shawl saturated with the rain and sleet, and her hand firmly grasping mine, and her mouth puckered with strange determination, she continued her beat outside the prison.

To and fro;

To and fro, unceasingly.

There was a policeman on duty at the prison gate, and from time to time she inquired of him if the trial that she felt such desperate interest in had yet commenced.

"Why did she not go into the court?" the man asked her.

"She might if she chose: it would be better than freezing out there in the wet and cold."

"No," said she, "I dare not trust myself," at the same time shaking her head so decidedly, that the policeman did not press his suggestion.

At length, about three o'clock in the afternoon it must have been, she inquired of an officer once again, and this time with a more satisfactory result.

"The trial of Henry Stedfast was just called," he said.

"Was it likely to last a long while?" mother asked.

"I should say not; the court won't be much occupied with witnesses for the defence," replied the policeman, with an unfeeling grin.

For a moment my mother regarded the man with a fierce scowl; but instead of abusing him, as I fully expected she was about to do, she shrugged her shoulders, and uttering a brief bitter laugh, turned away, still holding my hand tightly in her own, and made as though to continue her pacing up and down; then quite suddenly her strength seemed to forsake her, and staggering to the wall she leant for support against it, and there we stood.

We stood there without exchanging a word—I all the time wondering what it all meant—for more than half an hour, and until it was quite dusk. Presently there was a movement at the court door, and a bustling of people passing in and out, and my mother knew that the trial was over.

Rousing suddenly, she left me and hurried forward to ask the momentous question. It was not long before she obtained an answer.

I was close enough behind her to overhear it.

"Ten years," said the policeman she addressed; "he may think himself lucky it is not twenty."

I shall never forget the expression of my mother's face as she turned towards me. She was quite a young woman, and had about her the same air of superiority distinguishing her from the other women of our neighbourhood as marked my father as being different from the men. She had beautiful eyes, and I have no doubt at one time was a handsome woman. Now her eyes, always bright and flashing, seemed to glow as though there was fire in them, while her face was as white as paper, and her lips quite colourless. There was a feverish eagerness in her manner that frightened me.

"It is all over, Jack," she said, taking both my hands in her own, "it is all over, my poor boy. Good-bye!"

"Good-bye?" I repeated, in amazement.

"Aye, good-bye; I am going, Jack. I am no use now to any one. I never was —God help me! Why didn't I think and act so years ago?"

And as she spoke she again laughed that brief ugly laugh, and bit her white lip as though she would bite it through.

I began to cry.

"Come along, dear mother," I said; "come along home, and make a fire. I am so cold. So are you cold, or you would'nt shiver so."

"Cold, my boy? I'm burning! Never mind; I shall soon be cold enough. Don't cry, Jack dear. Here, take this," and she thrust into my hand the remainder of the shilling previously mentioned —a sixpence and twopence, "take this," she said, "it will prevent you from starving for one day. Good-bye for ever," and she plucked out of my grasp her apron that I had fast hold of, and turned away.

"I am coming with you, mother," I cried, "I can't find my way home by myself," and I ran after her, crying all the time.

"Follow me another step if you dare!" she exclaimed, stopping abruptly, and turning on me fiercely, "if you do I'll kill you!" Then, stooping down, she whispered.

"Jack, for your life do not follow me."

"We had reached the end of the Old Bailey at the Ludgate Hill end, and, as I was brought to a standstill by her threat, she darted across the road and into an alley on the opposite side of the busy thoroughfare, and was lost to me. For a few moments I felt stunned and stupefied, and then I broke into a passion of grief that must have very much astonished the people thronging the pavement, and, calling her by name as loud as I could halloo, "Mother, poor dear mother," I dashed across the road in pursuit.

In at one turning and out at another, without the least idea where I was going.

One moment on the pavement, the next in the road, through the mud and mire, fast as my legs would carry me. I kept on running, and howling, and crying.

Sworn at by omnibus-drivers for so nearly getting myself run over, jostled and cuffed by pedestrians for rushing headlong against them, down in the gut-ter, cruelly grazing my knees, up and down again, losing my cap, on and on till I approached Waterloo Bridge.

How much further I should have continued my frantic chase had Waterloo been a bridge free for any one to pass over, is more than I can say.

It was the toll-man who stopped me. There is a turnstile on the pavement through which passengers are passed as they pay the toll. I, however, was in the road, and had nearly passed the boundary, quite innocent of doing wrong, when the toll-man darted out of his little box, and held me by the collar in a twinkling.

"Hold hard, young fellow! Wanted to bilk the toll, did you? Come, stump up; a halfpenny, if you please, or you'll catch it!"

And without doubt I should have paid the sum demanded and passed on, had I been possessed of a halfpenny; but alas! in my mad race to overtake my fugitive mother, I had forgotten all about the eightpence—her parting gift to me—and somehow had lost it. But I was too distressed and breathless to enter on any explanation with the exasperated toll-man, who still kept his grasp on my collar.

Finding that I had not a word to say for myself in extenuation of what he regarded as a barefaced attempt at cheating him, he fetched me a stinging box on the ear, and turned me back towards the Strand.

## CHAPTER II.

I FIND A FRIEND IN OLD DAN OVERSHINER, AND AM INDEBTED TO HIM FOR THE FIRST OF A THOUSAND BENEFITS—I SEARCH FOR MY MOTHER IN THE DYER'S TANK IN VAIN.

I DID not know what to do; from every point of view I was a lost boy.

The chilling rain was still drizzling down. I had not the least idea of what part of the town I was in. The noise of the carriage traffic and the glare of the gas lamps dazzled and confused me.

I was bespattered with mud splashes from head to foot. I had no cap, and, though until this moment I had never missed it, I now discovered that in my headlong flight one of my old slip-shod boots had come off, and was now goodness knew where.

My trousers were torn and my grazed knees bleeding, my face streaming with tears and perspiration; this was the unhandsome figure presented to my gaze, as, halting before the plate-glass window of a haberdasher's, I accidentally caught sight of it there reflected.

Moreover, I was so fatigued with my long run, that now I had come to a standstill my legs trembled so that I could not set one before the other, and there happening to be a side door and a deep doorway by the haberdasher's, I slunk in and set down on the wet doorsteps to collect my thoughts.

Naturally they were chiefly concerning my mother. What had become of her? For a time I endeavoured to console myself with the reflection that after all she might have gone straight home when she ran away from me; but when I thought of her strange language my heart failed me.

If she were simply going home, why did she wish me good-bye? Why did she dare me to follow her, and threaten to kill me if I did so? Why did she give me that eightpence, all the money she possessed, as I well knew. More woeful than all, what did she mean by saying that she was burning hot, but would soon be cold enough?

I knew of something that was the coldest I had ever touched.

In the alley where we lived, some weeks before, a little girl had fallen unnoticed into a water tank, and was taken out dead. It was a little girl I used to play with, and, as she lay on the stones, I placed my hand on her forehead. It was colder than snow or ice, and, when I recalled my mother's terrible words, it came into my mind at once that the cold she meant was the cold of Polly Sabine's forehead, and that would only be unless she was drowned and dead as Polly was, and now lying in the dyer's tank.

Had I been in calm possession of my senses, it might possibly have occurred to me that my mother might be drowned, and still the dyer's tank be innocent of the shocking deed; but I was so overwhelmed with grief and bewildered, that I could think no other, and, with a vague idea that I might yet be in time to save her, I rose from my cold seat with desperate resolution, and enquired of the first person I met the way to Shadwell. I didn't know that he was a crossing-sweeper until I spoke to him, and then I saw that he had a birch-broom in his hand.

"Shadwell!" he repeated. "Why, what's up at Shadwell that you're going there through the rain without your cap, and with only one boot on, and your foot all a-bleeding." (It wasn't my foot, but the blood from my cut knee). "What's your hurry to get to Shadwell, young 'un?"

"To find my mother," I answered, hardly knowing what to say.

"And where's your mother?"

"She—she's lost, sir; but I think I know where to find her," and then I thought again of that dreadful tank, and my grief broke out again so violently that the old crossing-sweeper was quite affected.

"You've lost your mother a precious long while ago, judging from the looks of you, you poor little beggar!" said he. "It's a good four miles to Shadwell, but it's pretty nearly a straight line, that's one comfort for you. When was the last time you had anything to eat?"

I told him; though I did not think it worth while to inform him what it was, or under what conditions I had come by it.

"And when do you expect another feed? To-night?"

"I don't want anything to eat, sir. I don't want nothing but to find my mother," I answered. "Straight on I think you said Shadwell was, sir?"

"Yes; but don't you be in a hurry; let's see how much you have hurt your leg; you can't go on straight or crooked, don't you know, for very long, all a-bleeding like you are."

And by the light of the lamp at the corner where his crossing was, he examined my cut knee, and taking a ragged cotton pocket handkerchief from his hat, he tore a strip off it and bound up my wound tenderly as could be.

"Thanky, sir," said I, gratefully, as he completed the operation, "I can get on all right now, I think."

"Stay a bit," he returned, "I haven't quite done with you; I want you to *do me* a good turn now."

"I would if I knew how, sir."

"Oh, it isn't anything that you want apprenticing to learn how to do it; I only want you to give a hand towards changing my luck."

"Changing your luck, sir?"

"Aye. Dashed a farden have I took this blessed night, though I've been here this hour and more. You don't see how you *can* help me to change my luck. Well, I'll tell you, young 'un. It's a secret I found out many years ago, and I do believe I should have made my fortune out of it by this time, only somehow I could never get together capital enough to give it a fair chance.

"This is the secret.

"Whenever your luck runs out—and mind you, my boy, that is a misfortune that waits on nobs and great gentlemen as well as crossing sweepers—look out for somebody whose luck is at lower water mark than your own, and do your best towards giving him a lift.

"You'd hardly believe it now," continued the queer old fellow, finding that I had no comment to make on his wonderful discovery, "you'd hardly believe it. but I've tried it in better times and wuss times near forty year, and I never knew it to fail once. It has often puzzled me to discover the reason of it. More than anything it seems to me like pouring your last bucket of water down into a pump that seems pretty well sucked dry in hopes of setting it flowing again, only that one plan is a precious sight more certain than t'other."

Now I would wish the reader to understand that it was not from this once hearing the old crossing sweeper express his steadfast belief in the miraculous effect of doing as you would be done by, that I am enabled to set down his words at length as they appear. On the occasion of this our first conversation, as the reader needs not to be informed, I was in no condition of mind to pay attention to any lesson, moral or otherwise. To be sure, his unexpected kindness in binding up my cut knee inclined me to listen to him with some sort of respect, but all the time I was thinking about my mother.

The fact is, the first time of my meeting with old Dan Overshiner was not the last by many a one, and though it may appear somewhat premature to disclose it, when I come to tell you what a true and staunch friend he was to me (very often meeting with but a shabby return, I am ashamed to confess) it will not seem surprising that I should take so early an opportunity of acknowledging my acquaintance with him.

" The worst of it is," continued the old crossing-sweeper, stooping to whisper to me confidentially, as he ruefully chafed his frost-bitten nose with his broom-handle ;

" The worst of it is that want of capital I was speaking of; I haven't got the water, d'ye understand, to pour down the pump and set it going again; that's how it stands to-night."

Not knowing in the least what he meant, I could only shake my head.

" So I'm going 'tick,' with fortune in a kind of a way; going to try and get the luck changed on a sort of promise to pay afterwards," and he chuckled immensely at the artfulness of his design.

" Look here; you stop here a little while, and I'll go and give the crossing another touch up, and the very first copper I have given me you shall have to help you along to Shadwell, my boy."

So saying, the strange old fellow, buttoning the top button of his wet jacket with a determined air, spat on his palms, and rubbed them together, and went as vigorously to work on his crossing as though his " change of luck " was lurking somewhere between the chinks of the cobble stones, and he was resolved to hunt it out with his broom.

He found it before he was three parts across the road, not between the stones, but at the hands of a gentleman who at that moment stepped out of a glove shop, and who was especially grateful to the crossing-sweeper because of the splendid pair of shiny leather boots he wore. As he picked his way gingerly across to the opposite pavement, he dropped a coin into the old fellow's hand. His face was quite radiant as he hurried towards me.

" Here you are, young 'un," he exclaimed, holding out a penny for me to take. " Out of debt, out of danger, you know. Did'nt I tell you the luck would change? I shall be all right now, never fear. You may be off, now, as soon as you like—straight on, don't you know, and turn round to the left when you get to St. Paul's, and then straight on again."

I had taken the penny, but I didn't know what to do about keeping it; it seemed so odd to take a penny from a crossing-sweeper.

"'IT'S NO USE, JACK,' CRIED THE BURLY POLICEMAN WITH THE SLEDGE HAMMER."

"Thank you, sir," I said, offering him it back again, "you want it more than I do."

"How d'ye make that !"

"You just said that you havn't took a farthing to-night."

"Pooh ! that was before the luck changed. Don't you grumble; *I* don't, I shall be all right; I always know when I shall be all right by my feelings, and I feel like taking at least a shilling atween this and the time when the theatres shut up. Cut away, boy; you are only hindering me now."

And he bustled on to his crossing again; and I, much wondering at the strange man he was, went off with his penny. I had not gone far, however, when he overtook me.

"I say," said he, "of course it isn't any business of mine, but how are you going to spend it? You won't fool it away in sweetstuff, or that sort of rubbish? It would be a sin, don't you know, to spend a lucky penny in that way."

I told him that I had no thoughts of buying sweetstuff. Indeed, I had not thought of how I should spend the penny.

"I'll tell you," remarked the old fellow, after considering the important question for several seconds, "buy a penny pie. Keep on this side of the way for about five minutes or so, and you'll come to a pie-shop. Buy a beef 'un; there's more in the beef 'uns. They're rayther peppery, but that's so much the better a night such as this is. Good night."

And nimbly as his short legs would carry him, he was back to his crossing before I could thank him for his good advice.

I had no heart to adopt it, however. Arrived at the pie-shop the luscious pasties smoking in the window had no attractions for me.

Indeed, had I been so foolish as to have wasted my penny in one, there was a lump in my throat that would have prevented me from swallowing a bit of it.

I felt remorseful and guilty.

I had been wasting precious time talking with the crossing-sweeper about matters in which I felt not the least concern, while I should have been hastening home to my mother's rescue. And so upbraiding myself I broke into a dog trot, one shoe off and one on, up Ludgate Hill and by St. Paul's, and down Cornhill, and so to the east end of the town, never once stopping until I reached Rickett's Rents where we lived.

The house, the top floor of which we occupied, was at the further end. The window—*our* window—was visible at the entrance; but I scarcely cast a glance at it, fully expecting that it would be dark, as it was. The dyer's house, where the tank was, was about the middle of the row and the tank was in the yard.

I knew a back way to this yard that was surrounded by a wall that might be climbed, not easily, for it was at least ten feet high; but so strongly had the idea got possession of me that my mother had drowned herself in the tank that I was resolved to attempt it. And I did, and succeeded so far, but no farther, as the reader need not be told. It was about three feet deep and about two-thirds full of water; and all in the dark, and trembling in hope and fear, I leant over the edge and groped about with my hand, plunging in my arm as deep as the shoulder.

No mother !

"I shall soon be cold enough," she had said, and the water in the iron tank was so dreadfully cold, she *must* have meant it.

Perhaps she had sank to the bottom.

Then with desperate courage I drew myself up, and climbing over the edge of the tank, lowered myself down into the water that reached as high as my chest, and scraped the bottom well over with my feet.

But she was not there; and still standing in the water I leant my face against the side of the cold, wet tank, and shed bitter tears of sorrow and disappointment.

It never came into my head that since my mother was not where I had sought her, she might, after all, be alive and well. I never for a moment doubted that she was drowned somewhere (perhaps I may have heard her threaten that she would drown herself, in the course of one of her frequent quarrels with my father), and I would so much rather that she had done so here at home as it were, so that in one shape or another I might have seen her once again.

But now I felt convinced that I should see her no more.

Many a time, in the course of my strange and chequered young life, did the wicked thought enter my head what an excellent thing it would have been had I never emerged alive from that tank; and, indeed, it would not have been astonishing had such been the case. I was pierced and benumbed with cold, and so utterly dejected and weary, that I made but little effort to resist the fatal drowsiness that was creeping over me.

It may seem strange, but I do believe that it was the thought of dead little Polly Sabine that saved me. I don't think that I should have felt much terrified had I discovered my mother's dead body as I expected to; at all events I should not have run away from it; but as I stood there in the water, chilled to the heart and quite done over, a picture of Polly, with her awfully white and cold forehead and her long brown hair dabbling in reeking wisps on the pavement of the yard, was suddenly conjured up before my eyes, and I grew scared, and scrambled out of the tank.

I was over the wall in five seconds, and, reeking with water, I ran round to Rickett's Rents to the house where we lived. Like the rest of the houses in that disreputable neighbourhood, the door of it was conveniently latched, with a bit of string with a knot at the end of it hanging outside, so that I was able to gain admittance unknown to any of the other lodgers, and groping my way upstairs all in the dark, found my mother's room.

Casting myself down on to my miserable little bed that was made on the floor in a corner, too afraid even to take off my saturated clothes, there I lay with my face buried in the pillow, trembling and quaking, and with my mind in a whirl of confusion at the many strange things that had happened to me during the past few hours, until, soon after the church bells chiming midnight had startled the lonely stillness,

I fell asleep.

## CHAPTER III.

### IN WHICH I FIND MYSELF ALONE IN THE WORLD, AND NARROWLY ESCAPE MY FIRST TASTE OF "MONKEY'S ALLOWANCE."

IT was broad daylight when, aching in every limb, and with my clothes still damp and clinging about me, I awoke as forlorn and miserable a little wretch, I trust, as that morning might be found in the parish of Shadwell.

At first I could scarcely realize the true position of affairs, and starting up from my bed in the corner, rubbing my eyes, I cried out for my mother.

But she had not come home.

There was the bed, in which she should have slept, smooth and unruffled. There were the breakfast things on the table, just as they were left yesterday morning; there was the cup she had drank out of, half full of the coffee she could not drink, such was her anxiety to hurry down to the Old Bailey to hear the result of her husband's trial;

And when I called out "mother" no one answered.

I was not surprised at this when I became sufficiently awake to reflect on what had happened last night. Then something seemed to whisper unmistakably to me that I should never see her again, and as I looked around me in that squalid, solitary room, the whisper came again and more positively than ever,

"You will never see her again."

Hard, indeed, would it be to imagine a boy—a mere child—in a more wretched plight. Literally I was without a friend in the world.

My father must have had respectable connections somewhere. As I have before mentioned, he had nothing about him denoting him a low-bred ruffian; he was rather like a person brought up in decent position, but who, yielding to his natural disposition towards vice and depravity, had slid rapidly down the quagmire of ruin, and whether it was because his dishonest practices were suspected by the male inhabitants of the Rents that his company was avoided by them is more than I can say; I only know that it was avoided, and there was not a man there to whom I could in my distress say,

"I will go to him and ask him what I had best do; he was a friend of my father, and will be sure to tell me."

In the same respect I was as bad off on my mother's side, I regret to say.

At the same time I would have it understood that my mother was not an utterly bad woman. To be sure she was addicted to drink, but it is hard to say to what extent my father's cruelty was answerable for this. It was only at times that she got tipsy—when he goaded and taunted her and beat her with his white, bony fists. He would not let me go to school (the ragged schools were just springing up at that time, and goodness knows my tattered clothes would have qualified me for admission).

"Education be hanged," he would exclaim, "what's the good of it to such as us?"

" No, no, since he's bound to lead a dog's

life, it would be 'cruelty to animals' to have him taught that he is anything better than a dog. You'd have him go to Sunday school too, I suppose, and taught to be pretty and good, and to come home and preach to his naughty father, as *you* used to do one time-a-day."

Nevertheless, my mother declared that I should not go altogether ignorant. She bought me a penny spelling book, that likewise contained a history of Blue Beard, and finding that I was rather dull at learning, she hit on a rather ingenious method of bringing me along.

We used to take the alphabet three letters at a time, and when I had well learnt my lesson she would reward me by reading to me a bit of Blue Beard. And I well recollect that when I had reached as far as Q R S she had advanced in the story as far as where the azure-bearded monster came home and discovered by traces of blood on the key that his wife had been prying into the dreadful closet.

I begged her to go on, but she was inexorable; not another line until I was able to repeat three more letters along with those I had already learnt.

Usually it took me about an hour to get my lesson well by heart, but now taking the book I set to work, and in less than a quarter of that time polished off, not only T U V, but W X Y Z as well, to her perfect satisfaction, and had the supreme felicity of listening to the story of Blue Beard to the very end.

My father knew nothing of these lessons, however; they invariably took place when he was from home.

I believe, too, that with all her faults my poor mother was not a woman dishonestly inclined. I don't think that she was aware

that my father was a coiner of counterfeit money.

All I know about the matter is that she was always very anxious to impress on me how that it was impossible for any one to be happy who was dishonest, and that it was better to go in rags with a clear conscience, than to strut about with money to spend—a well-dressed rogue.

This set me thinking. My father was well-dressed; quite a fashionably-attired person compared with the other rough-and-tumble inhabitants of our court.

"Is father a rogue, then, mother?" I asked.

"Hush, Jack!" she replied, with a frightened air, and clapping her hand over my mouth (my father was at work in the back room). "It is very wicked to speak like that of your father."

"But why do you go in rags?" I continued. "Is it because you have a clear conscience that you always go about in that old gown?"

She laughed a strange, bitter laugh at this, and shook her head sadly.

"God help me!" said she, "the mire in the kennel is clearer than *my* conscience, I am afraid. But no matter for that, Jack —what I say is true, and you should always try and bear it in mind and abide by it."

I thought of all these things and a hundred others as I lay miserably crying in the corner where my bed was. What should I do? All I had in the world was the penny that the crossing-sweeper had given me.

I was shivering with cold, a frost had set in in the night, and the window panes were glazed and dim with it.

Sitting up in bed and looking about me, I saw on the table, left from yesterday's breakfast, which had been abandoned in such a hurry, a piece of bread and a little unmade coffee, and at once resolved to found something of a breakfast on these meagre materials.

What I wanted first, however, was a fire, and, as luck would have it, lying in the fender were some coals and wood.

Scarcely able to hold a limb still, I set about my job of fire-lighting, but, unfortunately, I was interrupted in the middle of it. Necessarily I made some little noise with the fire-irons, and this roused the person living in the apartment immediately beneath, who was the landlady of the house.

I was not so young and unobservant as to be unaware that there existed between this important lady and my mother a feud of the bitterest sort. While my father had his liberty, and was free to follow his nefarious trade, the profits of it were such as to admit of a punctual payment of rent, and so long as this was done the worthy landlady was civil enough and asked no questions.

But when the day of misfortune came, and she shrewdly foresaw that we were likely to be but unprofitable lodgers, her tone altered at once, and scarcely was a week's rent an hour due when she began to talk pretty loudly of the disgrace we had brought on a respectable house, and how that the sooner my mother suited herself with other apartments, the better it would be for her character and peace of mind.

Nor did it at all tend to mollify her when she discovered that my mother was surreptitiously conveying out of the house every portable article of furniture on which a shilling might be raised towards providing legal assistance for my father in prison.

Just as I had taken the bellows in hand, with a view to making the kettle boil, I heard her door open, and simultaneously the unpleasant tones of her shrill voice.

She was a very old woman, and very fat and short of breath, and to talk and ascend a flight of stairs at the same time was rather more than she could accomplish with that amount of speed her fury rendered desirable.

"So you managed to cheat me after all, did you?" she bawled. "You contrived to sneak in after I was abed and asleep, did you, jade? But it is the last time, take my word for it. I'll have no felon's cast-off in my house. If you had your deservings, Madam Mealymouth, you'd be served with the same sauce as he has been served with! You shan't get off yet, if there's a law to touch you. I'll have a policeman, and——"

By this time, wheezing and panting, she had reached our room door, and unceremoniously slammed it open.

But there was nobody within but miserable little me, squatting before the wretched fire-place with the bellows in my hand.

She stopped short in the midst of her fierce invective.

"Where's your mother?" she demanded, not at all moved to compassion at beholding my wretched plight.

"I don't know?" I replied, stoutly.

It wasn't likely I was going to tell her all I knew or suspected after I had heard her threatening manner and her talk of policemen.

"That won't do for me; she sent you here. Where is she? Where did you leave her?"

"I don't know anything about it," I repeated.

"You little liar!"—and she waddled

into the room, glaring with rage—" you little liar ! you know very well that she sent you here to see if you couldn't sneak out some more of the goods—*my* goods, such as the twopenny rubbish is as I've got a legal 'strain on for rent. Tell me this instant where the hussy is, or I won't leave a whole bone in your skin !"

And so saying, she grappled with me, and after a short tussle got possession of the bellows, seizing them by the nozzle, and flourishing them over my head.

Starved and shivering, and crippled of a knee, I was in no condition to accept combat, so parrying a vicious blow, I darted under her arm, and was down the stairs and out at the street door before she reached the first landing.

---

## CHAPTER IV.

IN WHICH I KNOW WHAT IT IS TO BE HOMELESS AND HUNGRY—I EXPERIENCE A HORRIBLE FRIGHT, AND MAKE THE ACQUAINTANCE OF GRANNY CORSON.

IT was on a Sunday morning, when, fast as I was able (for my injured knee, that the crossing sweeper had so kindly bound up, ached severely, now that I attempted to use it), I limped out into the world, in which I had now not one single friend.

As before mentioned, owing to my weary and exhausted condition, it was quite late ere I awoke, and now, by the time I found myself out in Shadwell Highway, the church bells were chiming for all good people to come to church.

I needed not this sound, however, to remind me that it was the Sabbath day.

Shocking as it may appear, I am bound to confess that, from my earliest recollection until a certain happy turn in the tide of my young life, I liked Sunday least of all the days of the week. Being as a rule pretty much at liberty to go where I pleased from the time I rose in the morning till night and bed time came round, it was my habit to roam about in search either of amusement or of something to eat, for it was not always that the cupboard at home was well stocked. But Sunday made me a prisoner.

Business is not half so squeamish as what passes as religion—not nearly so respectable and straight-laced. Let a man or a boy be never so ragged and poverty-stricken, he may elbow his way through the busiest thoroughfares from Monday morning until Saturday night, no one heeding him.

But poverty and rags must hide their heads on a Sunday.

So it is however, and so it comes about that a foreigner, perambulating our highways on a Sunday, would depart to spread in his own country the astonishing information that in England rags and beggary were unknown, and that the population all wore shiny hats, and spotless shirt collars; and that prosperity hung out at the waist-coat pockets of the males, in the shape of an ounce or so of gold chain, and was hoisted aloft in the hands of the females in the fashion of parasols of silk and satin, that must have cost at least a guinea each.

But now I was fairly driven out into the streets, Sunday or no Sunday; and out I must remain, in spite of the frowns and warning gestures of all the beadles and policemen that ever marched.

But I felt none the less miserable, because I was a prowler by compulsion. Every way I turned, the brightness and cleanliness seemed a fresh reflection on my own shocking shabbiness. The streets were so bright and quiet; the church-going people were all so smart and trim; the entire aspect of things was so chaste and proper compared with myself, that I felt as might a cock-roach or a spider that had blundered on to a delicate wedding-cake, and was too bewildered to know which way to turn to make his escape.

All that morning I sauntered on, aimless as a lost dog.

I still preserved my precious penny that the crossing-sweeper had presented me with, for the simple reason that having wandered into a somewhat respectable quarter of the town, there was no chance for me to spend it.

The shops were all closed, excepting the tobacco shops, and I was not yet sufficiently initiated into the ways of vice as to regard a "chaw," or a smoke of the noxious weed, as a handy substitute for food.

I was very hungry, and come one o'clock I grew downright desperate, and for this reason:—At that hour the bakers who had undertaken to cook the Sunday's dinners of their various customers, opened their doors, and the crowd gather-

ed about them entered, and presently emerged, every individual the happy bearer of a dish on which steamed with a delicious odour a joint of meat, baked over potatoes or a pudding.

And as I stood spellbound in an adjacent doorway, now and then would cross my nostrils a whiff of "stuffing" that nearly took my breath away.

I had never stolen yet, but I never was tempted as now, and whenever a small boy or girl crept slowly by my lurking place, burdened under their fragrant load, I certainly did feel a torturing inclination to dart out and plunge my hungry fingers into the baking-dish. But I suppressed the wicked impulse, and presently received my reward.

A motherly woman, living in the neighbourhood evidently, for she had flung her apron over her head by way of a bonnet, came toiling along, carrying an enormous shoulder of mutton, enthroned above half a peck of potatoes, brown and seething in the mutton fat, and a glorious batter-pudding.

Just as she got to the doorway where I was, a gust of wind whisked the apron from her head, and sent its ends plump into the baking-dish, where they lay in the gravy.

She was helpless to alter it, and so she applied to me.

"Drat the apron! and only clean put on to come out in! I wish you would take it out, little boy," said she.

As I did so, my longing fingers actually came in contact with the plump, crispy potatoes, and caused me to utter a sound that at once attracted the good soul's attention.

"Burnt your fingers, my dear?" she inquired.

"Oh, no, ma'am, it wasn't *that*," I answered with a sigh, and feeling the tears rise again to my eyes.

"I know what it is," said she, regarding me compassionately; "you are hungry. Lord help us, child, that face of yours would haunt me out of enjoying a mouthful if I didn't alter it. Here, hold your hands; they're hot, but you'll soon cool 'em, I'll warrant. There are enough to eat 'em at my house, I'll be bound, if there were twice as many; but never mind for that."

And so saying, she stood the big dish on the door-step for a moment, and picked me out three great smoking halves of potatoes, and placed them in my hands, and then catching up the dish again, was off before I could say "thank you."

But I thanked her in my heart twenty times.

Since that time it has been my good fortune to taste potatoes cooked in every imaginable savoury and delicate manner, but, one and all, they were tasteless and insipid compared with those out of that charitable woman's baking dish—luscious, hot, and saturated in excellence! Ah, never shall I forget their exquisite flavour!

Probably the remembrance of that little banquet lingers more affectionately in my memory because it was so long ere it was followed by another.

My baked potatoes devoured, I trudged on again, taking no heed whether I turned to the left or right until nightfall, and then I crouched under a truck I discovered standing in a stable-yard, and so passed the night.

I was indebted to a good ostler's wife for a slice of bread and a drink of coffee in the morning, and that, with as much more bread as my preciously-hoarded penny would buy, was all I had to sustain me in my aimless wanderings through another winter's day, bright as the preceding, as it luckily happened, but piercingly cold.

Come the evening, I found myself in the neighbourhood of Spitalfields, and close by some houses in course of erection.

With the brightness of the wintry day, its comparative warmth had departed, and it was as chilly as last night, and a few snow flakes began to fall.

The bleak, blank walls of the skeleton houses, with the great black holes where the windows were to be, and the yawning darkness of the open casements, were not very inviting to me; but my senses seemed as benumbed as my body was, and I groped my way in at one of the doorways, hoping to find some dry corner, sheltered from the wind, where to lie down.

And in this, at least, I was not disappointed.

Feeling my way with my feet, I presently came on some stairs, and, cautiously descending them in the pitchy darkness, I felt the wall, and then an opening.

Into this I groped my way, but had not taken three steps before a rustling sound, as though some live thing on the floor had moved, caused me to halt in a fright; but I stood still and listened, and, as the noise was not repeated, and the empty window sashes at that moment began to rattle, I was relieved to think that it was the wind that had occasioned my alarm, and stepped a little further into the place; and presently discovering, by the crackling sound, that there were shavings underfoot, I collected a little heap of them, and, carrying them to a corner, there placed them and curled down on them, nose and knees together.

I was very tired, and shut my eyes in hopes of falling asleep, but this I soon found was out of the question.

At the least sound made by the wind I opened my eyes wide, and my ears too.

To be sure, I could make out nothing but the wind, but there gradually crept over me a dread that I was not alone in that dismal place.

Almost afraid to move, I strained my eyes in a vain endeavour to pierce the inky darkness, but I might as well have tried to look through a stone wall.

It was of no use my trying to comfort myself with the reflection that if any one was there sharing my lodging, it was probably some poor harmless creature who, like myself, was glad of any shelter from the increasing inclemency of the unpromising night. If this were so, why did not my fellow lodger declare himself?

If there was any one in the half-built house with me, who was not afraid to do so, or who had not his guilty reasons for doing so, why did he lie lurking there without speaking? What was he lurking for?

As this thought came into my head, my mind reverted to all the hobgoblin stories I had ever heard of children kidnapped, of children burked, and of boys and girls who had been visible to friends and neighbours one moment, and the next spirited away mysteriously and suddenly and never seen again.

At last terror got such fast hold on me that, with an involuntary cry, I stirred myself to get out of the horrible place, happen what might.

But scarcely had I rose upright when my suspicion that I was not the only tenant of the kitchen received terrible confirmation, for there was an audible stirring of shavings close at hand, and, out of the darkness, came a voice, angry and snappish, though whether of man or woman it was impossible to say.

"Confound you! Is'nt it enough to come here disturbing me? Can't you bide quiet now you are here?"

I was afraid before, but now my heart beat so violently that it seemed as though I could hear it, and the perspiration streamed down my face, bitter cold as the night was.

More than ever I yearned to escape from the dreadful place, even though I passed the night in walking about the streets, but my feet seemed rooted to the ground, and I had no power to set one before the other; besides, even had I possessed the power of locomotion, I should have feared, under the circumstances, to have availed myself of it, lest I might stumble over the owner of the mysterious voice.

It came into my head that I ought to say a prayer, but I only knew one, and that imperfectly, and could in my fright recollect no more of it than "Our Father;" and this I repeated hysterically and louder and louder until the words became a shriek, and I cried aloud.

This roused the strange being in the corner at once.

"Stow that," exclaimed the voice, sharply; "if we have any more of it—so much as another word—it will be the worse for you, I can tell you. I can't see you, but I've got a chunk of wood lying handy, big enough to hit you wherever you are, and it won't come none the lighter for being stuck full of nails. Silence! d'ye hear?"

I was silent at once.

"Now, tell me what you are?"

"What I am, sir? I——"

"Are you a boy, or are you a gal?"

"A boy, sir," I whispered, tremblingly.

"I'm glad of that anyhow; I like boys better than gals."

And this last remark was accompanied by a cannibal clashing of teeth, that set my heart bumping harder than ever.

"Don't be afraid, I shan't bite you," continued the hidden mystery, with a chuckle that hardly reassured me. "How old are you?"

"I don't know, sir."

"Don't know how old you are? Don't tell me lies!"

"Seven, I think, sir—or very likely eight. I want to go now, sir, if you please."

"Want to go where?"

"I—I—don't know; anywhere!"

"Why don't you go home?"

"I've got no home, sir."

"No father or mother?"

"Yes—no—sir. I want to go now please."

"Yes, no, sir," echoed the voice, mimicking mine. "Now I know the sort you are, if I am not mistaken. Maybe we shall do business together. Let me have a look at you."

And then, as I stood there in a sweat of terror, and with my knees knocking together, I heard a sharp scratching along the wall, and instantly there was a light in the place.

I shall not easily forget the spectacle that was revealed to my amazed gaze.

The creature who had been talking with me was not a man at all, but a woman—a hideous-looking old crone, gaunt and bony, with a black cloak over her shoulders, and her enormous black bonnet tied over with a red handkerchief to keep the wind from her ears, as I suppose.

I could not see much of her face, for as she held aloft the lucifer match she had struck, she shielded her eyes with her skinny, dirty hand, and presented altogether a picture not at all calculated to disperse the troop of supernatural ideas her previous strange talk had conjured up.

As she peered at me from under her hand, the lucifer light faded and died out, leaving us in black darkness again.

"That'll do," said she, in tones of authority; "I've seen enough of you. You may lie down again."

"But I don't want to lie down, ma'am; I want to go," I cried, in desperation.

"And I want you to stay," she replied, in the same imperative tone. "I want you to stay till the morning, that I may see what you are made of. You've got no home, no friends, no father or mother; think yourself lucky that you met with me; it's the finest bit of good fortune that could possibly happen to a poor little lad such as you are. Come, lay down, now, and make yourself comfortable. I'll take care that nobody comes in to disturb you till the morning."

And as she spoke, I heard her rise from the shavings on which she was reclining, and after some little rustling and readjustment of her bed, she lay down again.

"There," said she, "*now* you're all right."

I could not see what this last movement portended, but I instinctively knew, and my heart sank at the knowledge—she had shifted her bed to the door, so that I should not make my escape!

Now what shall I do?

"THERE WAS NO ONE WITHIN BUT MISERABLE LITTLE ME."

To attempt to pass her by main force I felt would be an act of madness, for from the brief and imperfect glimpse I had got of her, although old she was evidently sinewy and strong. Besides, there was that chunk of wood with the nails in it she no doubt had shifted with her when she moved her bed.

Again I thought that I would raise my voice, and scream murder! thieves! fire! anything that would bring somebody to my rescue.

But on second thoughts it occurred to me that I had already halloed without any result, and that even if I did succeed in attracting the notice of a passing policeman, what sort of a story had I to tell him? No more than that while committing an act of trespass, I had discovered an old woman doing the same.

Clearly no good could come from such a move. And after all, what good could it do the old woman to harm me? It was not at all likely that I should close my eyes, and it would be quite time enough to hallo when I was hurt; and, somewhat comforted by these reflections, I plucked up courage, and slid down on my shavings again.

The old woman detected the movement. "That's a sensible boy," said she, in a kinder voice than she had hitherto spoken in. "Are you **hungry**?"

"Not very, ma'am," I answered, which was a very long way from being the truth. It was a long time since one o'clock.

"Not hungry enough to eat a nice bit of bread and meat?"

My famished appetite answered "yes ma'am," before I was aware of it almost.

"Here you are then," said she; "come and fetch it."

And then I heard a sound as of a wicker basket opening, and presently saw looming in the darkness, some substance of a whitish colour, and groped my way towards it. It was a thick slice of bread, with a substantial slice of meat a'top of it.

"Don't be afraid to eat it," said the old woman, "it is the primest of meat, and cooked at my own kitchen fire. You don't know me yet, youngster, Granny Corston does not always lodge in an out-house with a handful of shavings for her bed. She has a roost as snug as the best, when business does not call her away from home, as you will see perhaps. You may have part of my old cloak to cover you if you like to come and lie at this end. You would rather not, eh? Well, then, wrap this round your head; it isn't a nice night to lay your cheek on a cold flagstone."

And as she spoke, she tossed over to where I was lying a large cotton handkerchief, which I very thankfully put to the use she suggested.

As the reader may imagine, I was considerably astonished at these unexpected symptoms of her goodwill for me, and after smelling at the bread and meat, and tasting it, and finding it very good, I sat up eating it, hoping that she would presently begin to talk again, and enter into some explanation of the hint she had thrown out respecting the "comfortable roost" she enjoyed when not abroad on business, and which I might perhaps know more about. But nothing broke the silence but my own greedy champing; and when that was at an end, I lay down full of strange thoughts and speculations, and quite resolved not to close my eyes, and in the midst of my confident self-assurances that there was no danger of my doing so, I fell fast asleep.

## CHAPTER V.

UNVEILED BY ACCIDENT GRANNY CORSTON APPEARS TO ME IN HER TRUE SHAPE —I MAKE A DISCOVERY THAT MIGHT HAVE RESULTED IN MY MURDER— GRANNY AND I COME TO TERMS.

HARD as my bed was, I slept with tolerable soundness, although I had closed my eyes fully charged with speculation as to whom the hideous old woman in the cloak might be, and what object she had in view, in giving me food to eat and a handkerchief to tie over my head. Strange to say, that her picture vanished from my mind entirely when slumber took possession of me. Indeed my dream all night through was not of her, but of my father.

As I slept, was enacted over again the scene of his arrest. I heard, as I sat with my mother in the front room, the startling and sudden noise of the constable's sledge hammer battering in the back room door; and I saw them rush on him and secure him.

Likewise, I saw him—in my dream, that is—seize the little ladle and aim at me, with the molten metal in it. But now it did not miss me; it fell on my feet and sank into them, and set the rest of my body on fire.

And out of the fire a fine light smoke ascended, and the upper part of me, my head and body, seemed to rise and stretch out, so that I was lifted with the light smoke as high as the house tops; and I should have gone higher, and wanted to do so, only that the lead that had sank into my feet weighted me and kept me down, and my mother stood by wringing her hands and weeping; while my father clapped his hands and laughed to see my vain struggles to rise.

He clapped his hands so very loud that I awoke with, as I thought, the noise in my ears; but it was only the sound of a factory bell in the neighbourhood.

It was an odd kind of dream, and I think it none the less so at this distance of time, when I reflect on certain events that seem to bear so directly on what a superstitious mind might regard as its foreshadowing.

The factory bell was ringing, and I opened my eyes. I did not start up, however; I lay quiet, and for several seconds was filled with bewilderment as to where I was; which was no wonder, since, literally, I had never seen the place I was in. All that met my gaze was the naked and blackened joists overhead (it was a house half-built and abandoned, it seemed) and the raw brickwork of the walls all damp and mildewed. For the time even I forgot all about the old woman, till hearing a slight noise, I turned my eyes towards it and discovered her.

She was not on her bed of shavings by the door, however, but already up and busy; though at what, I could not make out. Her back was towards me, and her old black stuff cloak enveloped her from her shoulders to her heels. She was standing in a corner of the great kitchen most distant from that where I lay, and, with a stick in her hand, she was engaged in digging a hole in a pile of rubbish that was there heaped.

Now that it was daylight, I was astonished to find her only a little old woman after all. By the ghastly flicker of the lucifer match that had revealed her the night before, she had seemed twice her real size.

Daylight gave me courage too, and I felt not a bit afraid of her; indeed, had my terror of last night continued, there was nothing now to prevent my bolting, for the door stood open and unguarded, and fair in view were the stairs that would carry me to the open street; but I was curious to stay a little longer, and none the less so because of a discovery I presently made.

As Granny Corston for a moment shifted to one side, I descried close to her a black wicker basket of large dimensions, with a lid, and handles to carry it by, and beside the basket was quite a heap of broken victuals—bread, meat, and several lumps of pudding, both baked and boiled, and quite inviting to my hungry young eyes, albeit the scraps reposed on a no more dainty tablecloth than the dust and grime of the floor afforded. I felt wretchedly cold and stiff in all my joints, but as to my appetite, it was not at all sickly, and to see such a chance of presently comforting it, made me lick my lips. "She can't eat all that," I said to myself; "she's not a bad-hearted old woman; perhaps when she has finished that little job of digging, and sits down to her breakfast, she may ask me to have some."

Judge of my astonishment then, when having dug in the rubbish as large a hole as suited her, she turned about, and taking up the meat and bread and pudding by double handsfull, proceeded to bury it—stamping it in with her feet that it might lie close—as though it were no better than so much offal!

With amazement and indignation, I saw several excellent chunks of mutton and beef so disposed, to say nothing of a full half-peck of good honest bread and butter, until the heap was reduced to one meaty bone and a large crust. It was evident that unless prompt measures were adopted, this would share the fate of the rest, and my hungry belly groaned aloud at such a shameful sacrifice. Just as the wasteful old sinner was about to grasp my last chance in her dirty paws, I suddenly rose and darted forward.

Unfortunately, however, in my headlong haste, I stumbled against the wicker basket, and with a kick overturned it. A clinking noise followed, and there rattled out of it, besides a miscellaneous collection of tapes and bobbins and pieces of lace, a shining spoon and a fork, and a pepper box, of a metal as bright as that I saw my father at work on when I peeped through the keyhole.

The old woman was terribly dismayed at the sudden rumpus and clatter, and while I stood confused and not knowing what to do, she had caught up her crutch stick, and with a cry of affright retreated to the further end of the kitchen; but almost instantly discovering that it was I alone who had occasioned her alarm, her fright changed to fury, and, with terrible imprecations, she vindictively charged at me with the stick raised in the air. Thinking to mend matters, I hastened to stoop down and pick up the spilt goods, but this only further incensed her.

"Drop that, you little thief!" she yelled, and sprang towards me, and my bent position favouring her murderous design, I verily believe that she would have cracked my skull with the crutch handle, had not a nail, projecting out of the rough floor boards, caught the ring she wore on the shoe of her short leg, and capsized her just in the nick of time. By the time she had scrambled on to her legs again, I had the spoons and the pepper box, and the tapes and laces, in the basket, and handed it to her.

"I hope you haven't hurt yourself, ma'am," I said, apologetically; "here's your things, all right. I didn't mean to upset 'em. It was quite an accident."

Snatching at the basket, she dived her hand into it, and bringing out the spoon and the fork and the pepper box, thrust them into her bosom; and seeing that she was still trembling with rage, I turned towards the stairs, but she was after me in an instant, and caught me by the collar.

"Where are you going?" she abruptly demanded.

"You leave me alone. It's no business of yours where I am going," said I, endeavouring, but in vain, to wriggle out of her grasp. "You let me go. I'll halloo out for the police if you don't."

"To be sure you will. I know you, you little villain," she returned furiously; "you eat my bread and meat, and then you would turn the police on me because I won't let you rob me."

"I don't want to rob you. I don't want anything to do with you. You'll choke me if you squeeze your knuckles into my throat like that!" And as well as I was able, I shouted "Police!"

This brought about a change in the aspect of affairs immediately. Releasing her hand from my collar, she clapped it over my mouth, and with much more

strength than I should have thought her in possession of, she hauled me down the stairs again into the back kitchen.

"Look here, you rascal," said she, "I know what you want. Why didn't you ask for it when you bowled me out? Why didn't you cry, 'snacks?' I should have understood you then."

She was still shaking with passion, although she affected a milder tone as she made these strange observations.

Young as I was, my knowledge of slang was sufficient for me to understand that by "bowling her out," she meant that I had discovered something concerning her she had rather remained hidden, but what it was I had not the remotest idea; but why I should have cried "snacks," and what purpose it would have served, I was quite at a loss to discover.

As all I wanted, however, was to get away, I thought it as well to humour her.

"Very well, ma'am, I'll cry 'snacks' then, if you like. 'Snacks,' there."

"You are a downy one for your age you are!" said Granny Corston, grinning, spitefully, while at the same time she drew me to a dark corner and there produced from her bosom the spoons and the pepper box. "Make haste; how shall we 'whack it?'"

"Whacking," in my young mind, was only associated with one operation, and that a particularly painful one.

Why should we "whack" a pepper-box? I shook my head vaguely.

"I don't understand you, ma'am," I remarked.

"You'd rather have the ready for your share, eh?" continued Granny Corston. "Well, how much? Don't open your young mouth too wide; s'pose we say eighteen-pence, money down?"

And fumbling at a pocket in her shabby old frock, she produced a sizable leather bag, and turning her head for a moment, revealed a shilling and a sixpence in the palm of her skinny hand.

"Say the word," said she; "will this square it?"

All this time I had not the faintest idea what she was driving at.

It was quite evident that the shilling and sixpence was for me if I chose to accept it, but why or wherefore was a mystery; I had not earned it, I had done nothing to merit it—on the contrary, I had offended her so much that she had assaulted me with her crutch, and afterwards well nigh strangled me, and now I had but to "say the word," and she was willing to give me eighteenpence.

Many a time afterwards I had reason to wish that I had "said the word," and, taking her money, walked off without having any further dealings with her.

As it happened, however, in my boyish ignorance, I said other words that opened her cunning eyes to the true condition of the case.

"I shouldn't like to take all that lot of money away from a poor old woman such as you are," I remarked, modestly.

She looked at me suddenly and sharply as though she thought I was making fun of her, but, discovering no symptoms of anything of the kind, her face assumed a puzzled expression.

"I can't make you out at all," she remarked, presently; "what sort of a boy *are* you?"

"I'm a boy without a father or a mother, and I've got no home to go to, ma'am," I replied. "I am no other sort of boy than that; I told you so last night."

"But you did not tell me last night that you were a thief."

"I ain't a thief," I indignantly returned.

"Then what made you come stealing up behind me when my head was turned—when you knocked over my basket, I mean?"

"Only because I couldn't bear to see good grub wasted like you was wasting it," I answered. "I thought that I might as well have a bit of it as let it all be buried in the dust."

The old woman stared at me for several seconds, and then fell to chuckling as though what I had said very much amused her.

"Well, well," she exclaimed, chucking me under the chin, and assuming quite a motherly tone, "it is a shame to teaze a nice little fellow such as you are—a little fellow who can take a joke in such good part! You knew that I was joking from the very first, didn't you, now? So you thought it was a pity to see such good victuals wasted, eh?"

"A very great pity, ma'am," I answered more and more bewildered at her strange behaviour.

"But it isn't good victuals, my boy, Let's see, you didn't tell me what your name is?"

"Jack Steadfast, ma'am."

"That's a good name—a good honest name. I like everything that seems honest; it goes down so much better in this wicked world, eh, Jack? No, you were mistaken; that stuff you caught me burying was fit for nothing else—only dogscraps and stale bits put by for beggars."

"I wouldn't mind eating it, ma'am. I could eat that lump of bread now, if you'd let me."

"But I won't let you. I make it a rule

to feed my boys as I feed myself, on everything of the choicest and best; good juicy steaks at breakfast, and roast and boiled at dinner, and never particular to a shilling or so if they want to go to the play at night. That's how I treat *my* boys—as long as they behave well, of course. When they turn round and think to be cleverer than their granny, they get into trouble. Its a strange thing but they do," said she, with peculiar emphasis, and regarding me meaningly; "they get into prison or something. I've noticed it a dozen times."

"Serve them right too, ma'am, if they are so ungrateful," I remarked, taking quite an interest in the old lady's account of how she treated her boys.

"That's how I came to be all alone now," she continued; "the last boy I had to lead me about liked his job at first, and did very well, but he grew too clever, and was glad to take to his heels and leave me in the street, a poor old blind woman, to find my way home as I best could."

I could not help laughing at this.

"What poor old blind woman?" I asked, looking full at her dark optics that twinkled like glass beads. " *You* are not blind!"

" Not just now," she replied, chuckling, and winking one of her beady eyes knowingly, " not just now, Jack; it is only when I am out looking sharp after my living that I am blind. It is then that I want a boy to lead me about. D'ye see?"

And the wicked old wretch chuckled and winked again, as though making quite sure that I must have taken her meaning by this time. But I had not.

" I never heard of any one being blind one time and able to see at others," I remarked; " how is it, ma'am?"

"Oh, come, come," said she, suddenly becoming grave, " I like a nice innocent little boy, but I can't abear a fool. You don't believe that all the people you see begging about the streets with their eyes shut are blind?"

" They might as well be blind, if they keep their eyes shut, ma'am."

" To be sure. Only they wouldn't have the blessed privilege of opening their eyes at night to laugh and make merry over the gulls they had been bleeding all day. Come, let's have no more making pretence, and acting ' Goody Two Shoes.' *You* know what I mean well enough. Let's talk about business. You have no home, no place to lay your head, no means of buying your next meal?"

" Only a penny, ma'am," I answered ruefully.

" Are your parents dead?"

I hesitated to answer this question. " My father isn't," I presently said.

" Where is he then? There, don't turn red and stammer; you are not the first bright boy whose father got himself into quod. I'm right, eh? I knew I was. Well, I don't think any the worse of you for that."

I had not said that my father was in prison, or in " quod," as she, in her cant language, put it; but to be sure I had turned red and stammered when she asked me the question so abruptly, and so the secret leaked out. Nevertheless, I felt very much obliged to her that she thought none the worse of me on that account, and I told her so.

" Now, how long have you been knocking about?" was her next query.

" Only since the day before yesterday morning, ma'am."

" And you've kept honest of course, and been living like a prince, eh?" She said this with a sneer, as she glanced over my woefully shabby exterior.

"I've kept honest, ma'am. I mean to keep honest," I replied ; the word reminding me of that good maxim my poor mother so frequently impressed on me. "It is better to have a clear conscience, ma'am, and ragged clothes, than——"

"Than what?" sharply inquired the old woman, whose angry glance had cut my quotation short.

"Than — than do what isn't right. ma'am," I answered meekly.

"And isn't it right to fill your belly when you are hungry?"

"There can't be any mistake about that, ma'am." I answered heartily.

"And to go bed warm and snug o' nights?"

"Oh yes, ma'am, that's right enough."

"And to have good strong boots to your feet and a warm jacket to your back? Isn't it right to get all that if you find the chance?"

"I wish that I could find such a chance, ma'am."

"Why so you have," returned Granny Corston, "you've got it already to your hand."

"Whereabouts, ma'am?"

"Here. *I'm* your chance. Should you think that a poor, ragged, homeless boy, with no better prospect than starvation or the workhouse before him, would be doing a bad turn for himself if he got all the good things I mention and ever so many more that I have not mentioned, as his wages for no harder job than leading a blind woman about the streets?"

"What would she do while he led her about, ma'am?" Somehow I felt that under all this splendid offer there must be something ugly that did not appear, and which I should afterwards find out.

"While she begged from house to house," replied Granny Corston, bluntly, "but p'r'aps you've got too much pride to undertake such a job?"

"Not I, ma'am," I hastened to explain; "but would he have nothing else to do besides ringing at the gates and knocking at the doors?"

"Not much else. Nothing else that a sharp lad with his wits about him and who valued his situation, need make any trouble of," returned Granny Corston, vaguely. "Come, make your mind up. Plenty of good victuals, warm lodgings, and always a shilling in your pocket. Decide at once, because I want my breakfast. A good mutton chop and a round of toast, and a pot of fine hot coffee, isn't to be sneezed at such a morning as this. Say the word. Are we to breakfast together, Jack Stedfast, or shall I bid you good bye?"

Poor little fellow! Ignorant and hungry little wretch that I was, how could I withstand such prodigious temptations? I cannot plead that I was entirely ignorant of the danger there was in coming to terms with the old hag. Had I simply believed all that she said I should not have felt that indescribable dread of her, or that strange heart-beating, while I rapidly made up my mind.

"I will go with you, ma'am!" said I buttoning my tattered jacket desperately.

## CHAPTER VI.

THE OLD LADY TAKES ME INTO HER CONFIDENCE AND RELATES TO ME THE STORY OF THE PERFIDY OF HER LAST BOY, TOM.

GRANNY CORSTON received my descision with evident satisfaction.

"That being the settled, then," said she, the sooner we get out of this dismal hole the better.   Stay a moment, though. It will be as well, p'r'aps, if we are not seen leaving in company.  You go out first, and if you should see a policeman, or a boy about your own size, only better dressed, and with carotty hair, and a Glen garry cap on, let me know.  Hark; you hear that milkman?  Well, if you see either the policeman or the boy, squall out 'milk!' as though you were mocking him."

But there was no occasion for resorting to the cunning artifice the old woman suggested.  I found the street quite deserted, and presently Granny Corston stealthily emerged from the half-finished building, signing me to follow her.

After a while she halted at a low-looking coffee-house in a back street in Spitalfields, and we entered it together.  Since the appearance to breakfast of a ragged, capless, little urchin, and an old woman who looked no better than a beggar, excited no surprise, the character of the establishment may be easily guessed. Nevertheless, materials for good feeding were there to be had in abundance for ready money, and to do her justice, the old woman was as good as her word.

Before we had been in the place ten minutes such a breakfast as, in all my life, I had not set eyes on was smoking before us, and I regaled in a manner that was as foreign to me as it was delightful. Granny Corston was especially kind over the meal.  She helped me to the largest eggs, and the fattest rashers, and with her own hands sweetened my coffee.  I began quite to like her.

After breakfast she confided to me the story of the ingratitude of her last boy, Tom, and how it had came about that she, a person with a good home to go to, and with plenty of money in her pocket (when she took out her bag to pay for the breakfast, I saw that there was gold as well as silver in it), was glad of a night's shelter in the empty house where I had discovered her.

She pretended to relate the incident in a chatty, off-hand sort of way, but I have no doubt that she had more meaning in doing so than appeared on the surface. Probably she thought that as our compact was now fairly entered on, she might venture to break the ice, as the saying is, and give me a glimpse of the foul water into which it was her design that I should plunge.

"I'll tell you how it happened, Jack," said she, leaning forward over the little table that stood between us, and speaking in so low a whisper that it would have been difficult for any one sitting in the next box even to have overheard her, "I'll tell you how it happened.  I never suspected Tom for a moment, but took him to be as honest a boy as ever stept. Honest towards *me*—you understand, Jack?—who had found him just as I have found you, and took him in hand and fed him, and clothed him, and would have made a man of him, if he had behaved as he ought. We'll, we worked together till last evening. We'd been about all day—just as you and I might—and we hadn't done bad."

" That you hadn't ma'am," I observed. " *I* saw what a prime lot of good grub you had. Did you have all that give to you?"

" Yes, my dear," she replied, leering knowingly, and whispering still lower. " All that lot of grub, as you call it, and a pretty pepper-box to season it, and a silver fork and spoon to eat it with."

" Had the fork and spoon give you?"

" Hu-s-sh! No, no, Jack, we wasn't beholden to anybody for giving us them— we found 'm. Tom found 'm—just as you might. Tom led his poor old blind granny down an area—nice and quietly, don't you know, so as to be humble and not disturb anybody, he, he!—and knocked at the kitchen door, and nobody answered. So, —just as you might, Tom turned the door handle softly and peeped in, and, what should be lying just as handy as though it was placed there for us, on the dresser, but a pepper-box and a fork and spoon. It wasn't *our* fault that the servant had forgot to put 'em away, was it, now?"

" No ma'am," I answered faintly, and conscious of that heart-quaking again.

" To be sure not. Well, Jack,—just as you might, Tom said to himself, ' It's a shame to let such things lay about neglected; I'll take charge of 'em!' and he

had hardly said the words before they hopped off the dresser into his blind old granny's basket that happened to be opened. Ha, ha! it isn't often you hear a better joke than that, eh, Jack?"

There was a drop of coffee remaining in my cup, and, feeling a queer rising in my throat, I hastily raised it to my lips to gulp it down, but it went the "wrong way," as people say, and set me coughing and choking at a rate that made it quite impossible for the old woman to say whether or no I saw the joke or to what extent.

" Oh, yes, my dear," continued the old hag, when I had recovered my breath, " Tom was a clever little chap, and we should have gone on smoothly for ever and a day if he hadn't wanted to be *too* clever. It was all the worse because he was mean enough to take advantage of my affliction; for you must know, Jack, when I get my eyes well turned back for business, it isn't always that I can recover the use of 'em in a moment. Tom knew this, the little villain!

" Well, it was just growing dark when we came to a house that looked likely, and —just as you might—Tom unlatched the gate and led me in. This time the kitchen door was open, and, after softly asking if they had a stale crust to give his grandmother, eighty-six, and blind; and getting no answer Tom stept inside.

" I had such confidence in him that I thought I could have trusted him in any one else's kitchen for an hour if needful, and there I stood with my blind eyes, waiting for him. But I can tell you, when I put on blind, my ears are all the sharper, and, presently, along with Tom's returning footsteps, I heard the clink of money, and I got a little sight, just in time to see the rascal slip two half-crowns into his waistcoat pocket. 'There's nothing there,' he says, 'come on;' but he wasn't going to cheat me like that, and I pounced on the pocket; and while we were hauling one way and the other, out comes a servant and collars us both, and called out to somebody else to fetch a policeman, as he had caught a couple of area sneaks. That was a pretty fix, hey, Jack? And all through that mean young scamp.

"But I turned the tables on him.

" 'You're quite mistaken, young man,' I says to the servant, with a face as long as that of a Methodist parson's wife. 'It is true I am only a poor old soul, selling staylaces, but thank goodness I'm honest. I was coming to see if I could turn a penny with the servants, when I saw this boy stealing out of the kitchen, putting money in his waistcoat pocket; you'll find it there now if you look,' and I laid hold of him.

"He! he! you should have seen Master Tom's countenance, my dear, as I said this!

" 'So that's how the cat jumps, is it?' said the servant, 'we'll take care of you, young fellow,' and he left go of me to get a better hold on Tom.

"But Tom was like an eel, and wriggled out of his grasp in a moment, dodging the servant round the garden shrubs. You wouldn't believe it, but the hardened ruffian was not yet satisfied with the harm he had done me.

" 'She honest?' he bawled out, 'why she's the greatest old rip in the parish! She pretends to be blind! She's a cadger! She's a thief! Look in her basket!'

"But luckily for me, the servant had dodged him out at the gate by this time, and ran after him full speed, and as there was no use in my staying there, to invite people to poke and pry over my basket, I went off another way, and being so far away from home, I turned in for the night, where you found me.

"There, now you know all about it."

And as she uttered these last words she regarded me meaningly, as though she would have said—

"There, now you know who I am and what I am, and the sort of service I expect of you if you go along with me."

I felt that she expected me to make some remark, to inquire what would probably become of Tom, or something of that sort, but I felt sick and bewildered, and sat hanging my head and unable to say a word.

Had the wicked old wretch then put the question to me—"Will you come with me or no?"

I don't think there would have been much hesitation about my answer; but it was terribly plain to me that she regarded that part of the business as settled. I *had* come with her, and she had paid me wages in advance in shape of a breakfast, and imparted to me the secrets of her trade.

Then, again, see what her treatment of Tom had been!

Undoubtedly, Tom was a bad one, but the terribly clever way she had contrived to snare him in his own trap, showed her to be a woman who was not to be trifled with; and as I felt her sharp eyes fixed on me, I grew each moment more afraid of her.

"Come along, Jack," she abruptly exclaimed.

"'I'LL TELL YOU HOW IT HAPPENED, JACK,' SAID SHE."

"I'll buy you a cap and a jacket," said she, "as soon as we can find a shop;" and so she did, giving the large sum of four and sixpence for the one, and two shillings for the other. Better still, she invested a further sum of five shillings in the purchase of a pair of boots for me; a favour for which I had especial cause to feel grateful, for, as the reader may recollect, I had lost one of my old shoes during my unsuccessful chase after my mother. Now there could be no mistake about my having accepted the situation she had offered me.

They were her clothes I had on, and nice and comfortable they were that bitter cold morning—and if I ran away from her she might call after me "stop thief!" I thought at the time when in the coffee room she said aloud "we must get home, Jack, or grandfather will wonder what has become of us," that it might be merely make-belief before the people there, and that soon as we got outside we should straightway begin a day's business of the sort she had described with such terrible distinctness; indeed for some little time after we were in the street, I from time to time cast glances at her eyes, expecting each moment to see them "turn up" in the strange manner she had indicated as the first step towards the shameful cheat to be practised.

Nothing of the kind happened, however, and from the decided way in which she took street after street, and road after road, it became evident to me that we really were going "home," wherever that might be. But who was "grandfather?" I relished the business less and less, the more I thought about grandfather and pictured the sort of man he was likely to be.

Very few words were exchanged between us, though our walk extended to an hour or more. At last we arrived at a quarter of the town that was quite new to me. "We shall soon be home, now, Jack," said she, "there's Westminster Abbey."

And we went up the broad road and towards the magnificent building in question. However, we soon got out of this respectable locality, and after entering in at one narrow alley, and emerging at another that was narrower and dirtier, we came on a sort of market-place.

"This is Strutton Ground," said the old woman, perceiving that I was looking wonderingly about me, "and over the way is Penny's Fields, and there we are at home."

As I need not remark, "Penny's Fields" were no fields at all. It was a sort of square of tumble-down dilapidated houses, some utterly ruined, and with their doors, and windows boarded up, and all of them "shored up" with massive baulks of timber. That familiar spot Rickett's Rents was bad enough, but it, was quite an elegant retreat compared with Penny's Fields.

The roadway was a morass of black mire, relieved here and there by the green of vegetable offal cast from the windows and the white and yellow of broken castaway crockery. Pavement there was none, nor pathway; but where it should have been before the houses there were any number of half-naked, squalid-looking urchins playing and quarrelling in the mud, while their parents smoked short pipes, and lounged and gossiped out at the windows, or lolled negligently against the black and greasy door-posts.

Picking her way amongst the urchins

in the kennel, by whom she was recognised and cheerily hailed as old Granny, Mrs. Corston presently paused at a door, and opening it by means of a piece of cord conveniently suspended outside, entered, bidding me shut the door and follow her. As we were ascending the dark and ricketty stairs, presently was heard the shrill, screaming voice of a child, and a cry of " Oh, don't ! pray don't !" This brought me to a standstill.

"Why don't you come up? What's the matter?" Mrs. Corston coolly asked.

"There's somebody being beat up there," said I. " Can't you hear 'em hollerin' out ?"

" I'll make 'em holler to a new tune when I get at 'em, the squeaking little vermin !" exclaimed Granny, maliciously. " That's that aggravating little wretch, Luce, I'll wager. All right, my beauty, if you knew the tickling that was in store for you, you'd make less noise, I'm think·ing."

I do think that I should have dared everything and run away, now matters arrived at this pass, had not Granny, as though she had suspected some such design on my part, got behind me and sent me on before her. " Up you go to the top of the next flight," said she, and up we went as high as the garret floor; and there arrived, she abruptly turned the handle of a door and pushed it wide open.

As long as I live I shall never forget the sight that was then revealed. The room, which was spacious as to depth and width, though so low-roofed that a tall person could not stand upright in it, was dark except for the little yellow, fog-like light that came in at such of the tiny window panes as were not blocked up

with rags and paper, while the walls and ceiling were black almost as a chimney back.

The place was not scantily furnished, however; there were chairs and tables enough, besides a large old-fashioned four-post bedstead in one corner. But it was not the aspect of the room, nor its furniture that chiefly claimed my attention; indeed, it is improbable that at that first view I should have been aware even that there was such an article as a four-post bedstead in the room, had it not been for the circumstance of a child being tied to one of the posts—a little girl about my own height, but woefully thin and pale.

She was drawn up tight to the post by means of a leather strap, such as labour-ing men sometimes wear round their waists. Her back was towards us, and above her dirty old ragged frock, where her poor little bony shoulders were visible, were several wheals such as might be made with a cane, and quite sufficient to account for the screams and imploring cries we had heard while ascending the stairs. She had long, fair hair, but it was all massed and tangled over her head and about her pitiful, tear-stained face.

Close by her, taken by surprise, and with the instrument of torture still in his hand, was " grandfather," as grotesque and hideous an old monster as is possible to imagine. Mrs. Corston was old and horrid, but the man she called her hus-band looked old enough almost to be her father.

His head was quite bald, except for a few dark grey bristles that sprouted here and there out of his unclean surface, and his face wrinkled with age, till it more than anything else resembled that of an ourang outang, while his toothless jaws had so contracted together, that there was not a quarter of an inch of space between the tip of his hooked nose and his nether lip. He wore neither waistcoat, nor coat, nor neckerchief, and his dirty shirt, all open in front, revealed a chest, hairy as the back of a street mongrel, and of about the same texture. To complete the repulsive oddity of his appearance tied about his waist and trailing down to his slipshod heels, was a coarse cotton apron, of a blue and white check, such as washerwomen wear.

Stranger than all, and contrasting strongly with his ancient, apish aspect, on the mattress of the enormous four-poster were three little children, the youngest a mere infant of nine or ten months, holloweyed and ravenous-looking, and sucking desperately at a cracked and empty feeding bottle. As for the other two, the eldest might have been five years old, and the other, three; and this one, a boy, a curly-haired little creature, whose natural prettiness was powerful enough to shine through all the dirt and rags that enveloped him, soothingly held one of the imprisoned hands of the poor girl next to the bed post.

Discovering who it was that had opened the door, the old man recovered from his momentary astonishment, and dropping his cane, came shuffling towards Mrs. Corston, peevishly whining like an idiot. It was easy enough to see that he had grown almost into second childhood.

"You're back again, Sally—back again, at last," said he; and embracing the old woman before she had time even to divest herself of her bonnet, he imprinted a kiss of welcome on her wrinkled visage. "I'm so glad, Sally. I thought you had left your old man, and gone away quite!"

"No, you did'nt," responded Mrs. Corston, ungraciously, as she disengaged herself from his embrace; "you are an old fool, I know, but not fool enough to think that I would go away and leave you. It's time that I did come home, I can see. What's the rumpus, now? They're all alive, still, hang 'em!"

"I wish you'd smother, or drown 'em or something," whined the old man, wringing his hands; "they're killin' me by inches with their squallin's and their teethings, and their woracious appetites. There's one on 'm nearly croaked since you was gone."

"Well, and who hindered it?" demanded the old crone, darting a fierce glance at the bed-post captive, as though she made sure of discovering the culprit there.

"I did, my love, I did. I was compelled to; you'd a done it, if you had been at home."

"Should I?" returned the old hag, mockingly. "Well, how was it? Which one was it? They all look bright and hearty enough now, cuss 'em."

"Oh, yes, my love, they're all right now, the danger did not last long. It was the baby swallered the injerrubber of the feedin' bottle; got it stuck in his hungry young throat till he was black in the face. We got it up agin with the scissors. He's all right now, 'cept for a soreness where the pints of 'em nipped him."

"And what was Luce doing to let him swallow it?" Mrs. Corston was determined to get at poor Luce, somehow.

"What was she doing? what she's always doin'. Neglectin' the 'ouse and larkin' out in the street, o' course."

"I wasn't," sobbed the poor child, "it was when you sent me to the Black Bull to—

"Beg me a short pipe," promptly interrupted the cunning old gentleman, "so it was, but you know how she stays on her errands. She is wuss than all of 'em put together."

"She always is, always was, and always will be, the jabe," exclaimed the old woman, furiously, and hobbling across the room to where the poor little captive was, she fetched her a stinging box on each ear, and then taking up the cane her worthy husband had laid down, said she—

"I may as well settle her score altogether, now I have commenced. What else has she been doing?"

"Oh, nothing new," mumbled the old monstrocity; "nothing new, only her old trick of stuffing 'em with the wittles I gives her to eat herself till they are uncomfortable and cross. She doesn't give it 'em because she likes 'em, no fear o' that; she ses she wishes that she was dead, and she does it to starve herself to death; just to spite us. She *will* do it. I whack her and whack her and whack her, but it's all no use, she *will* do it!" And the hideous old man began to cry, wiping his eyes on the dirty chek apron.

"She will do it, will she?" cried Mrs. Corston, flinging off her cloak, the more conveniently to grasp the cane, "p'r'aps

a little of *my* physic will prevent it; it's stronger than yours, daddy."

Hearing this and with a woeful knowledge of what it portended, poor Luce uttered a piteous cry, and turning her head, looked appealing towards me. All this time I had remained just on the spot to which I had advanced when I followed Mrs. Corston into the room, amazed and spell-bound.

That look of the little girl, however, roused me; I made for the door, in which the old woman had turned the key, and unlocked it. The cane was already raised in the air; but this unexpected movement of mine arrested it.

"Hullo! where are you off to?" cried Granny Corston.

"I am going down to call somebody to you," I replied, my indignation lending me boldness. "I didn't know what a wicked old woman you was, or I never would have come home with you. I'm going to fetch somebody that will save that poor little girl from being whacked." And I made a bolt for the stairs. But it was so dark that I was afraid to set one foot before the other; and while I groped hesitatingly, Granny Corston darted out after me, and collaring me by my new jacket, hustled me back into the room again.

---

## CHAPTER VII.

IN WHICH I MAKE THE ACQUAINTANCE OF LUCE, AND THROUGH HER GAIN FURTHER KNOWLEDGE OF THE BUSINESS CARRIED ON BY THE MESSRS. CORSTON.

IT seemed that it was not until the old woman had asked me where I was going, and I had raised my voice in reply, that Daddy Corston was made aware of my strange presence. When his wife dragged me back into the room, there he was in a fine pucker to know who I was, and what I wanted.

For the present, however, Mrs. Corston was too bent on revenge for the unwarrantable interruption of which I had been guilty, to reply to his questions. Unfortunately for me, she still had the rattan in her hand; and as I struggled on the ground and fought and kicked to elude her grasp, she laid into me with it with all her might and main, while the babies on the four-poster, moved by the novelty of the exhibition, swelled the bawling chorus of which I was the leader; and poor Luce, aware that I had incurred granny's displeasure on her account, could do nothing but cry out "Pray don't, Granny, pray don't! Beat me, Granny; don't beat him!"

As for Daddy Corston, knowing nothing about me, but concluding that I deserved all that I was getting, and perhaps a little more, he danced about us, cutting it in with a cuff whenever he found a chance. He was incautious enough, however, presently to approach too close; and in my plunging fore and aft, he all unexpectedly received a kick in the pit of his stomach that disabled him during the rest of the combat, which ended only with the exhaustion of Granny Corston's breath. She reserved a little of it, however, to give her strength to hand me into a sort of ante-room on the landing, into which I was thrust, and before I could turn about I heard the key grate in the lock.

My fury, however, if not my strength, was equal to the old woman's, and feeling for the door—for the place was quite dark—I set up a battery against the door, at the same time bawling to be let out at the top of my voice. But I soon found reason to abate my transports. Kicking against the hard oak panels produced no other effect than bruising my toes, while

a cry louder than mine own caused me to cease my row that I might listen. There could be no doubt it—it was the little girl's voice. My interference had caused more trouble than good. If Mother Corston had exhausted her strength over me, she had mighty soon recovered it, as poor Luce's screams attested. Never in my life did I feel more savage and vindictive, and regarding Daddy Corston as the main cause of the disturbance, in the wickedness of my heart I fervently hoped that he might never recover from the effects of that kick that had sent the weak old ruffian sprawling on his back.

My vain fuming was presently interrupted, however. I could hear the sound of footsteps and sobbing approaching, and then the key grated in the lock and the door was opened.

"There! go in there and cry it out together, like a pair of blue hen's chicks as you are!" It was Granny Corston's voice that spoke. "Go in and tell the devil's cub of what a nice dressing I've given you, and what *he* may expect if he sets his back up against me."

I slunk to a corner as the form of the vindictive old witch hove dimly in sight, but the push she gave the little girl as she spoke sent her staggering against me. Then the door was slammed to and locked, and we were left alone in the dark. Perfect strangers as we were, we were at least brother and sister in affliction. Luce began to console me as soon as Granny Corston's retreating footsteps were heard.

"Did she hurt you much, boy?" she asked in her soft and tender voice, as finding my hand, she pressed it in her own. "Oh, I am so sorry; it was all through me, and it was so kind of you to take my part. But it is of no use; anybody who take's my part gets into trouble, so pray don't do it again, will you?"

"Won't I!" I returned, recklessly, "you'll see if I don't. She's a spiteful old cat, that's what she is, and as for him, only hope—"

"Hush, they'll hear you; pray, don't," and she placed her hand over my mouth; "they'll hear you if you talk so loud; you don't know what they are as well as I do."

"I don't care if they do hear me," I replied, raising my voice still higher, for I was still smarting from the savage cuts the old woman had dealt me. "Why should I care?"

"Oh, don't, don't!" the little girl whispered, imploringly, "you'll have her here again, and she may bring the whip instead of the cane. Ah! you don't know how the whip hurts!"

"But I don't belong here!" I cried. "Hang her, what right has she to wallop me and lock me up?" And roused to fury by a recollection of the indignities I had recently been the victim of, I am ashamed to say I launched into a torrent of as much foul language as my gutter experience had made me master of, inveighing against Granny Corston and all her belongings. Luce, who had hitherto held my hand with a grasp in which there was confidence, dropped it at once.

"I'm very sorry," she said, "but—but I didn't think you was *that* sort of boy."

"What sort of boy," I asked, considerably astonished.

"A swearing boy;" she replied, and then she hastily added, "Don't mind me, little boy, I—I did'nt know, you know. It isn't your fault, I dare say. Only don't say wickeder words than you can help, please."

I don't think I should like her to have seen how I reddened at hearing her say that. It seemed so strange that she, brought up in such a place, should have an objection to bad language; but it flashed to my memory this was not the only instance in her strangeness with which our brief friendship had made me acquainted. It was hard to imagine any one more thin and hungry-looking than she was, and yet had I not heard old Daddy Corston accuse her of giving her food to the little ones? These and other reflections caused me to pause a considerable time before I could make up my mind what to say next to her. She spoke first, however, creeping up to me so softly that I did not hear her until she took my hand again.

"Don't be cross with me, little boy," she said, softly.

"I ain't cross—leastways with you. Why should I be? I don't want to use any wicked words. I shouldn't, only she made me so savage whacking me for nothing. And what did she want to whack me for?"

"I don't much mind it, poor Luce answered, with a woeful sigh : "I'm used to it. They don't beat me hard enough, I think, sometimes. I know how wicked it is, but I do wish they would beat me hard enough to kill me! Oh, I am so tired of my life, little boy! So—so tired!"

I was lounging against the wall, balanced between sulkiness and an unaccountable yearning towards her, when she uttered these words, and immediately afterwards I was aware from the sound, for I could not see her, that she had sank down on her knees and was pressing my hand to her wet face. I felt tears of a new sort in my own eyes.

"Never mind; don't cry; though I don't wonder at your being tired of your life if you never have any other sort than the bit I've seen of it. I should have hated *my* mother if she had served me so."

"But she isn't my mother," Luce answered, hastily.

"Your grandmother, I meant, I——"

"Nor she isn't my grandmother. It wouldn't be so hard to bear if she had a right to beat me."

"And does she beat your little brothers and sisters?"

"They are not my brothers and sisters, poor little things; they are not brothers and sisters at all. They are all as strange to each other as I am to them. Ah! if their mothers knew how they were treated. If I knew where they lived I would go and tell them. I would—if Granny killed me for it!"

"How do they come by 'em, then?"

"Hush!" Luce said, "I musn't tell."

Suddenly a terrible legend, current among the juvenile population of Rickett's Rents, came into my mind.

"I know how they get 'em!" I remarked, sinking my voice to a whisper, matching her own.

"How?"

"They kidnap 'em," said I. "That's it! That accounts for it. You're a kidnap, a 'spectable kidnap, that don't agree with their ways."

"No, no; not so bad as that; at least it does not seem so bad. They are nurse children," replied Luce.

"Nurse children!"

"Hush! Yes. You won't tell if I tell you?"

"Not if they was to beat me all to bits," I answered, valiantly.

"Well, then, they put advertisements in the newspapers, and mothers who have children they want took care of, give 'em to Granny Corston, and she brings 'em here, and Daddy Corston nurses 'em, and I help."

"What makes you give 'em your grub?" I asked; for that was a matter I felt very curious about. "I shouldn't, if I was you."

"Ah! yes you would, you couldn't help it," returned Luce, confidently. "You couldn't sit and eat by the side of a hungry baby!"

"Well, they do look awfully hungry. That's what made that young 'un swallow the indiarubber, I reckon. They can't expect 'em to live if they don't feed 'em."

By this time we were seated side by side on the ground, all in the dark. When I made this last remark, Luce put her arm round my neck and drew my head close, so that she might whisper fairly into my ear.

"Don't talk loud about that, whatever you do!" said she, in a voice of terror, "that is the worst of all, the very worst. I am afraid even to think of it."

"What is the worst of all?" I whispered back again. "Tell us; I won't split; don't you be afraid."

"They *don't* expect 'em to live," replied Luce.

"Do they expect 'em to die, then?"

"They like 'em to die," said Luce, in the same dreadful whisper, "they don't try to hinder 'em. They're always dying here. I couldn't count up the names I've read on the little coffins, there's been so many of 'em."

There was a pause in our conversation after this. Bad as had been my previous opinion of Granny Corston, now it was heightened ten-fold.  To be sure, of my own knowledge, or from which it was in the power of my youthful mind to gather from Luce's strange revelations, it was difficult to fix any particular crime on the old woman in connexion with the babies; but the terrible fact of coffins innumerable carried empty into that front attic and carried out full, considered together with its other features—the filthy old four-poster, and the ragged, dirty little children crawling over it, and the dreadful old man in the check apron—brimmed up the measure of my alarm to overflowing, and there and then I resolved to make my escape at the earliest opportunity.

"How long have you been here?" I asked the little girl.

"Oh, a long while—years and years. I'm ten now; I wasn't six when I was brought here; that was when my mother died," and here she broke down again and sobbed so that I could scarcely pacify her.

"And don't they expect you to die?" I asked.

"We won't talk about that now," she rejoined, suddenly drying her eyes.  " I'll tell you about that some day if you stay here.   What did you come here for? What is your name?"

"Jack."

" My name is Lucy—they call me Luce. The other boy — her boy, I mean—is named Tom."

"So she told me."

"Do you know Tom?"

" I've heard about him," I replied, feeling rather uneasy at the direction to which her questions were evidently tending.

"Then you know the sort of boy he is ?"

" No, I don't ; I only know what she told me."

"Did she say he was a bad boy ?"

"She said that he was good and he was bad ; it was a kind of mixed up character she gave Tom."

"Ah, he's a dreadful boy," said Lucy, shaking her head.  "I shouldn't like him to know that I said so, because he's so spiteful; but he is a very dreadful boy.  I don't think that you could like him."

"Why don't you ?"

" Because I think that I could like you."

" But what's that got to do with it ?"

"Well, I don't think I should feel like that towards any one that could like a boy like Tom," replied my queer little companion.  "It's a dreadful thing for him; but I think that he is the wickedest boy that ever lived.  I'm more afraid of him than of the great, rough men who sometimes come here.  He tells lies because he likes 'em better than truth, I think.  He takes delight in telling lies to get me beat, and then he stands and makes faces, and mocks me when I am obliged to cry out."

"Then I am sure that I shouldn't like him.   But you needn't be afraid ; it's very likely that you won't see Tom again."

"Where is he then ?"

"I don't know for certain; I think he has run away."

" I'm glad of that," said Luce, after a pause ; "he can't run to worse than he leaves behind; it's dreadful here."

"Too dreadful for me," I returned. "They want me to take Tom's place; but it isn't likely after the way she's served me."

"To take Tom's place !" she repeated in tones of alarm.  "What, to do as Tom did?"

" I suppose so."

"What *altogether* as Tom did ?  You don't mean that ?"

"I don't know about the *altogether*," said I, reddening again, and feeling much ashamed. "Perhaps I haven't heard altogether about it."

"I'm sure you haven't," said Luce, earnestly, "or you wouldn't think about it. You couldn't do as Tom did without being a thief, and you can't be a thief, unless you're bred up to it. I've heard those dreadful men who come here sometimes to borrow Tom say so very often. *You* wasn't bred to be a thief, were you ?"

"'Tisn't likely," I answered, my very ears tingling. "My mother taught me very different from that. But what do the dreadful men want with Tom that they come here to borrow him ?"

Luce was about to answer, when there was heard a noise of trampling upstairs, and laughter, evidently that of a boy. My first thought was that this was Tom come back again; that somehow he had overcome the little difficulty Mrs. Corston had given me the particulars of, and he had returned to renew his duties. I was delighted to think so. Now there could be no obstacle in the way of my going about my business ; the old woman did not want two boys.

"That is Tom, isn't it ?" I asked Lucy.

"No ; Tom never comes in laughing ; he is a sly and quiet boy. That's Nat ; he's always laughing. Jerry Tyler is with him I think."

"Who are they? Do they work here ?"

"I don't know what they are. They bring things here to sell. They are not nice boys. If I were you——"

But Luce was not allowed to give me her advice as regarded "Nat" and Jerry Tyler. At that moment there was a noise at the door of the room we were locked in, and then the door was opened.

"Come out, you lazy slut !" exclaimed the harsh voice of Mother Corston. "You'd like to idle there all day, I'll be bound."

And Luce crept out, and the door was once more slammed to again.

---

## CHAPTER VIII.

I EXTEND MY CIRCLE OF ACQUAINTANCE, TAKING INTO IT "NAT" AND JERRY TYLER—OUR LITTLE TEA PARTY, AND THE CONVERSATION THAT ENLIVENED IT.

As for me I remained a prisoner all through the remainder of the morning, and far into the afternoon. I will not trouble the reader with an account of what my reflections were; indeed, did I try to I doubt if I should succeed, for two simple reasons, that they were so many and so various. I know this, however, that they were none of them of very engaging complexion, nor could they well be when their main sources were melancholy and dismal apprehension.

What would my mother think could she know of my miserable situation? It was only natural that my mind should dwell pretty constantly on my mother, and more than ever since she was away from me. I considered the probabilities of my ever seeing her again, either here or hereafter; for to tell the truth, the treatment I had received at the hands of Granny Corston, together with my protracted incarceration in that dark and dismal chamber, and the little girl Lucy's talk about coffins, had set me in the humour to regard my speedy death and burial as by no means improbable events.

In my extremity of horrible cogitation I conjured up all manner of dreadful possibilities. I had heard of kid-nappers, and I had likewise heard of body-snatchers, and the awful use to which "bodies" were occasionally put. Was it possible that Luce in her innocence had altogether mistaken the vocation of Mr. and Mrs. Corston? Considering what a dreadful pair they were, was it not highly probable that they were in the "body" trade, and found it more convenient to steal live babies and starve them to death, and to inveigle unsuspecting boys with the same appalling end in view, than to confine their operations entirely to churchyards?

I had no means of ascertaining how the time was going, and though I could hear, now and then, the sound of doors opening and shutting, and the confused hum of talking in the front attic, it seemed to me that it must be midnight and past, and that their design of depriving me of my life by keeping me without food was well advanced.

Full of these terrible forebodings, I was indeed astonished when, all on a sudden, the door was unlocked, and a cheery voice addressing me as his "tulip" inquired if I had not had enough of "Pompey's Hole," and if I didn't think I should feel all the better for a "feed." It was not the voice of Granny Corston that thus invited me, but a youthful voice; and hurrying out of the dark room the owner of the voice stood on the threshold to receive me.

"Come on, my kiddy; tea's ready, with a mild bloater for a relish. Make haste; there's only one soft roed 'un, and Jerry'll be sure to nail him if we ain't quick.

By this time I had emerged from the dark closet and stood on the landing; and then, to my amazement, I perceived from the murky yellow light that still struggled through the patched staircase window, that it was but as yet early evening. The lad who addressed me was a slim youth of about fourteen, decently attired and of a rather genteel appearance, save for his short-cropped bullet head and a flashy yellow silk neckerchief that was loosely twisted about his throat; the other lad he alluded to as "Jerry" must have been the one Luce had mentioned.

"Stir your stumps, the tea's getting cold," said he, as he commenced a descent of the stairs and beckoned me to follow.

"I don't want any tea," I replied, so far true to the good resolution I had been fostering for hours,—namely, to make my escape as soon as ever a chance presented.

"You don't want any! How's that? Your stomach can't be so werry much overloaded."

"I want to go. I've had enough of this place. I'm going."

"Going? Where to?"

"Anywhere, I don't care; I won't stay here."

"WHY DON'T YOU COME UP? WHAT'S THE MATTER?"

"You never mean to say that you would go without bidding your granny good bye! D'ye want to break her 'art?"

"Let her break her heart if she likes," I replied, moodily, "I want to go, I tell you."

"Let her!" repeated my new friend, holding up both his hands in mock amazement, "what! yer kind old granny who bought you that nice warm jacket; who stood a stunning breakfast for you when you was perishin'; your tender-'arted old granny wot has been goin' about with tears in her eyes cos she was obliged to wallop you for your good! Oh! I'm ashamed of yer."

A loud peal of laughter followed this strange speech, and a voice near at hand called out from the landing next below—

"Cut it, Nat! How can a feller toast a bloater without blacking it agin the bars, if you makes him laugh fit to bust hisself? Come down here, young 'un, don't you mind what he sez."

And as he spoke the young gentleman who tendered this kind invitation came up a few stairs and revealed himself. He was apparently younger than the other lad, and of different build, being short-necked and bulky. He held a red herring impaled on a toasting-fork, and, that amusement might be agreeably combined with amusement, his lips bore a dirty short pipe at full blast. There was no use holding out against this double invitation. At all events, in going down the stairs I must get nearer to the street door, and down I went and discovered the lad alluded to as Jerry standing hospitably at the threshold of the back room. The place was meanly furnished, but a big fire crackled merrily in the grate (contrasting to advantage with the great snow-flakes that came drifting with the wind against the window), and on the table were spread ample materials for a rough and ready meal.

"Don't you mind what he sez," repeated the boy with the short pipe, in allusion to his friend; "he sez anything but his prayers. Come on in and have a warm and a regler good tuck in. Don't you fret yourself about old Mother Corston; *he* knows what she is as well as I do. She's a regler old tiger cat when you strokes her the wrong way of her fur—not that she's a bad un at bottom, mind yer; she stood this tea, and she didn't forget you, neither. Afore she went out she sez to Nat, ' When it's all nice and ready, let him out, and make him comfor'ble.' ' But,' sez I, ' If he's such a hobstinate young genelman as what you says he is, and won't be made comfor'ble, wot are we to do then? ' Why, then,' sez she, ' let him go.' "

"That's what I want to do," I remarked; but not, I must confess, without a yearning glance towards the seat by the cosy fire-place that Nat had placed for me.

" ' Make him take off the things wot I bought for him—his cap and his jacket and his shirt, and his boots—and let him go,' " continued Master Tyler, not heeding my interruption. " ' Never mind how hard the snow is pepperin' down,' she sez, ' don't you be so soft 'arted as to trouble yerselves about his poking away in some cellar or somethink, and being found froze and stiff to-morrow morning; make him take off the cap, and the jacket, and the shirt wot I bought for him and turn him out.' "

"She did not buy me a shirt," I indignantly replied; "it is my own shirt I have got on."

"Well, we know nothing about it; it might be your own jacket as well, for all we know; we only give you her messidge," remarked Master Jerry, with edifying candour. "I tell you what though, young un," he continued, as he drew me into the room and shut the door, "if you're a goin' or if you are a stayin', you're a muff if you don't pitch into the wittles. That's a precious sight a better way of taking revenge on her than sulking."

There was no denying this; half an hour could make no difference to me; and if I was to be turned out without a jacket and cap, or a shirt even, on a bleak snowy evening, I should have a better chance of bearing up against it with a belly full, than empty.

"Besides," reasoned my grosser inclination, "it is only fair that you should eat at her expense if you are hungry; she has kept you shut up for her own pleasure; if you had been at liberty you might have picked up a meal, and so been independent of her." And, smothering my conscience under this spacious bolster, I accepted a seat on the stool that had been placed for me in a warm corner, and very speedily was deep in the enjoyment of the viands my young friends had prepared.

During the meal their conversation was lively and various. They talked of their many enjoyments, of going to the play, and the "stunning" pieces they had there seen, as well as of the sumptuous cook-shop feasts they invariably partook of when the play was over. They bragged of the bran new suits they had at home, and, to show themselves lads of wealth, displayed a handful of shillings and halfpence.

Likewise, to exhibit their contempt for money, they made bets. Nat wagered Jerry half-a-crown that he couldn't balance a fish-bone on his chin, and Jerry losing, he tossed over the sum of two and sixpence to his friend with as little concern as if it were three farthings. Jerry produced a wonderful clasp knife that comprised within its buckhorn handle a miraculous assortment of cutlery—a corkscrew, a screwdriver, a pair of tweezers, a button-hook, and half-a-dozen other articles.

"Tom gave you that, didn't he?" Nat carelessly remarked.

"Yes, he's bought a new un; one with a spring back and a dagger blade," Jerry replied; "awful feller to waste his money, Tom is, isn't he?"

"Oh, I don't know, a cove ought to spend his money when he gets plenty of it," Nat responded. "What's three or four bob to a chap like Tom? He isn't a poor chap like you or me!"

(Poor chaps like them! with at least ten or twelve shillings each in their pocket!)

"He didn't use to be," said Jerry, "but I reckon he won't cock it over us now when he meets us. That's the wust of Tom," continued Jerry, turning to me, "jest because his situation was as good as mor'en a pound a-week to him, he must always be a ridin' the 'igh 'orse. I hate such ways; don't you, young 'un?"

With a nod I signified my assent.

"Ah! it's all very well to talk," said Nat, "but there's no mistake: when a cove wot's always been poor finds hisself a genelman, with lots of tin in his pocket to treat hisself to anything he fancies, it does alter his feelin's. Why, look at Jack—look at *you*, Jack. You think that *you* couldn't look down on us poor coves wot has to work hard for a livin', but you see if you don't think different before you've been in Tom's billet a month."

"Well, he may," remarked Jerry, shaking his head doubtfully; "you've got your 'pinion on it, Nat, and I've got mine."

"Human natur *is* human natur, don't you know?" said Nat, sententiously.

"There ain't no question about that," responded Jerry, "and that's a chalk on my side, in a manner of speaking. Tom always was a toff, don't you recollect, even afore he got to be granny's boy and to be so jolly well off. When he had hardly a bit of 'at to his 'ead he would always wear it cocked a' one side; and many a time I've knowed him spend his last penny in hair 'ile. Now I looks at Jack, here, and I don't see nothink of that in him."

"Except respectin' the hair 'ile," grinned Nat, pointing at my head, which from long neglect was as rough and untidy as a crow's nest, "he's rather extravagant in that article."

"That's the wust of you, Nat," said Jerry, in tones of solemn remonstrance. "You must cut in with a joke, no matter how serious is the toepicks. As I was sayin', I can picter Jack dressed as nobby as ever Tom dressed, but I can't picter Jack a toff. I thinks I sees him now," continued the imaginative young fellow, waving the smoke of his pipe from before his eyes, and leaning back in his chair that he might obtain a full and uninterrupted view of me; "I thinks I sees him now, moulted out of them rags, and wearing a spicy little cut-a-way coat, and fashionable cut corduroys, and shiny boots, and a sprigged weskit with the

silver chain of his watch hanging all across it, and with plenty of money in his pocket to spend or to toss with—all just like a genelman. I can picter Jack all that, and it seems only nat'ral; but, as I said before, Nat, and as I sez again—I can't picter Jack a toff."

"Well, well, we shall see," returned Nat, still dubious, but evidently more than half convinced, by his friend's eloquent arguments; "if it's in him he'll precious soon show it, that's a certain thing."

And these were *my* prospects my friends were discussing with so much frankness and freedom! I, the homeless, friendless, ragged boy, was the envy of these two comfortably established young fellows who could afford to wear good clothes and to carry money in their pockets. In less than a month, so they were good enough to foretel, I should be the proud possessor of a sprigged waiscoat and a watch, to say nothing of shiny boots and a cut-a-way coat of the approved cut!—Always supposing that I became Granny Corston's boy; which meant—— !

It made me catch my breath to think *what* it meant. "Better rags, and a clear conscience," my poor mother had tried hard to impress on me; and I felt quite sure that I should be miserable to do as Tom had done, in spite of all the cut-a-way coats and shiny boots that ever were made. Then, again, what had Luce said on the subject? I would sooner believe poor Luce than either Jerry or Nat, and she had set it down so perfectly out of the question that I could take Tom's place altogether. Besides—and the idea came into my head quite suddenly—if it was such a fine thing to be Mother Corston's boy, how was it that she had not conferred the favour on one of these, her young friends, rather than on me, a strange boy, picked up in an empty house?

"What are yer thinking about, Jack?" Jerry asked presently.

"He's a thinking of **what coloured kid gloves he shall wear on Sundays when he comes into** his property," suggested Nat.

"No I wasn't," I replied; "I was thinking how strange it was that one of you two didn't try after Tom's place, since you knew it to be such a good un."

Nat looked at Jerry, and Jerry elevated his eyebrows and puffed very hard at his short pipe.

"And well enough you might think it strange," he presently replied: "Nat couldn't take it, he's a size too large for the area business; but it would have suited me to a T. Why didn't I try after Tom's place? why, cos I never had the chance; I never heard that he left till this arternoon; and I come rushin' here at once, making cock sure o' getting the job. 'Oh, it's gone,' I'm told! Got told flat to my head that the boy what had been took on was twice a nicer cove than I was—more 'spectable lookin'! Strike me! I never felt so insulted in all my life; arsk Nat wot I said at the time. 'Sez I, I ain't going to be put on one side like that, and, nicer or nastier than me, the new feller will find his nose flattened within two minutes of my meeting him.' But, there, I ain't a chap to bear malice, wot I said was in the 'eat of passion. Give me your hand, Jack; we can't all of us be top sawyers." And he seized my hand and shook it cordially, with a sigh of amiable resignation.

"Well, you may have **Tom's place for me**," I remarked; "I don't want it; I don't think it would suit me."

"Well, there's no knowing," replied Master Jerry, after a pause, and an exchange of glances with his companion, "I ain't a selfish cove, but, after what you've heard me say, you won't be surprised if I tell you that I hope it *won't* suit you. The first day will show you; then you'll give a week's warning, I s'pose?"

"No," said I, "I am going at once. It's a mistake. I ain't the sort of boy she wants; I—I couldn't do it."

"You couldn't do what?" Jerry asked, taking his pipe from his lips in apparent amazement.

"I couldn't be a thief," I boldly replied.

Both boys broke into a fit of laughter so uncontrollable that they were obliged to grasp each other for support.

"Oh! hark at him!" exclaimed Nat, when he had recovered his breath a little. "Innercent! why, sugar and cream is fire and brimstone compared with him. Why, that's the very thing! That's what makes the old woman so sweet on you. You couldn't be a thief! of course you couldn't. It was because Tom couldn't keep his fingers from picking and stealing that he got the sack. The old woman told you about that, didn't she?"

I must confess that this argument bewildered me considerably; but the good resolutions I had formed in the dark closet were not entirely dissipated.

"I'll turn it over in my mind," said I, and come back and tell her to-morrow if I'll take Tom's place. I *must* go now," and I rose and put on my cap.

"Go, then, and be jiggered," said Nat, scowling; "it's nothing in our way to keep you here. Pull off your jacket and shirt, and go at once; it ain't above twenty degrees over freezing pint outside."

"Don't be hard on him," pleaded Jerry,

"you was a young 'un yourself once, you know, Nat. If you *will* go, Jack, I don't mind if I stand a corker before you do; the doctor recommends it to anybody going out in the cold, don't you know."

"What's the use of talkin' Greek to him?" laughed Nat, his good humour returning as suddenly as it had vanished. "A corker is a drop of rum, Jack; it's good against cramp in the stomach and rheumatism and that. We've got to go out in the cold as well as you, so we means to have a drop."

And as he spoke he produced from a cupboard a black bottle, and pouring a drop out in a teacup kindly offered it to me. I had never tasted rum, and certainly it smelt very nice. Besides, there was no denying that the two young fellows had displayed towards me an amount of disinterested kindness not commonly met with, and already I had offended one of them by my perversity; therefore I took the cup and at a gulp drained it, and, much to the amusement of Nat and Jerry, did nothing but gasp and cough for a minute afterwards.

They likewise helped themselves out of the black bottle, and, wishing me luck, tilted the rum down their gullets with no more concern than though it had been water. The spirits seemed to inspire Jerry with even a larger amount of good feeling towards me than previously possessed him. Regarding me compassionately, he observed—

"It *do* seem a precious shame to turn a fellow out without his jacket and shirt such a bitter night as this is."

"What's the use of talking, you know it's got to be done; if he's obstinate," said Nat, shrugging his shoulders, "how can we help it?"

"I was thinking, since he *won't* stop, that if we knew the way that Granny was likely to come home, we might go with him and meet her, and ask her to let him keep the togs; blest if I wouldn't sooner fork out the tin and pay her baek for 'em, and be the money out o' pocket."

This generous avowal on Jerry's part affected me much. I never thought that I should do so, but, with tears in my eyes, I took his hand and pressed it in gratitude.

"Come on then," said Nat, "I know the way she'll come, if that's all; only don't blame me if you gets into a row, that's all."

And off we set. The rum I had drank revived my spirits wonderfully. It was indeed a freezing night; the pavement was slippery as glass; and an icy sleet was fast falling. We walked along steadily for some time, till Nat, descrying a friend on the opposite side of the way, crossed over to speak with him, and in a few minutes overtook us. We went as far as Strutton Ground, where the market stalls and the marketing people were, and there Nat paused.

"It's no use going any further," said he, "she is sure to come this way. Let's have a game of 'touch' to keep ourselves warm."

Undoubtedly the rum had to do with it. I made no objection. Our game consisted in evading the touch of each other as we dodged in and out of the mob; it was capital sport and kept one fine and warm. Presently, however, I felt a "touch" of an unusual heavy character on my shoulder, making me alive to the fact that a fourth person had joined in our game. It was not the touch of a boy, however, but of a tall man, with his coat buttoned up to his chin. We were not in the mob, then, but on the dark and unfrequented side of the road.

"I want you, my lad," the man said, and tightened his grip on my collar.

"What for? what do you want him for?" asked my young friends, running up, with an excellent imitation of wonder in their eyes; "he ain't done nothink."

"I'll have you too, if you don't make yourself scarce; you're all three in it, I'll wager."

I was at first too alarmed to speak; but now I tremblingly asked what I had done.

"Oh, nothing uncommon," sneered the tall man; "only picked a pocket."

"You've made a mistake, sir."

"Oh! Then what do you call this?" And as he spoke the tall man thrust his hand into the loose pocket of my jacket, and drew therefrom a long bead purse with money in it.

While for an instant I stood dumbfounded, Nat gave a whistle of astonishment. Jerry Tyler, however, showed more self-possession. With a sudden spring he ran forward, and with his bullet head butted the tall man with great apparent violence in the stomach, so as to cause him to bow down in dreadful pain.

"Now's your time!" whispered Jerry, plucking me by the sleeve, "run! Follow us, and don't loose sight of us."

---

## CHAPTER IX.

"EVIL COMMUNICATION" TELLS ON ME WITH DEADLY EFFECT—I STRUGGLE AGAINST THE SOPHISTRY OF NAT AND JERRY, BUT AM FINALLY VANQUISHED, AND EAT AND DRINK AND MAKE MERRY WITH THEM.

The vigilant member of the detective police force whom Master Jerry Tyler so unceremoniously assaulted, must have been very badly hurt, since, after the terrific ram he received in the region of his stomach, he was incapable of retaining his hold on my collar, and it was the easiest matter in the world to wriggle out of his grasp. Then he staggered against a lamp-post, doubled up, it seemed, in great agony, and unable to do more than gasp and moan.

"Follow us quick, and keep us in sight!" were Jerry's rapidly uttered words of advice, and I, in my fright, and scarce knowing what I did, obeyed them. Perhaps it should rather be said that, following my instinct of self-preservation, I did as I saw them doing, and exercised my legs to the best of my ability that I might not be left behind.

It was not easy to preserve a rapid flight over the circuitous route the two lads adopted. Not easy for me, at least; as for them, they seemed thoroughly well acquainted with every nook and blind alley that came in their way, and took them one after the other without hesitation or stumbling, while I sustained many awkward tumbles, and bruisings, and buffetings through coming in collision with obstacles, animate and inanimate.

Still I continued to keep them in sight, until, by a roundabout course, we finally arrived at our original starting-post, Penny's Fields, and at Granny Corston's abode.

Nat was leaping and skipping nimbly up the steps, and had the door open in a twinkling, making room for the breathless Jerry to dart past him into the passage. I was about to follow, when I was caught roughly by the arm.

For the moment I thought to be sure that it was the detective policeman, who had recovered his wind and overtaken us, and was ready to sink in terror. But it was'nt his voice that spoke.

"Hullo, my covey! What's your game? You don't live there."

"It's all right, Bob; let him go; it's all right; he's one of us," Nat hastily explained.

"If it's all right it is," returned Bob, releasing my arm. "I didn't know him, and I knows it isn't always pleasant to be seen home by strangers," and laughing at his little joke, he went his way.

We had hurried up stairs and reached a room on the third floor. Nat was the first to speak.

"A pretty thing you've done for yourself," said he, addressing Jerry. "I reckon you'll be sorry for this night's work, Jerry, my boy; I reckon we all shall."

"Well, it can't be helped," responded Master Tyler, wiping his perspiring brow on his coat cuff. "What's done can't be undone, can it, Jack?"

"Oh, ah, it's all very well, but runnin' risks for strangers—for strangers wot,

now they're rescued, can only sit like a stuck pig without so much as a thanky for the cove wot saved 'em! I ain't a jealous chap, Jerry, but I don't believe as you'd a' done as much for me!"

"I wouldn't a' done as much for my own mother unless she deserved it, Nat," replied Jerry, with the air of a person who is not unaware of his superior virtue. "In my 'pinion Jack did deserve it; it was done beautiful. Who was it you eased of it, Jack?"

But as yet I was too aghast to answer questions, and could only look from one to the other.

"Oh! he don't understand; he's not aware of what you've done for him! Oh, no, not in the least! He's a rare grateful cove, isn't he?" exclaimed Nat, sneeringly "We shall see what the perlice say about it in the morning."

"It was that blessed old weasel, Sergeant Nipper, wasn't it, Nat? It was all so sudden that blowed if I hardly saw who it was."

"No occasion to see him, I knowed his voice in a moment. D'ye think he twigged us, Jerry?"

"Rather! When I butted him and he looked down, his glarin' eyes were fixed on mine quite close."

"Ah, then, you're as good as nailed!" exclaimed his friend, sinking, with much dejection, into a chair. "You might just as well take a cool walk in the mornin' up to the perlice station and give yourself up."

"I know it," Jerry replied; "but what was I to do? Was I going to see a pal what could do his work in that there style collared off—nipped in the bud, in a manner of speakin'—without having a go in for his rescue? No, not if it had been

Sir Richard Mayne himself!" And, having delivered himself of this heroic sentiment, he flung down his cap and regarded me admiringly.

I was so utterly breathless and exhausted, that as yet I could not speak. My limbs, my heart, my brain even, seemed to tremble, so that I was only able vaguely to understand what was going on around me.

"I ain't sayin' a word agin the style of the work," remarked Nat; "at the same time there's no denyin' that Jack is a precious artful cove."

"I admires him for it; I likes him for that better'n anythink!" said Jerry, emphatically.

"Oh, rubbish!" responded Nat. "If he's got talents, wot call has he got to be ashamed on 'em? Why didn't he, instead of snivellin' and makin' believe to be wantin' to go home to his mother, like a good little boy, why didn't he up and say when we was chaffin' him about Tom— 'Look here, my fine fellows, I don't know this Tom what you're speakin' about, and I don't know you two either, but if you think I'm a green hand, you was never more mistaken in all your lives.' That 'ud have been straightfor'ard, and we should have knowed the sort of customer we had to deal with."

"That's the beauty on it," returned Jerry; "if he'd been a bounceable cove, he might have said—'Don't talk to me; I can give you a chalk and beat you hollow' — as you could, couldn't you, Jack?"

"Beat you at what?" I asked, bewildered.

"At anythink—from fakin' a cly to crackin' a drum; or, as they say in perlite circles, from pickin' a pocket to burglariously enterin' a dwellin'-house arter

dark. Blest if I can make it out," he continued, regarding me admiringly; "you must have gone to school werry young!"

I was still so amazed with the strange occurrences of the last half hour as to be quite unequal to comprehending the full meaning of what both boys were saying. I must have been bewildered indeed however, if I could not understand the drift of the last observation of Jerry Tyler.

"Beat you at picking pockets! What do you mean?" I cried. "You don't mean to tell me that you think that I can pick pockets?"

"Cert'n'y *not*," replied Jerry, with much gravity; "I don't think that such a nice little boy as what you are could be guilty of such a thing. I've got no reasons for suspectin' you in the least."

"I should be sorry if you had," I exclaimed, earnestly.

Nat looked at Jerry and burst into a loud laugh.

"You admires him for that better'n anythink, don't you, Jerry!" he remarked, ironically.

Jerry's mirth, however, was so uncontrollable that it was several seconds before he could reply.

"How can I help admirin' him?" he cried, at length. "Who can help it? Look at him—isn't it beautiful? Look how nat'ral he can bring the tears into his eyes! Look at his innercent starin'! Look at the Sunday-school egspreshun of his ole mug! Lor', it's the richest thing I have seen this many a day! You're a downy one, Jack, and no mistake!"

"I don't know what you are laughing at," I remarked, sorrowfully; "I see nothing to laugh at—rather the other way."

JACK STEDFAST; OR, WRECK AND RESCUE.    59

Master Jerry was set off again in a fit of laughter, in which his friend now joined. "The simple-'arted little kid!" he cried. "What jury—fathers of families, don't you know—could find it in their 'arts to convict him?"

What could I think, or say, or do? In my own mind I knew that I was quite innocent; but brazening my innocence out of countenance were the hard facts that a purse had somehow found its way into my pocket; that somebody, to all appearance a detective policeman, had found it there, and that my new-made friend, Jerry Tyler (who once before that evening had displayed for me a touching instance of friendliness), had not scrupled to jeopardise his liberty that I might escape the vengeance of the law.

It did not then appear to me what, doubtless, has already appeared to the discriminating reader, that from first to last it was a villanous trap—that nobody's pocket was picked (at least, not at that identical moment, though, doubtless, the long bead purse was the result of some robbery perpetrated by a member of the gang in the course of the evening), and that the "detective policeman" was no other than the friend with whom Nat had crossed the road to speak when we started from Penny's Fields, on our way to meet Granny Corston, and that Master Tyler's assault on the supposed detective was of a piece with the rest of the cruel sham.

Indeed, if I had suspected the true condition of affairs, what evidence had I to produce in support of any accusation I might make? But, as before stated, I had no suspicion. I only found myself face to face with certain evidence that was as inexplicable as it was astounding,

and I could do no other than bury my face in my hands and give way to a passion of grief.

"Now what's up?" Nat asked. "Lordstruth! it's as good as a play in five acts."

"Oh, pray let me go!" I cried. "Perhaps they may find who that purse was stolen from; whoever it was, they'll know whether it was me who took it."

"Oh, come stash it now," remarked Jerry, pretending to check a violent inclination to renew his fit of laughter.

"Yes, that's enough of it," his friend chimed in; "we've had a pooty exhibition of what you can do in the artful line. Now let's be serious and talk about bisness."

"Yes; it isn't a laughing matter, is it?" pursued Jerry. "You see I'm in for it, Jack, as deep as you are. Aiding and 'bettin', don't they call it, Nat?"

"Robbery and instructin' the perlice in the executing of their duty," returned Nat, coolly; "that's what you're in for, Jerry, my boy. It 'ud be about a twelvemonth's hard for you, and a six on the mill for Jack; that's how I reckons it up. It ain't a nice thing for a feller to have hanging over him. We'd better take Granny's advice on the subject, I think."

"But I have done nothing!" I exclaimed; "it is all a mistake, it is indeed."

"Wot's all a mistake?" inquired Nat, opening his eyes wide.

"What a aggravatin' feller you are!" remarked Jerry; "why can't you be serious? A joke's a joke, but hang it all, you know!"

"I'm not joking," I cried, desperately. "I did not steal the purse. I never put it in my pocket. I swear that I didn't!"

"That's what I should do if I was took before the beak," sneered Nat, "and much good might it do me. You might jest as well swear that you saw it jump out of an old woman's pocket into yours."

"So he would," said Jerry, "he's got cheek enough for anythink."

"But it is as true as that I am sitting here alive," I persisted. "Until the policeman found it there, I knew no more about it than you do."

Nat now lost his temper, and frowned ominously.

"Here, I ain't going to stand any more of this, don't you know," he exclaimed, sulkily. "This smells like peaching, this does. P'r'aps you'd like to turn round on Jerry, what was your friend, and swear that *he* put the purse in your pocket! P'r'aps, since you're so werry fond of swearing, you'd even like to go as far as to take your oath that you rather think that *I* had a finger in it." And the honest young fellow laughed derisively at the preposterous suggestion.

"I couldn't swear who put it there," I replied; "I only know that I did not."

"Yah!" put in Master Tyler, "you'll get *my* monkey up if you go on blubbering and acting the virtuous boy any longer. Look out, or you may be made to toot to another tune."

I was in a pretty predicament; all my endeavours to set myself right seemed rather to increase than to mitigate my difficulties. It was quite certain that my two friends believed me guilty, and to be sure, proof was terribly strong against me. I sat silent awhile, still hiding my face and crying.

"Don't stay here if you don't like to," observed one of the lads; "nobody wants to tie you here; you ain't such cheerful company."

"Oh, no, he *daren't* go out," cried the

other; "he won't do that for all his blubbering, you see if he does."

"Why shouldn't I?" I asked.

"Because you're a jolly sight too wide awake. Because you know the meaning of 'companion of thieves,' and 'well known to the perlice.'"

"Are you thieves?" I asked, feeling my cheeks grow pale.

"What bosh! Of course we are!" replied Nat, speaking for himself and friend. "Ask the perlice—ask Sergeant Nipper, the detective, what dropped on *you*. 'They're two of the cleverest young thieves in Westminster,' he'll say. He *has* said so, right to the beak's head, when we've been standing uncomfortably close by to hear it," grinned Master Tyler. "Oh, you've no call to feel ashamed of the company you've fell in with, I can tell you."

I understood the matter perfectly well now—or at least, I thought that I did. In the eyes of all who knew me I was a thief. Heaven only knew the nature of the strange accident that had made it appear so, but so it was. In the opinion of the law I was a thief, and a companion of thieves—of two of the cleverest young thieves in London, as Sergeant Nipper was ready to take oath. Jerry was quite right, I *dare* not go out into the street just at present; if I did, all innocent as I was, I should be pounced on by the police and conveyed to prison.

"I never knowed such a leaky cove as you are," persisted Jerry, as I gave way to a fresh torrent of tears. "*Now* what's the matter?"

"Oh, I'm so miserable, I can't help it!" I answered, sobbing more violently than ever. "I know I am in danger "

"FOLLOW US—KEEP US IN SIGHT," WERE JERRY'S RAPID WORDS."

"Try a little drop more rum, there's some left in the bottle," suggested Nat; "not that you deserve it—— But there, we shall know one another better by-and-bye."

I was so wretched that had they offered me poison I should have drank it. As before, we had each a drop of the fiery liquor, and then it was agreed that before any steps towards avoiding the mischief we had fallen into that evening was taken it would be better to consult Granny. And that important subject being for the time dismissed, Nat's good-humour was restored, and he suggested a game of dominoes. I could not play, but I sat by the fire and watched them, and, so speedy is the corrupting influence of evil company, that as the game progressed I found that I could at first smile and finally laugh outright at the funny things Nat gave utterance to.

The old woman not returning, Jerry went out and brought in a large basonful of roast pork and baked potatoes, and a pot of beer, and we partook of supper quite harmoniously; and what beer was left served my young friends to wet their pipes while, after supper, they told stories, chiefly of their own and their companions' dishonest exploits. They were all funny stories, tending to show how they were only fools who drudged from morning till night that somebody else might fatten on their earnings, and with what impunity a lad might, if he chose, and had the pluck, lead a life of ease and plenty, "working" when it suited him, and lying idle when he pleased.

"It can't be so very hard, when purses tumble out of one pocket into another, by a mere jostle of the elbow in a crowd," remarked Nat, winking at Jerry.

"Pish! let Jack alone, he doesn't need telling how easy it is," returned Master Tyler, laughing. "We should find ourselves on the last form in the school that Jack was the cock of. That's what I said before, and that's what I'll say again."

And did I again strenuously protest against the dreadful insinuation that I was a thief? Alas! dear reader, pity my tender age, and the crushing difficulties that beset me. Make due allowance for the assumed frank good nature, and the specious arguments used by these youths, so old in the ways of crime and iniquity! I did not protest against the insinuations; I did not acknowledge its justice; I merely laughed, and took another pull at the beer: and hearing me laugh, Jerry and Nat laughed too, very heartily, and slapped shoulders, as though something very good had been said or done.

"What did I tell you, Jack," cried Nat, "didn't I say we should understand each other better by-and-bye? You was shy at first, that was what it was; though 'pon my word at the time I thought you was as soft as you pretended to be."

"I didn't," reiterated his companion; "I saw what he was from the first; though, mind yer," he continued, somewhat altering his tone, and speaking slower and with more distinctness, "if it had a been that Jack was innercent always before to-night, it wouldn't make a bit of difference. It don't make any difference, if a fellow makes the 'quaintance of the perlece once or a hundred times. All he's got to do is once to put his foot in it—just as Jack might to-night, for we all has our beginnings, don't you know—and to be seen in the company of what the beak honours us by speaking of as suspicious characters, and it's all over with him. If he was ever so dead set against prigging he'd be bound to keep on with it when he had once over-toed the mark. Nobody can be 'known to the perlece,' and honest at the same time! You know that, of course, Jack."

"It's all the same to me now," I replied, with wicked recklessness.

"Course it is; that's jest what I say," remarked Jerry, with much satisfaction in his voice. "And, now since we've had such a comfor'ble evening, with such a werry pleasant wind up, I think we'd better go, Nat. Ours is werry 'spectable lodgings, don't you know, Jack, and we ain't allowed the viciousness of latch-keys. I should pitch down on the old sofey in the corner if I was you, and let Granny wake me if she wanted me, when she finds her way home."

And after an affectionate "good night," and a friendly promise to see me some time to-morrow, my plain-spoken and obliging young friends took their departure, locking my door and leaving the key outside, for fear, as they said, any other lodger in the house might disturb me.

## CHAPTER X.

### FROM BAD TO WORSE.

THE fire had burnt down to white ashes in the grate, and there was not more than an inch of candle left, therefore it seemed that I could not do better than take the advice of my friends, and lie down on the old horsehair sofa that stood in one corner of the room. I listened intently for the return of Granny, but beyond the occasional wailing cry as of a baby in pain, not a sound was to be heard, and I had no better company than my own reflections.

They were neither creditable nor wholesome, I am ashamed to confess. Jerry Tyler's parting words, "it's all over with you when once you put your foot in it," haunted me long after the two young thieves had taken their departure. "It's all up trying to be honest when once you are booked as being known to the police." It was like the dismal tolling of the bell that foretold the approaching dissolution of all my brave intentions and good resolutions.

It was nothing to the purpose, or so it appeared to my ignorant young mind, that these said good resolutions of mine were not murdered in cold blood and by my own hand, as the reader is by this time aware; so far from that being the case, they had been most cruelly assassinated by my enemies. But I could draw no comfort from the distinction. As far as results were concerned, it could matter little whether I voluntarily abandoned the path of rectitude, or was entrapped thereto by a villanous combination over which I had no control.

Hard fate had bound me 'prentice to a trade I hated, and to a master from whose service I could not run away.

I *had* put my foot in it with a vengeance. I was a thief. The police, to whom, according to Jerry Tyler, I was by this time well known, were prepared to swear it. I had but to show myself in the street to be at once pounced on and borne away to prison! It was, indeed, all over with me.

Had I a friend to counsel me; had honest little Luce even been at hand to explain matters from her simple point of view, I might have obtained a clue to the true position of affairs, and been brought to see clearly that it was *not* all over with me. That although I had done wrong in yielding to the temptations Jerry and Nat had spread to catch me, although I should have resisted their kind-seeming invitation to sit and drink with them and listen to their wicked tales, that at present I had slipped but a little way, and might easily regain my footing. That even though through a terrible mistake I might be clapped in gaol, still there was truth in the words of the preacher poet, who said—

"Stone walls do not a prison make,
Nor iron bars a cage"

for the innocent, however they may become entangled in the meshes of adversity.

But I knew nothing, could think of nothing but Jerry's awful words; and, what was worse, the more I thought of them, the more I was convinced of their truth. There was no use in holding out, I was "in for it." To be sure it was a comfort to think that it was not my fault,

and that if I could have done as I liked I should have steered clear of the ways of thieves and thieving; but the power of doing as I liked had slipped out of my hands, and like a poor mariner wrecked on a barbarous shore, there was nothing left me but to consider my future means of living.

One thing at least was certain, it was possible to be jolly, though dishonest. In their own sleek and contented persons, Nat and Jerry presented unmistakeable evidence of this. In my time I had known many boys as honest as I was; but it had never been my lot to discover amongst them one with half as much money in his pocket as Jerry had, or even with a comfortable suit of clothes to his back.

I never knew a boy who had been to see so many plays as Jerry had, or who could boast of such a luxurious experience in the ways of eating and drinking. Indeed, all the honest boys I had ever known were ill-clad famished boys such as was I, glad to obtain a meal of a quality that Jerry Tyler could afford to turn up his nose at.

Ah ! my dear readers, the pages of a story—albeit such a one as this, which tell of adventures and incidents that are mainly true—are not best adapted for sermonizing; but a few words in season should never come amiss.

Rely on it, that never does the father of lies and deceit show himself in his truest and most detestable colours as when he finds opportunity for taking by the hand and whispering in the ear of a silly young waverer between right and wrong. It is his prime chance; the means by which he gets recruits for his terrible legion. His power, as a magician, is beyond conception. By a wave of his wand he can make ways that are slippery as ice, and yawning with hideous chasms, appear smooth and easy, and inviting to the feet as a dasied lawn; he can conjure before our eyes a smoke through which poisoned berries please the sight, and allure the appetite more enticingly than ripe peaches hanging in the shade of a sunny wall.

So, poor little wretch that I was, I found it as I lay all alone in that den of infamy. The inch of candle was not yet burnt out, but was still gasping for breath, as it were, in its socket, and with it flickered to death my strength of purpose to keep as good as I was able, and presently, with "I don't care—where is the use?" on my lips, I sank to sleep.

And such being the grim key that locked me in with slumber, no one will be surprised to hear that I did not wake in a more creditable temper. It was Granny Corston who came and woke me.

"You were so sound asleep last night, Jack," said she, "that I thought it a pity to disturb you. Come along, breakfast is waiting."

She spoke quite kindly, and as though there had never been the least difference between us. The sight of the hideous old hag at once reminded me of our encounter of yesterday (I had not seen her since, it will be remembered), but the thoughts of it did not rouse me from the sullen fit of "devil may care ism," into which I had fallen.

"All right!" said I; "I'm quite ready for breakfast."

The old woman regarded me with pleasurable astonishment.

"Come, now! that's spoken like a sensible boy," said she. "I like to encourage sensible boys." And she gave me a shilling.

I dare say she was as much astonished that I dropped the coin into my pocket without so much as a thanky. But I wasn't in the humour to thank anybody or anything; only just to go on taking things as they came.

I followed her upstairs to the front attic, where the four-poster and the babies were; and the first object that met my gaze was old Daddy Corston, still with the check apron on, and looking for all the world as though he had neither changed his clothes nor gone to bed since I saw him last; certainly he had not washed himself. He did not have a cane in his hand, however, but a toasting-fork, with a rasher of ham on it.

Seeing me, he grinned maliciously; and I knew that he was thinking of our battle of the day before; but I returned his glance with one of dogged defiance, and, without a word, took my seat before a well-filled plate.

Yet with all my wicked bravado I was somehow afraid to look round. I had not yet seen Luce, but I *knew* she was somewhere about, and presently casting a sheepish eye towards a corner, there she was with one of the little squalling babies in her lap mocking it with the ceremony of washing, her materials being a morsel of yellow soap and about a pint of dirty water in a cracked yellow pie-dish. Heroic ruffian as I was, it was an inexplicable relief to find that the back and not the face of the poor little girl was towards me.

Coffee and rashers and eggs were plentifully provided for me and my master and mistress; but the farce of washing at an end, Luce took her breakfast, surrounded by her three miserable little charges squatted on the floor, with the lid of an old deal box as a table. Neither rashers nor coffee fell to her share, however. A lump of dry bread and a tea-cupful of milk were apportioned her, that she might manufacture "sop" for her famished young brood, and out of the ingredients mentioned, and a jug of hot water, she had to contrive a meal for herself as well as for them.

Once she came to our table staggering under the burden of the second-sized baby, and humbly begged a little more hot water, and for an instant our eyes met; only for an instant, for the next mine drooped shamefully, and I bowed my head over my plate that she might not see the colour my face had suddenly turned. I am afraid, however, that I felt angry as well as abashed. "Confound her!" I thought to myself, "what is it to her, that she looks so sad and sorry at me?" I should have felt much more at my ease with rollicking Nat and lively Jerry Tyler as my breakfast companions.

The meal concluded, Granny beckoned me into the adjoining attic.

"I ain't going to quarrel with you," said she; "what I'm going to say to you is for your good. I've been told about what happened last night."

"Well, what of it?" I answered doggedly.

"It was neatly done, and I like you none the less for it, Jack, but, as *my* boy, you mustn't repeat it."

I knew what she meant of course, but I made no attempt to set her right. "I don't care" was the benumbing influence that possessed my stubborn heart, and I made no struggle against it.

"It mustn't be repeated," said I, echoing her words; "I hear you."

"Because if it is, you'll find yourself in the same wrong box that Tom finds himself in by this time. You understand?"

"What's become of Tom?" I inquired.

"There was only one thing could become of the ungrateful villain," replied the old woman, "he is cooling his heels on the treadmill by this time. Tom had skilly for breakfast this morning instead of the tuck-in you've just had. Ha, ha! he's a penitent thief by this time, I'm thinking!"

"But won't he split on you?" I asked.

"Split on *me!*" repeated the old woman, regarding me in amazement.

"Ah, why not? You split on him," I replied, recklessly.

I fully expected that the old hag would have flown into a rage at hearing me so candidly express my opinion, but she took it quite calmly, though a sinister twitching of her thin lips accompanied her answer.

"I'll tell you why Tom don't split on me, Jack. I'll tell you why *you* wouldn't do it if you was in Tom's place."

"I'd like to hear."

"Because you would not be such a fool. Because when you came out of prison you'd be glad to find somebody at the gate to meet you; somebody bearing no malice, and ready to take you home, and feed you, and make you comfortable."

"To be sure, I should be glad to find that if I was in Tom's place," said I; "but what has that got to do with *you?* You wouldn't take me home—you won't take Tom home, shall you?"

"To be sure I shall. This is Tom's home—this is *your* home. No, no, I punish a boy when he deserves it, but when I once take him in hand I never turn my back on him—never!"

And the old woman chuckled, and regarded me in a way that made me feel uncomfortable, in spite of "I don't care!" and my wicked resolution to be nothing else than a hardened ruffian. Such a vouchsafing of perpetual attachment from such a person was ominous.

"However," continued Granny Corston, resuming her customary hypocritical whine, "we shall get along together very nicely, I'll be bound. You do well by me, Jack, and I'll do well by you. You can do well enough by me if you like. Your little clever bit of business last night convinces me of that."

She laid particular stress on the latter part of this sentence, and looked at me sharply as though she thought I should have something to say in allusion to it. Undoubtedly the wicked old wretch knew all about it—nay, afterwards I found out that she it was who had planned the cruel imposition from first to last.

But I had no suspicion of this at the time, and the only reason why I preserved a surly silence when she alluded to the shocking business, was because, as I said before, I had sullenly resolved that it was no use kicking against stone walls—I was "in for it," and must make the best of it.

"We begin business together to-day," she presently remarked.

"All right," I answered, listlessly.

"Yes. You know the sort of business I mean—that I explained to you yesterday."

"Very well."

"And as I was saying, Jack, you will have nothing to do—at first, that is—but to lead me about, and open gates, and help me down area steps; nothing but that, and keep your ears and eyes open, for any useful article lying about, and for servants coming down stairs. D'ye understand?"

I did, and was glad I was *not* expected to go straight at the trade of thieving. However, I simply replied—

"All right, I'm ready when you are; when do we start?"

"As soon as we're dressed we'll be off,—but you must change your clothes, you know?"

"What, ain't these good enough to go begging in?" I asked, in considerable astonishment.

"Good enough! to be sure they are, you young simpleton; but is there nothing else to consider?" replied Granny Corston.

"Nothing that I know of," I replied, wondering what she could mean.

"You soon get over a fright," and she regarded me a little suspiciously; maybe, perhaps, she thought that I had my doubts of the genuineness of last night's business, and was leading her into a trap. "Don't you know what would happen to you, before you had got as far as Parliament Street?"

"I shouldn't find another purse in my pocket, I hope."

"I hope not; but you would find a policeman's hand on your collar. A pretty mess you'd get into, if there was no one to look after you! You must change your clothes altogether, and wear a different sort of cap from that you wore last night. You'll find all you want in that bundle in the corner. Be quick; it is time we were off."

And the crafty old woman who was solicitous for my welfare, hobbled out, and left me to attire in my new rig. It was not handsome, but it was at least warm and comfortable; and, besides the clothes, there was a good pair of boots—a better pair than it had been the good fortune of my feet ever before to make the acquaintance of. Just as I had finished my array, in came Granny Corston, attired in the old patched cloak, and the enormous bonnet, just as she appeared to my appalled vision when in the empty house she struck a lucifer and revealed herself. I was not afraid of her now, however.

"Come along, Jack," said she, "you had better walk a bit behind me till we get out of this neighbourhood; if any one speaks to you, don't take any notice."

She had with her the well-remembered black wicker basket, out of which a few tapes and bobbins were innocently hanging. Dutifully obeying her injunctions, I walked a few paces behind her. No one took any notice of me, however, until we reached the Strutton Ground end of Penny's Fields, when there stood Master Jerry Tyler, lounging against the wall, and discussing a morning pipe with a friend of about his own age and stamp. Taking off his cap, he bowed until his nose was within a foot of the cobble stones, at the same time audibly whispering behind his hand to his companion,

"The Little Wonder, you know—the chap we was all talkin' about last night."

The person addressed was so startled by the astounding announcement, that his short pipe was nearly jerked out of his mouth; had I been a giant in a show-booth, or a young Indian prince, he could not have regarded me with more apparent awe and admiration.

"Mornin', Jack," exclaimed Jerry, speaking aloud, "if I had my slippers on I'd shy one on 'em arter you for luck.

Ta, ta! be a good boy and do all yer granny tells yer." This last item of counsel being accompanied by a wink and the application of his finger to his nose in a manner that would have highly incensed Granny, had she seen it.

Granny turned her steps towards Chelsea, and I followed, wondering when the business I was engaged for would begin. I was not kept long in suspense. Arriving at a quiet square, she suddenly halted and beckoned to me, and making up to her I was for the moment startled at the alteration in her face.

Hideous as it was at its best, it was now ten times more so. By some villanous manœuvre, of which long practice had made her perfect mistress, she contrived to turn back her eyeballs until only the white was visible, while at the same time she drew down the corners of her mouth as does a person in the extremest depth of grief.

No wonder that she excited compassion! I will not attempt to describe what were my feelings as I gazed on the wicked old impostor. I felt ashamed till my eyes filled with water that I should be a partner in such infamous deception. It seemed worse than downright highway robbery.

For an instant I had it in my mind to run away, but the impulse was speedily checked. Who and what was I? Was I not a boy well known to the police? Was I not at that very moment disguised in clothes that did not belong to me in order to put the emissaries of the law off my track? Was I not absolutely at the mercy of the unscrupulous old woman who stood before me? As I thought of all this, the rising tears were quenched in my bitterness of spirit, and "don't care" again resumed its sway.

"Are you there, Jack?"

"I'm here."

"Lay hold of my arm, my dear boy; guide your poor old blind grandmother from house to house that she may beg her bread." This she said in a whining, tremulous voice, such as I speedily discovered was her "business" voice; and then suddenly assuming her natural tone, she continued—

"Now let us see what you can do. Bear in mind the three simple rules—be very humble, tread lightly, and keep your eyes open."

## CHAPTER XI.

### IS CHIEFLY DESCRIPTIVE OF MY CAREER AS "GRANNY CORSTON'S" BOY.

NEED I describe how as a novice I acquitted myself as the guide of Granny Corston, imposter, cadger, and thief?

With the reader's kind permission I will spare myself that pain. My only consolation—and it is indeed but a poor one—is, that on that first day, and on many succeeding days, in the performance of the shameful duty that was imposed on me, I adhered strictly to the plan of operation as originally arranged between us; in other words, as Granny Corston's boy, my hands were innocent of actual theft; her's were not. Never a day passed that did not see the convenient wicker basket the repository of some plunder or other.

At first the old wretch's dexterity amazed me. My business, as already hinted, was to lead her down kitchen steps and to kitchen doors, and, knocking meekly thereat, beg of whoever responded to buy a stay-lace or a piece of tape of my poor grandmother, who was blind and starving, while she made capital of me by imploring, in the name of Heaven and all the angels, a morsel of bread to succour her poor little grandson, who had not tasted food since an early hour yesterday morning. If the person we were imposing on was charitably inclined and talkative, she was edified with the story of the grandfather who had died of dog-bite, with a graphic description of his final sufferings.

Even this branch of the old woman's trade was despicable and disgraceful enough; but had she been content with what profit it brought, she would not have done badly. So accomplished a cadger was she that as sure as she got audience of a soft-hearted cook or house-maid, a gift of a penny or some food was certain to follow.

As regards the latter, we would rather have been without it: indeed, it was the most troublesome part of the business, for the false bottom of the wicker basket contrived for its reception was not very commodious, and whenever, thanks to the tiresome bounty of good folk, it was full, there ensued a waste of sometimes an hour in hunting about for some retired spot where, unobserved, we might waste or destroy the wholesome food that many a hungry person would have run a mile to secure a portion of.

Never was Granny Corston so cross, never was her mouth so full of oaths and curses, as when, moved by her lies and her whining, people opened their cupboards, instead of their purses, for her relief.

Granny Corston, however, got most of what she wanted when there was nobody by to listen to the tale of her distress and relieve her. When I knocked at a kitchen door and no one opened it from within, it was my duty to raise, the latch, and peep into the interior.

If nobody was there, the old woman recovered her eye-sight at once, and slipping in, she stole whatever portable of value happened to be within easy reach, and immediately slipped out again; and such an adept was she at these nefarious tricks that many a time when, out of the spite I felt towards her, I rejoiced to think that she had experienced what she called a "bad day," I was disappointed to see the array of articles she would produce from the depths of her basket. They were not always of silver. A carving knife or steel would not be rejected, or a pair of snuffers or scissors, for want of anything better.

Her avarice made her daring at times. I have known her extinguish a lighted candle for the sake of appropriating the plated candlestick that contained it.

That was a narrow escape for her, for before she had time to hobble back to the door, outside which I was standing, the servant came down the stairs, and had the candle been alight as she had left it, she must have detected the thief, who was crouched by the side of the dresser. But as soon as she put her head in at the door "Drat that boy!" she exclaimed, "how many more times am I to clout him for carrying my candle guttering out in that wood shed?" And vowing vengeance against the boy, she hurried off to find him, while Granny slipped out and hurried me away in a twinkling, telling me the funny story with great delight as we went along.

On another occasion her desperate greediness might have brought about a dissolution of our partnership in a rather awkward manner.

As before mentioned, I would never witness any of Granny Corston's larcenous exploits; whenever she trespassed over a threshold I invariably turned away until she re-appeared again. Somehow I found a sort of salve for my conscience in the act.

One afternoon, however, finding her chance, she entered a kitchen and did not emerge again as quickly as usual, and this, coupled with the fact of a child suddenly setting up a loud squalling, caused me to peep in. By the fire-side was a cradle with a baby in it and the old woman was hastily busy stooping over it.

Presently, to my horror, she turned about with her wrinkled old face distorted with rage, and catching up a knife that lay on a table, stepped back to the cradle. I could not see murder done, so pushing open the door, I rushed at her, and, clasping my hands about her arms, pinned her fast.

"Come away!" I cried, in a loud, frightened whisper. "You shan't do it! I'll scream out for help if you don't come away!"

For a moment she was startled by the sudden attack, but recovering her presence of mind, she looked over her shoulder, and said in a cool way,

"Aye, aye, come away, Jack, come away quick, or I don't know what I might be tempted to do."

"What's the matter, you imp?" she exclaimed, when we were a safe distance from the house. "What did you interfere with me for? Have you gone mad?"

"I ain't mad enough to stand by and see you murder a baby!" I replied.

For a moment she stood still regarding me quietly, with her bright, beady eyes, and then such a fit of chuckling overcame her as caused her to lean against the wall for support. We had finished work for the day, and were on our road home, and there arrived, before Nat and Jerry Tyler, who happened to be there on business, she related how nearly I had caused her arrest for murder just because she had used a knife to cut a ribbon she could neither untie nor break, and, as she spoke, she exhibited from her basket a baby's silver-mounted coral with the severed ribbon still attached to it.

I saw it all now. It was her rough hauling at the string that had awoke the child and caused it to scream out, and her explanation of what then followed tallied with what I had been eye-witness to.

Of course Nat and Jerry laughed outrageously at my blunder, as they would have done at nothing at all, if they had thought that by doing so they would please Mother Corston. The miserable lickspittles! For all their bragging and vaunting, they were mortally afraid of the old woman.

Jerry was a stout, bull-necked young fellow, strong enough to run a race with Granny Corston a pickaback, but I had seen her crack Jerry over the head with her crutch stick, and wring his small nose between her finger and thumb, and he no more dare resent the indignity than an unbreeched urchin dare question the right of his school dame to chastise him.

"*You*—you gaol fledgling!" Mother Corston would scream out in her passion. "You, who I can clap behind a prison grating any hour, by merely holding up my finger—aye, and keep you there—you dare hold out against *me!*" And the stout Jerry had not a word to say in reply, but hung his head and skulked out, scowling.

I fell rapidly in the esteem of Messrs. Tyler and Nat. It soon became evident that their respect for Tom was based on a more solid foundation than regard for his talents. I have no doubt that the sleight-of-hand accomplishment that led to his ignominious dismissal served to line his pocket in a way that made him a very agreeable companion to the young fellows of his acquaintance. But beyond the few sixpences that Granny at odd times gave me I was without money. They couldn't make it out at all. "It's *you* that's blind, you young fool!" Nat one day savagely remarked, "blind as a brick-bat. Granny ought to lead *you* about, and not you her," while Jerry tauntingly dubbed me the "honest prig."

Meanwhile I went along moodily from day to day, never speaking until I was spoken to, and with never any other than a surly answer for anybody. If I felt resigned to my situation, it was the resignation of helplessness.

One day, however, there came a change in the aspect of my affairs.

"'BUT I HAVE DONE NOTHING,' I EXCLAIMED."

I had returned in the morning from my solitary rambling, moody as usual. My bed-chamber was a sort of cock-loft over the back attic, reached by a ladder in a corner of that apartment. Ordinarily a bit of bread and meat and a little jug of beer were left for me in the attic, and I free to go to bed as soon as I chose. On this occasion, however, on opening the door I saw that there was company—two men besides Granny Corston.

The fellows I had never seen before, but as soon as I set eyes on them, what Luce had told me of the "dreadful" men who sometimes came to borrow Tom flashed to my mind. Two more sinister-looking ruffians I had never seen. Their clothes were well enough; indeed, more than anything they resembled in dress the men of the Sunderland and Shields colliers who used to come ashore at Wapping from their vessels in the Pool. It was their faces that were so repulsive. Scowling, big-jowled, with their small eyes deep set in their heavy brows, and their great ears jutting out from their short-cropped sconces; they made as pretty a pair as ever claimed the hospitality of Newgate. A glimpse of them was enough for me, and I was for closing the door and hastening down stairs again, but Granny Corston sharply called me back.

"Don't go down again, Jack, you are wanted here."

"They can't eat me," thought I, and I returned, though not without a foreboding that something the reverse of a pleasant sort was in store for me.

## CHAPTER XII.

INTRODUCES TWO INDIVIDUALS, WHOSE INTIMATE ACQUAINTANCE IT IS MY MISFORTUNE TO MAKE—THIS IS A SHORT CHAPTER, BUT THE READER MAY PROFITABLY LENGTHEN IT BY READING IT TWICE OVER.

"SHUT the door," said Granny Corston, as I sidled into the attic. "There he is, make the best and the worst of him ; it is the best I can do for you, my jockeys."

One of the "jockeys," regarding me contemptuously, shrugged his shoulders, and expressed his opinion of me in a dissatisfied grunt. The other one put out his great hand and pulled me towards him, and after scrutinising me narrowly, turned me about as though I were some animal he was examining with a view to purchase, and spanned me across the chest and shoulders.

"He'll do as to size," he remarked, turning to his companion.

The other shook his head doubtingly, but taking a foot rule from his pocket, he, too, measured my breadth.

"That's right as far as it goes," he grumblingly assented ; "but it isn't much towards it. Thundering little, *I* call it, towards it, for a tenner."

"That's the lowest," chimed in Granny

Corston, "and half of it down before he stirs a peg."

"I wouldn't haggle a minnit, missis, if it was t'other one,—what was the kid's name? beggar him, I forget it."

"What, young Tom Kipling?" said his mate. "Yes, I'd prefer Tom myself, I must say. This one might do for a common job, but, you see, this one we've just took in hand is rather a delikit job."

"That's the worst of you thick-headed fellows," remarked Granny Corston, bluntly. "You've got a delicate job in hand, and you don't know the right tools for it when you see 'em!"

"We like tools we are used to the handlin' of, Granny," laughed one of the ruffians, significantly. "Young Tom was a good bit of stuff; there was no mistake about Tom. That boy 'll make a name one day, or my name ain't Bender. However, that's neither 'ere nor there. What we've got to consider is this 'ere boy, and, to speak my mind, I don't like the cut of him."

Young as I was, I felt complimented rather than otherwise at the ill-looking rascal's free-spoken opinion.

"Why not?" his friend asked. "You hear what Granny says. He's warranted stanch."

"Why, as to that, Toby," exclaimed Mr. Bender, with an ugly laugh, "there won't be no choice from him atween being stanch and having his blessed young neck twisted, if so be we close the bargain. But what I mean—— blest if I know how to give it a name! But, somehow, he ain't got the look of *our sort*."

"What rubbish! Don't you mind what Bender says," remarked Toby, patting my head encouragingly. "You'll be as good a scholar as the best of us. I'll

wager, when you've had good schooling. Better make a deal of it, Bender."

"Oh, I'm agreeable to anythink," returned the obliging Bender, and with that, he pulled out of the pocket of his trousers a leather bag and clapped it down on the table with a metallic chink.

"Five down, and five on return, I think you said, Granny?"

"Five on return, if it's not later than the night after to-morrow," replied Granny. "you must pay extra if you keep him longer. He's worth a pound a day to me, every ha'penny on it."

"That's right enough," said Bender; "you'll have him back in good time, no fear."

"And another thing I must mention," said Granny, significantly. And she drew Toby to a corner and there whispered into his ear.

"Get out!" exclaimed Toby, with a half laugh, in reply to the whisper. "You ought to know Bender; his bark is worse than his bite always. The night after to-morrow, safe and sound, and without a scratch, I'll warrant."

"Then I'll take the money," said the old woman. Whereon, Mr. Bender, with a discontented growl about whispering of some coves behind other coves' backs, untied the leather bag and counted down five sovereigns into Granny Corston's eager hand.

As the reader must have remarked throughout this haggling and bargain-making for my services, I had no voice at all. It was quite clear that the old woman regarded me in the light of an ordinary article of commerce that she was at liberty to handle as she saw her profit. By this time I had kept the company of miserable young thieves long enough to be aware that this was the ordinary way in which this peculiar business was conducted. The prime aim of boy-thief trainers and "keepers" is to get them so tight in their clutches as to make it impossible for them to demur to any proposition that may be made respecting them, no matter how much of peril there is involved.

They never know—these youthful aspirants to fame, who hope one day to wear the laurels that have descended from the renowned Jack Shepherd, and once pressed the bullet-head of that tremendous thief—they never know what it is to go to bed in the certainty of a night's repose; at any hour their sleep may be broken in on by the dazzling flash of a lantern, and they may be hauled, shivering, to a stone-paved police-cell.

But I had better get back to Messrs. Bender and Toby, lest I incur a charge of sermonizing.

"Then I'll take the money," said Granny Corston, and, having done so, the two men rose, and finishing between them the brandy that remained in the bottle on the table, buttoned their heavy jackets and put their caps on.

"Now, young'un," exclaimed Mr. Bender, "you come with us."

Of course I expected this after what I had heard, but thought it better to demur, or, at least, to appear surprised.

"I don't want to go with you, sir; I would rather stay here."

Mr. Bender regarded me for a moment ferociously from under the peak of his shaggy cap.

"Now look here!" he exclaimed, taking my arm in his rough grasp, "I don't make no secret of what I'm going to say, d'ye see? I sez it before the woman what you

belongs to. Nobody asks you what you wants and what you'd rayther do; you'll have to put off them there airs and graces till it's more convenient to indulge in 'em. I've hired you and I've paid for you; you're *mine* till the day arter to-morrow; mine to do as I like with, d'ye understand?"

It was evident, from his tightening grip on my arm, that he expected an answer.

"Yes, sir, I understand." And so I did, but it was only to strengthen the resolution I had come to.

"That is well. Now look here, if you cut up ugly you'll catch it hotter than you ever dreamt of. If you do your best you'll get a whole sovereign to do what you like with. You're goin' with us and you've got to do jest what you're told, and you ain't got to ask no questions; d'ye understand?"

Again I replied in the affirmative.

"Very well, then; we may as well be off at once," remarked Mr. Bender.

Still with his hand on my arm, though in an assumedly negligent manner, we went down stairs, accompanied by the man called Toby, and into the street, at the end of which, to my surprise, was a light cart and horse in charge of a boy of the neighbourhood, and which, as it appeared, belonged to my new friends. "Jump up," said Mr. Bender; and I jumped up, and was driven rapidly away. And after a half-hour's ride in the direction of the Surrey side of the Thames and through Camberwell Gate, we stopped at a house in a dark street.

"Jump down," said Mr. Bender, who had already alighted. The door of the house was opened and we entered, while Toby went away with the vehicle.

A woman, who might have been Mr.

Bender's wife, brought a light into the parlour.

"Supper's ready, Phil," said she, "will you have it up now?"

"Stop till Toby comes back. D'ye want any supper, boy?"

"No, thank'ee, I'm not hungry," I answered.

"More for them that are," returned Mr. Bender, gruffly. "Go to bed, and make the most of it; you'll be out all night to-morrow night."

The woman who had brought the first candle appeared with another.

"Second floor back," said she, laconically; "you'll find the door open. Mind how you put the light out."

I took the candle and went up stairs and found a room-door open, as she said, and entered. It was a very comfortable bed-room, far more so than mine at Granny Corston's; and, still labouring under a dread of Mr. Bender's threatening manner, I got to bed, extinguished the light as directed, and, with my mind in a wondering whirl as to what would be the upshot of this new adventure, and what was the nature of the business that would keep me out all to-morrow night, soon fell asleep.

Next morning I lay awake a long while before I was called. I have alluded to a certain resolution I had made as soon as I knew that I was to be hired out to assist the two ill-looking men in some undertaking they had in hand. I could have no doubt that they were of the sort that Luce had described as "dreadful," and that their occupation was one that conferred on them the full merit of the title.

What I resolved on was that, come what might, I would disappoint them.

The ruffian known as Toby had prog-nosticated that I should be as apt a scholar as any of them, when I had been long enough at school. But, then, he didn't know how little the schooling I had already received agreed with me. I was utterly sick, as well of my governess as of my fellow pupils. I yearned for a change —for anything to break the miserable monotony of my existence. It is true I had clothes to wear, and food to eat; but that only made matters worse with me. If I had been famished and ragged, as of old, I might have sought excuse therein for obtaining a meal dishonestly. But, to be a well-fed, and warmly-clad thief, or at least a thief's assistant, was a reproach that grew on me heavier day by day.

It is a terrible pass, that which a boy arrives at when he dare not face and return the frank and honest-eyed salute of another boy. Once, when I was taking my customary and solitary walk, I was overtaken by a gossiping boy, who worked at an oil-shop, and who carried on his shoulders a basket with half a hundred-weight of goods in it. He was older than me, but not much bigger; and I wouldn't have given my cap for his entire rig, it was so shabby. But, I tell you what! I would have given all I possessed in the world to have been able to look as he looked, and talk as he talked.

When I got back to Penny's Fields I found that there was a "raffle" going on in the parlour, and a company of about twenty boys and young men assembled, with pipes and beer, and making as much noise as though they were the jolliest dogs in the world.

"Here's another member. Jack'll be in it; come on, Jack!"

"What, young Surly! we don't want him," exclaimed another; "the looks of him is enough to turn the best beer sour as vinegar."

I should have gone in, I think, had I been cordially invited; but as it was I turned away full of bitterness, and with tears in my eyes, muttering to myself, "What good am I? I'd better be like them, and jolly sometimes, than always miserable." I did not think so at the time, but I am sure it was the most fortunate thing that ever happened to me, that I was *not* cordially invited to that raffle. Downcast as I was, it wouldn't have taken much persuasion to have turned the balance in which I was trembling.

I had been miserable ever since, and longing for a change. Now it was at hand, and luckily it came in so ugly a shape that it bid fair to scare me altogether from the treacherous path I had trodden of late. "You are a doomed boy!" was the dismal reflection that haunted me. "You'll go on and on until you end in becoming a great hulking ruffian such as you see prowling about the Fields." Now, at a single jump, I had made the acquaintance of two of the worst-looking villains I had ever pictured, and if I didn't mind I was to be their confederate. "Should it be?" I asked myself, thinking of my mother, of Luce, of all and everything better than myself I had ever met—including even the oil-shop boy, and I resolved that it should *not*, come what might.

I had no plan of escape. To run away simply I knew would be useless. The vague idea that possessed me was that in the course of working out their scheme, whatever it was, and at which I was to assist, I might, at a bold stroke, succeed in breaking away from the men whose

unwilling companion I was, and at the same time prove to the persons against whom mischief was designed that I was really anxious to be released from the life I was leading. This being the case, there was left nothing for it but to put as good a face as possible on the matter, and bide my time.

I ate my breakfast to the satisfaction of Mr. Bender and his friend, and the latter presently complimented me on the evident improvement in my temper, at the same time informing me, that if I did "the right thing," he shouldn't be at all surprised if his mate gave me thirty shillings, instead of a pound. To which, without flinching, I replied, that I had quite made up my mind to do the right thing.

Nothing worth recording transpired until the afternoon, when Mr. Bender and his friend, coming up to my bedroom, to which I should have said I was confined, and puzzled me with the enquiry what sort of a climber was I? To which I replied, that I knew nothing at all about climbing.

"D'ye think you could manage to climb down a chimbley?" was Mr. Bender's next astounding question.

"I dare say that I could if it was big enough," I answered; and at the same time the meaning of that mysterious measuring of my breadth by the two men the night previous dawned on me.

"We mustn't depend on 'daresay,'" returned Mr. Bender. "You had better come up stairs, and do a little practising."

So we went up stairs, and clambered through a trap on to the house roof.

"I s'pose we shall catch it from Granny if you spile your togs by gettin' 'em all over soot," remarked Mr. Bender, with a grin; "you'd best take 'em off; it will make it easier for you. Though that won't do by-and-bye," he continued, turning to his companion; "you had better buy him some sort o' rig—something tight-fitting, Toby. There won't be an inch of space to spare in t'other hole, I can tell you. Now, young un, off with your clothes!"

"What, all my clothes?" I asked, alarmed at the cool proposition.

"All on 'em! of course; you'll come clean with scrubbing, you young fool."

Fortunately for me, it was now the warm spring time of year, and the afternoon was sunny. I had made up my mind to a certain course, and was determined not to stick at trifles. I pulled off all my clothes to my bare skin, while, assisted by Toby, Mr. Bender was busy removing a chimney-pot from a row close at hand. Beckoning me to where he stood, he pointed to the sooty hole.

"Get down here," said he.

It looked such a little hole—scarcely larger than a dinner plate.

"I can't, sir," I replied, "I couldn't if I was to squeeze ever so tight."

"Don't tell me you can't," replied Mr. Bender, "I know better. Pop in now, or I'll ram you down head fust."

It seemed impossible; but Mr. Bender looked as though he meant what he said, and I could but try. It was much easier than I thought. I slipped through until I was as deep as my armpits, and my hands grasped the rough mortary edge.

"I shall fall if I go any lower, sir!" I exclaimed, in a fright.

"You will if you ain't keerful," coolly returned Mr. Bender; "if you ain't keerful you'll go whack down fifteen foot, and break your legs on the iron grate at the

bottom; so, mind yer! Draw up your legs, and press your knees each side of the chimbley, so as to hold tight, and then put your arms in and plant your elbows the same way, and wriggle down Quick now! d'ye hear?"

And to expedite my movements, Mr. Bender administered a gentle kick with the toe of his boot to my hand grasping the edge of the chasm. I did as directed, and found that, excepting for a sensation about my elbows and knees, as though the skin was being rasped off, it would not be impossible to overcome the difficulty. About the centre of the narrow sooty way, however, there was a curve, and there I stuck.

"Get on!" the hollow-sounding voice of Mr. Bender called down the hole; "what are you stopping for?"

"I can't get any further, sir," I called back, though not without difficulty, for, opening my mouth, it was at once half filled with soot. "I can't go any lower, there ain't room."

"Good Lord, Bender! what a spree if the young beggar warn't able to get either up or down!" I heard the charitable Toby exclaim, with a laugh.

"I'll make him move, I'll warrant," growled Mr. Bender, and the next moment I was painfully conscious of a sharp blow on the top of my head, caused by a jagged bit of old mortar he had viciously thrown down.

"Now p'raps you'll get on; there's some bigger bits up here if you don't," exclaimed the cruel ruffian.

I made a desperate wriggle and overcame the obstacle, though at the expense of setting my left elbow bleeding. I could feel the blood trickling down to my fingers. But that only made me set my teeth closer in determination to make the villains repent of their treatment of me if I found the chance.

By the time I had reached the empty grate of the room to which the chimney belonged, the two men were there to receive me, and I thought that funny fellow Toby would never leave off laughing at my deplorable figure. " Oh lor ! it's as good as a pantermine !" he exclaimed, holding his sides, though, as I need not say, with my eyes and mouth choked up with foul soot, and my grazed and painful knees and elbows, I was not quite of his opinion. Mr. Bender appeared better satisfied than his behaviour during the performance of the feat led me to expect.

"There ! I told you you could do it !" he exclaimed, grinning. "You'll do it easier next time, now you know the dodge. Tell yer what, Toby ; we must get him a bag or a stocking or something to pull over his head. It won't do for him to find himself down in the old cripple's room too blinded to see what he's about."

Every word that Mr. Bender uttered I carefully noted, though I affected to be only concerned at the disagreeable prospect of having to "rehearse" again immediately.

"Couldn't I have the bag or something you was speaking of now, sir ?" I pleaded. " I can hardly breathe, let alone see."

So far Mr. Bender relented. He sent Toby downstairs to ask the missus for one of them old "padding socks" of his, and presently Toby returned with the "padding sock," which the innocent reader may be informed is a thick woollen sock made large enough to pull on over a boot, and is used by housebreakers, the delicate nature of whose business makes it essential that they should tread without noise. It was quite large enough to make me a cap that would cover head, face and all, and with a bit of rag bound round my bleeding elbow under Mr. Bender's direction, I again ventured the sooty descent, and this time, as he prognosticated, with much more ease than at first.

Then I was allowed to wash myself, and put my clothes on; all the time wondering what Mr. Bender could mean by that strange observation of his respecting the "cripple" that I should possibly encounter, when, by-and-bye, I put in practice my lessons in the art of chimney-shooting.

## CHAPTER XIII.

### I TAKE A MOONLIGHT TRIP WITH MESSRS. BENDER AND TOBY.

I WAS not to be kept long in suspense.

It was approaching towards dusk when Mr. Bender called me down into the parlour, where, with his mate, he sat indulging over a glass of grog and a long pipe. He appeared to be in an affable condition of mind.

"Have a wet, Jack?" he exclaimed, offering me the rummer.

"Thank you, I don't like spirits."

"A good job for you if you never do; many a bright feller's been brought to the dogs through drinkin'!" and, wagging his head sagely, Mr. Bender raised the grog to his lips and drank two-thirds of it.

"Now to biness," said he. "There's nothing spiles a kid so much as praising him up, but I feel it my duty, Jack, to tell you that you've astonished me. I've been a considerin' over it since your second touch at the chimbley, and my werdict is that you'll do."

"I told you so from the werry fust," remarked Mr. Toby, smiling in self-satisfaction.

"That's the werry reason why there was no occasion to tell me so agin," observed Mr. Bender, with a reproving glance at his friend; and then, turning to me, he continued,

"Yes, you'll do, Jack. There'll be another chimbley for you to climb down to-night."

"What, here, sir?"

"Here be hanged! It would pay to hand over ten pounds for you to come a gettin' down *my* chimbley, wouldn't it? No, it's down a strange chimbley."

I nodded that I understood so far.

"Down a chimbley that leads to a room what ain't empty."

"Not an empty room, sir?"

"No, somebody lives in it, somebody whose acquaintance we want particularly to make!" grinned Mr. Bender. "He's a cripple."

"That's why we are 'bliged to get at him down the chimbley, Jack," remarked the facetious Toby, "being a cripple he can't come down and open the street door for us."

"But I should be afraid," I exclaimed. "If I got that way into his room he might kill me, very likely."

"Don't I tell you he's a cripple?" returned Mr. Bender, with an ugly frown. "Open your ears, now, and I'll tell you how the case stands. This old chap what we're speaking of is a diamond polisher. He's one of the cleverest in the trade, and does work for some of the best shops, though he's got no use in his legs, and can get about no faster than a tortoise. He won't trust anybody to sleep in the house with him, he's such a suspicious old warmint; not even the man who works with him all day, though when the man leaves in the evening it takes him half-an-hour to creep as far as the street door—which is iron lined from top to bottom—to bolt and chain it after him."

"Likewise the door of the room what

he works in, and sleeps in, is plated jist in the same way, so that the knowingest cracksman going can't hope to touch it," chimed in Mr. Toby. "He locks and bars himself in this room, and he thinks that he's all right; d'ye understand?"

"He thinks that he's all right," I repeated, with my heart quaking at what evidently was in store for me."

"Yes, he thinks so, but he's mistaken," remarked Mr. Bender, bestowing on me a wink full of meaning. I nodded, not knowing what else to do. "We are going to prove to him to-night, that when he thinks he is all right he was never more mistaken in all his life."

I couldn't say a word in reply, again I nodded.

"We know all about him," continued Mr. Bender, "we know that he keeps his work—the diamonds he's got to polish—in a black japanned box, in a drawer in his work-bench, and we know that the drawer is never locked."

"The drawer is never locked?" I repeated.

"It is that box that we wants. You are going down his chimbley to get it for us. You are going down the chimbley with a little bag round your neck, and you're going to slip the japanned box into it and climb up again to where we are, on the roof; and if you does it clean and neat, you are going to have thirty bob all for yourself to do as you like with."

"Besides the certainty of other jobs which will pay you werry nearly as well," chimed in Master Toby.

I was so completely dumbfounded and horror-stricken, that for several seconds I could do no more than gaze from one to the other.

All along I had been making up my

mind for some desperate undertaking—an undertaking in which the two burglars would join—such as breaking into a house where there were people to be alarmed and put on their guard by a bold movement on my part. But in the present case, as it was put by the two ruffians, of what avail would be all my honest intentions?

There could be no doubt that when a man took all the precautions the cripple took, to guard the property in his possession, it was hardly likely that he would permit it to be taken from him very readily. I felt quite sick with terror.

"I—I'm afraid, I don't think——"

"You don't think what?" interrupted Mr. Bender, abruptly; "out with it."

"I don't think I could do what you ask, if I was to try, sir."

"If you was to try! that's good, too!" And Mr. Bender laughed ironically. "Of course you'll try, and your best, too, or it will be the wust for you. I'll chance the rest; you do your best and I won't grumble."

"Besides," chimed in his companion, "you don't know what you're saying when you talk about not being able to do it; you have done it, or as good. And as for being afraid, why there's no more call for fear than there would be in robbing a bird's nest."

"Not a bit!" growled Mr. Bender; "he's a cripple, don't we tell yer, and can't get along faster than a snail. Why, before he could get out of bed, you could do the trick and be up the chimbley again twice over. That's supposing he wakes, which he won't do if you're careful. Besides, a thousand words won't fill a bushel—you've got to do it."

My will was good to dispute this point

with Mr. Bender, but I saw how useless it would be. If I meant to carry out the desperate resolve that had upheld me since last night, it must not be by openly thwarting the will of the ruffians in whose hands I was.

Tremendous as were the odds against me, still there was a chance.

Even if things came to their worst, and I was compelled to descend the chimney to the diamond-polisher's room, I might possibly make a friend of the cripple. At all events, there was no other hope for me that I could see.

And taking this view of it, I said no more, but in silence listened to the minute instructions Mr. Bender had to give me, as to the position of the cripple's bed, as well as of the bench, in the drawer of which the precious japanned tin box was deposited.

How the robbers managed to obtain such exact information is, of course, more than I can say, but Mr. Bender was actually able to inform me that no doubt there would be found nothing on the hob but the saucepan in which the old diamond polisher boiled his gruel, and that I must be careful that I did not kick it over into the fender.

After making me repeat word for word the instructions I had received, so as to make quite sure that I was master of them, I was dismissed to my bed-room to wait for night.

What was my condition of mind during the four hours that intervened between that time and ten o'clock I will not attempt to describe.

Once only were my meditations disturbed by the entrance of Toby, who came and rummaged for something he wanted in a box full of the strangest looking "tools" I had ever seen. It was growing late then, and the moon was shining in at the window. Wishing to maintain a show of sociability, I remarked that it was a fine moonlight night.

"Curse the moon!" replied Master Toby. "I shouldn't wonder if it spoilt our plant to-night after all."

But I didn't curse the moon. Maybe there was a chance for me in this direction! Would the expedition, so full of peril for me, be postponed on account of the inconvenient fineness of the night?

Alas for my vain hopes! Within half-an-hour Toby looked in and told me to look sharp, for the cart was at the door.

"Slip into these togs," said he, throwing a bundle into the room; "they'll be handier than them you've got on."

I opened the bundle and discovered a greasy old suit of corduroy of the tight-fitting pattern, known as the "skeleton," together with a small bag of light gauze with a piece of elastic run in the hem of it, and the use of which I was at a loss to understand. Mr. Toby, however, enlightened me.

"You'd no occasion to put that on now, don't yer know," said he, looking in again, and impatient at my delay. "That's to put over your head by-and-bye; it'll keep the soot out, and you can see through it all the same. My eye, Jack! you do look a swell!"

I thought so too, and wondered at the figure I should cut riding out in a cart on a moonlight night.

But I need not have troubled myself on this score. I was not to ride on the cart seat. There was a couple of sacks on the floor of the vehicle, and bundling me in, neck and heels, Mr. Bender threw the sacks over me and told me to lie quiet.

"WITH A CRY OF MORTAL DREAD, HE SAT BOLT UPRIGHT."

Which way the cart was driven was, of course, under such circumstances, impossible for me to say. It was driven for a long time, however—an hour or more. Then the horse, which had been at a sharp trot all the way, was brought to a walking pace; presently it stopped entirely and the two men got down.

Mr. Bender came to the tail-board of the cart.

"Don't move," said he; "don't stir till we come back; we ain't going far, not a stone's throw, so no tricks mind."

I think, had Mr. Bender known how seasonable his warning threat was, he would have put it in a stronger form. Soon as the horse began to walk, betokening that our journey was drawing to an end, I lay in a perfect ague of fear, trembling in every limb. Laying his hand on the sacks that covered me, the burglar discovered this.

"You're cold," said he; "here, take a mouthful of this."

And taking a flask from a side pocket, he unscrewed the top of it and held it to my lips. I don't know what was the liquor it contained, but its reviving effect was wonderful. It made me feel quite bold.

Bold enough almost to disregard Mr. Bender's threatening words, and scramble over the back of the cart and run for my life. But one consideration restrained me.

When Mr. Bender was feeling for the flask, he displayed, as though by accident, the butt end of a pistol protruding out of the side pocket. If I scrambled out and ran, what was easier, nay, what was more probable, than that a ruffian of his mould would send a bullet after me and then drive away with his companion, leaving me to die in the road?

I so far disregarded his injunction, however, as when he was gone, to raise my head and peep out. It was not so light as it had been, for now the sky was clouded and the moon frequently quite obscured.

I could make out, however, by the splashing sound, that the dark lane we were in skirted the river. Indeed, far away over a broad black waste, there appeared the arched twinkling lamps of a bridge.

In about ten minutes Mr. Bender appeared again.

"Tumble out," he whispered; "no funking now. It will be all over, and we shall be spinning home again, in ten minutes if we have any luck."

He lifted me out of the cart, and taking my hand, ran along with me noiselessly until we came to a wall, and there we found Toby.

It was the side wall of a house—a low house of two floors—and Toby held in his hand some sort of rope contrivance that seemingly was attached to the top of the wall.

"All right and tight?" asked Mr. Bender, in a low voice, as he took the cords and gave them a shake.

"Right as a trivet; I've been up as high as the parapet, so I know," returned Toby, confidently.

"Up you go, then, Jack! Mind what I told you about funking! Right to the top; I'm after you."

There was no use in hesitation. The ropes I had noticed formed a ladder that led somewhere on to the roof above.

Screwing up my courage, I placed a foot on the bottom round while the men held the ladder away from the wall, and the ascent was not very difficult. When

I reached the summit there was moonlight enough to show me that the ropes were hitched over the edge of the stone coping by means of strong iron hooks.

I stepped on to the roof, and the next moment the grating of the hooks against the stone told me that Mr. Bender was coming up the ladder, and in five seconds his bullet head, surmounted by a close-fitting seal-skin cap, appeared in view.

The roof was of the pattern technically known as the " ridge and furrow," and atop of the ridge was a row of fine, square, old-fashioned chimney pots.

Mr. Bender, first pulling a pair of " padding socks " over his hobnailed boots, noiselessly crawled up the slanting tiles, beckoning me to follow him.

I did, with legs that shook so, that some crumbs of mortar, displaced, went rattling down with a hollow sound into the gutter, causing Mr. Bender to turn his head and shake it at me with a threatening scowl.

Presently, however, we both stood, crouching against the chimney-stack.

" Where's your cap?" Mr. Bender asked, in a business-like tone.

I produced it from the pocket of the corduroy trousers.

" That's the ticket; have it ready to slip it over your head. Here's the bag to put the box in; let it hang round your neck and open like that, it will be handier; and see here, I've got another little contrivance what'll help you."

For an instant I could not make out what the contrivance was.

It was a broad strap with an iron buckle, and in the strap were two strong loops of leather. Mr. Bender fastened the strap round my waist, buckling it behind.

This arrangement completed, he produced from his capacious side pocket two long pieces of stout cord. Observing my look of astonishment he remarked, with a grin—

" You needn't look so scared, Jack, I ain't going to baulk Jack Ketch of what'll be his job one day if you are lucky. These are only a pooty little pair of reins. I'm a goin' to fit on to you."

My hopes, glimmering but feebly before, now sank dead, as he proceeded to attach the one end of each cord to the loops in the waist-straps before mentioned,

" There !" he remarked, pleasantly, as he pulled at the strings, to make sure that they were secure, " it isn't many coves as would take so much trouble over a boy wot was only engaged for a odd job, eh ?"

" What are the strings to be used for ?" I asked him, although I had a foreboding that I knew too well.

" What are they for ?" replied Mr. Bender. " Well, they're for all sorts of useful things. You'll find 'em handy when you're down the chimbley, don't you know and have nailed the swag; you might feel flustered and ork'ard about climbing up again, but I shall be able to help you. I shall bide up here, and I shall hold the cords in my hands—they're long enough, d'ye see, to let you cross the length of the old man's room, and when you're ready just you give your end of the strings a jerk, and up you come in a jiffy ! Don't you think it a clever dodge ?"

I could not speak, my heart was too full; I nodded my acquiescence as to the ingenuity of Mr. Bender's plan, but tears of bitter disappointment started to my eyes. Now, indeed, there was no hope for me—I was at the burglar's mercy.

I was to be held in leash—driven in harness to the devil, Mr. Bender holding the reins !

## CHAPTER XIV.

IN WHICH I QUALIFY MYSELF (THOUGH AGAINST MY WILL) FOR MR. BENDER'S PRAISE AND ADMIRATION.

"WHAT are you tooting about?" Mr. Bender asked, suspiciously, as he applied his thumb to my eyes, and found that they were wet; "d'ye mean to sprout the white feather at the last minute?"

With desperate resolution I dried my eyes.

"I'm all ready, sir; I'm all right," I answered.

"Oh, there's no mistake about you're being right," returned the burglar, in a growling whisper; "you won't get away, if that's what you mean. These cords are strong enough to bear you; and, cuss me, if I wouldn't drag you through a hole no bigger than the neck of a wine bottle rather than let you go."

Suddenly I recollected that, in changing my clothes before we started, I had not neglected to shift my knife from my own pocket to one in the trousers of the skeleton suit.

But, alas! so dazzling was the gleam of promise that the recollection afforded me, that, inadvertently, I clapped my hand where the knife was. Mr. Bender detected the movement instantly, and clapped his hand over mine.

"What's the matter?" he asked. "What have you got there?"

"Nothing, sir; only—only my pocket-knife, sir."

"Ah, you'd better leave it with me," grinned the ruffian; "a bold young cove like you might go a slittin' the old gentleman's wizen, if he cut up rough,

and we don't want to make a murder job of it if we can help it. Take it out."

There was nothing for it but to give it to him, and to place myself in his hands, helplessly and entirely.

I can't say that it cost me a severe pang to do so, now that matters had taken the unexpected turn they had. Everything seemed to go so completely against me that I quite gave up, and didn't care what became of me.

"Come, we haven't any time to cut to waste," said Mr. Bender; "there's the moon a-breaking out again; confound it, be quick. You'll find the chimbley a little wider than the one at home, and easier to get down."

With the courage of despair I climbed lightly to the chimney top, and pulling the gauze cap down over my face, lowered myself in at the mouth of the pot.

"Hold hard!" exclaimed Mr. Bender, in a low whisper; "let's be quite sure you haven't forgot anything; "whereabouts is the work-bench?"

"At the further end, right hand side of the fire-place."

"And where's the drawer?"

"Underneath t'other side of the polishing lathe."

"Good; and whereabouts is the head of the bed?"

"Against the wall, in the centre of the room, in a line with the fire-place."

"All right. Now be off, and remember this," continued he, impressively; "I'm up here, and I've got yer."

I was but too painfully aware that he "had me," and that I must do all that he bade me. There was a terrible fascination about the ruffian, when you came face to face with him, that was more sufficient to vanquish any amount of self-will a boy, young as I was, might possess.

I set my teeth together in grim despair, and, stealthily as a cat, made the descent.

As Mr. Bender had informed me, the chimney was of larger dimensions than the one I had practised in at the burglar's abode; moreover, it was not so choked up with soot.

But he was out in his calculation respecting the gruel pot.

It was not on the hob, it was in the fender; but when I set my naked feet on the grate, it was so hot, that a slight expression of pain escaped me. My head, however, was too far up the chimney for any one in the room to have heard it.

The burning pain caused me more unpleasant sensations than one,—the hot stove betokened that the occupant of the room had, not long since, used it for his fire.

Was he now a-bed? and, what was of much more importance to me, was he fast asleep?

I listened intently, but not a sound was to be heard but the breathing of the burglar, who evidently was on the alert to listen his hardest at the mouth of the chimney.

Screwing up my courage, I slipped down off the hob into the room.

The moon shining out from behind a cloud bank, and, shining in at the window, revealed to me the contents of the chamber quite distinctly—as distinctly, that is, as was possible to my vision, impeded as it was by a veil of gauze begrimed with soot.

I could make out that the place was scantily furnished, and that on the truckle bed an old man was sleeping, his gaunt shape fantastically visible through the thin bed-covering, and his grey head reclining on the pillow.

So quietly had I executed my task so far, that he had not moved, but still slept on, his sharply worn features and his closed eyes dimly revealed in the moonlight.

Hazily showing by the bedside, exactly in the position in which Mr. Bender had described it, was a work-bench, with a polishing lathe attached to it.

At the end of the bench, just beyond the lathe, was a drawer with a key in the lock of it, and, so close to the bed, that the old man might have reached it easily with his outstretched arm.

Close against the old diamond polisher's head, and shining distinctly in its little pink pocket against the wall, was his old-fashioned silver watch, and, in the dead stillness, it seemed as though its ticking must wake him, were he sleeping never so soundly.

Indeed, so profound was the quiet, that I stood as I had alighted on the hearth-rug, afraid to move a step forward; but a gentle jerking of my leading-strings roused me to desperate action.

Acting on the instructions I had received, I dropt softly down on to my hands and knees, and, Mr. Bender slacking out the cords as I crawled, I gained the bedstead, and then the bench.

A little further, and I was well under the drawer in the bench in which the precious box was deposited.

I reached up my hand, and quietly pushed at the back of the drawer.

It yielded, it was not locked.

With my heart running a race with the loud-ticking watch, I worked the drawer gently forward, until it stood out half way.

Then I raised myself a little, and, feeling over the edge of the open drawer, my finger-tips encountered the cold smooth surface of what I was seeking.

But it gave me no thrill of delight, but a horrible and deadly sensation—very, indeed, like that which followed my touching the forehead of drowned little Polly Sabine, and I paused in a sweat of terror.

But had Mr. Bender been by my side instead of on the house-roof, he could not have exhibited a more intimate knowledge of my movements.

Again he gently agitated the cords, and I heard them stirring on the ground like snakes disturbed in their sleep.

I rose half up, and the next moment the jewel-box was lifted from its resting-place; it was in my hands; it was safely deposited in the bag of wash-leather that hung round my neck!

Then came the snapping of the screw—the screw that a turn at a time had wound up my courage since I parted with the burglar on the house-top.

It was as though I had been blindly groping in the blackest darkness, and a dazzling light had suddenly shot down on me.

*Now*, then, I was a thief—a robber—a house-breaker!

A burglar as bad as the two men whom half an hour since I felt good enough to despise!

I felt as though I should choke—as though I was in deep water, and the weight in the bag about my neck was a great weight of lead, bearing me down and drowning me.

I couldn't bear it. I gasped, as though for breath, and, with a cry, sank with my face to the mattress on which the cripple was lying.

The sound awoke him instantly, and with a cry ten times louder than mine own—a cry of fright and mortal dread— he sat bolt upright in his bed, and as I hastily raised my head our eyes met.

I can only imagine how his horror must have increased at the grim figure I appeared to him in the dusky light that filled the room, my tight-fitting suit, powdered over, and patched with black, and my hands clasped together beseechingly.

He was about to cry out again, and shrink away from me as though to escape out of the bed on the further side, when, in my flurry and bewilderment, in my terrible anxiety lest we should be overheard by the burglar I knew to be listening at the chimney-pot, I ventured to pluck him by the sleeve with one hand, while I clapped the other over his open mouth.

But he contrived, nevertheless, to pull my hand aside and shout, "Murder! thieves!" pretty loudly.

At the same instant, I was made aware that the alarming sounds had reached Mr. Bender's ears, for the cords attached to my waist-strap were shaken violently.

"Pray don't make a noise, sir," I whispered, loud as I dared, and clambering up on to the bed to bring my voice closer to his ear. "Pray be quiet. I'm only a poor boy that can't help himself. I can't hurt you; I wouldn't if I could."

But the poor old gentleman was too affrighted to understand a word that I said, and kept continually bawling at a rate that must speedily have alarmed the neighbourhood.

"You will spoil all if you won't listen to me," I cried, in despair. "I am not what I seem—I am not, indeed!"

And, thinking to lessen his fright, I tore the gauze covering from my face.

"You are a thief—a burglar! What else can you be? Help! Police!"

"No, no, I am not. Hush! I must not speak loud, or he will hear me."

"Ha, you mean your fellow robber!" And then, with a desperate attempt at calmness, he continued,

"But, for once, you are mistaken! You will not find enough in this poor little place to repay you. What could you expect to find here, eh?"

"Never mind that," I urged, earnestly (for Mr. Bender from time to time was impatiently shaking at my leading-strings), "never mind that. I am not a thief. They wish to make me one, but they shall not if I can help it."

And I burst into a passion of tears that did more than anything else to convince the old fellow that I meant what I was saying.

"If you can help it!" he repeated, in amazement. "How came you here, if you couldn't help it? Answer me that. Boys who don't want to rob, don't break into people's houses in the dead of night."

"But I was forced to it, sir. Oh, pray help me! He is waiting on the roof now, expecting me to climb up the chimney again."

Unfortunately, however, for the success of my plan, the uncertain moon just then shone broadly on the window, and by its light the old man saw the wash-leather bag round my neck, and, as I suppose, recognised the shape of the square bulk within it. Then he cast a startled glance to the drawer in the bench, and saw that it was wide open.

Instantly his assumed calmness gave place to despair, and, with the furious yell of a madman, he flung himself towards me so savagely, that involuntarily I started back, and with such precipitancy, as to lose my balance and go toppling off the bedstead down on to the floor, at the same time uttering a loud cry of fear.

Mr. Bender must have heard both, and was evidently thereby thrown into a state of great alarm.

Giving a sudden tug at my reins, that drew me at least a yard over the floor towards the fire-place, he bawled down the chimney, with a most unearthly and startling effect—

"Quick, Jack, quick! Have you got it? Pop it in the bag, Jack."

I could only reply by a loud cry of distress, not knowing which way to turn or what to do.

"Hang you! do you want all the parish to hear you?" came the bellowing voice down the chimney again. "Clout him over the head with the poker, you young fool! Muzzle the old hound somehow! Oh, Lor', I wish that *I* was down there!"

From his first hearing the mysterious voice overhead, the desperate fury of the old diamond-polisher had increased, and he bawled "murder" and "police" unceasingly.

And here the great precautions he had taken for his security told seriously against him, for the window was tightly hasped, and the door, as before mentioned, was cased with iron-plating, and chained and bolted.

He might almost as well have been in a box with the lid shut down, for all the sound that could escape from the chamber.

However, the old man did something else besides cry out.

He had shuffled, as well as his crippled legs would let him, off the bed, on the side opposite to that I had tumbled from, and was wriggling his way towards a corner cupboard. Presently he reached it and opened the door, and instantly I espied, lying on a shelf within it, a table knife.

The sight of it nerved me with desperate hope; could I get hold of it, there might still be time for me to release myself from the cords that held me, and then I might set my burglar companions at defiance.

I sprang forward, just as Mr. Bender, with an awful oath, was commanding me to come up with or without the box, unless I wanted to be left behind.

Just, however, as I reached the cupboard, and stretched out my hand to take the knife, with a cry of exultation the old man turned about, and instantly a sudden flash dazed my eyes, and a tremendous bang sounded in my ears, and I felt a burning sting in my left thigh.

I was shot. It was to procure a pistol that the old diamond polisher was in such haste to reach the cupboard.

"D—— me! he's shot the boy, I think!" I heard Mr. Bender's rough voice exclaim; and then in a sharp, imperative tone, he continued, "Now for it, if you can; up you come!"

I was so bewildered with pain and fright that I was conscious only of that commanding voice, and instinctively obeyed it. As well as I was able I staggered towards the fire-place, and, somehow, contrived to place my feet upon the hobs.

Certainly I had not sense enough to know what I was doing, or, without doubt, I should have disencumbered the wash-leather bag of its contents, and so appeased the terrible fright of the poor old man whom I had robbed, and who, crying till his cracked voice was hoarse, "Thieves! thieves! thieves!" came writhing along the floor after me.

By the amount of cord he was able to haul up it was evident to Mr. Bender that I was doing as he told me.

"Now, then, help up, if you've got any life in you, cuss you!" he exclaimed, applying his gigantic strength to the task of pulling me up.

I tried, but my strength failed me completely.

"Hang your arms down straight, you lazy whelp, if you can't do any better," roared Mr. Bender; "I must have been an idiot to have trusted such a little cur."

The burglar cursing me a'top, and the plundered old man shrieking out mad imprecations after me at bottom, and me dangling bleeding and half stifled in a sooty chimney, leave on my memory a picture I am not likely ever to forget.

Had there been another loaded barrel to the pistol I have no doubt that my unhappy legs would again have suffered; but it was not so, and having crawled as far as the grate, all the furious poor old fellow could do was to beat the hobs and bars with his naked fists, and shriek and implore us not to rob him.

But, in a few seconds I was high out of his reach, and, by a few more vigorous pulls, my head and shoulders appeared out at the chimney pot.

"Curse you! it would have been an infernal good job if you were shot dead!"

This was the salutation with which the

burglar greeted me, as, taking me roughly by the shoulders, he lifted me out on to the roof.

But judge of his amazement, his inexpressible astonishment and delight, when he discovered that my errand had not been profitless,—that the prize was secured and lay snug in the wash-leather bag.

"My eyes! here's a stroke of luck!" he involuntarily exclaimed, as he dropped me down on to the tiles while he lugged the bag from my neck. "Bust me! if I ain't struck all of a heap!"

"What's the matter? Be quick. You'll repent if you don't, I tell yer!"

It was Mister Toby that spoke.

Alarmed for the safety of his friend, he had climbed the rope ladder and now appeared with his uninviting countenance just visible above the stone coping.

"Matter? Here, step up, and lend a hand, Toby. He's got it, by ——!"

"To be sure he has," growled Toby, thinking that his friend alluded to my injuries, and, in his own mind, was disposed to resent what he considered the unfeeling tone in which Mr. Bender made the announcement. "I knowed he'd get it. Didn't I hear the barker? There's no call for you to be so jolly pleased about it; we shall catch it from Granny."

"Hang Granny! that isn't what I mean. He's got the box, man—brought it up in the bag with him."

"No!" replied Toby, in ecstacy, as he skipped nimbly on to the roof.

"Fact, by ——! Isn't he a young trump! D—— if I could believe it! Stuck to the old hunks and fought him for it. I heard 'em, and, like a thickhead, thought that the little 'un was piping (betraying us). There's a boy for you! Cuss me, if I ain't proud on him!"

This little conversation, of which, in my half-insensible condition, I was a passive hearer, occupied much less time in its delivery than it takes the reader to read it; and, while they talked, they were busy as they could well be, for all the while the old diamond-polisher was shrieking up the chimney.

"He is hurt," Toby tenderly exclaimed.

"Oh, blow it, Bender, here's one leg of his corduroys completely sattirated!"

"His thigh's broke, I think," replied Mr. Bender, handling me as considerately, and carrying me in his great arms as easily, as though I were a baby. "But he shan't die for want of physicing—hang me, if he shall! I'd sooner have give a fiver than it should have happened, though! Leave him to me, Toby; I don't want no help. Down you go. Say when you're down, and hold the rope. Quick! My eyes! the old gentleman is keeping it up, ain't he?"

"Shall we leave the ladder?" asked Toby, as Mr. Bender reached the ground with me in his arms.

"Oh, hang the ladder, it can't tell tales! Now for the cart, and home in less than an hour!"

And that was the last of my recollections for a very considerable time.

## CHAPTER XV.

IN WHICH I RETURN TO CONSCIOUSNESS AND RENEW MY ACQUAINTANCE WITH LUCE, TO MY ULTIMATE PROFIT—IT IS TO BE HOPED.

WHEN I came to my senses, I found myself lying in that identical back attic in the old house in Penny's Fields where my hiring had taken place, and where I first made the acquaintance of the two burglars, Bender and Toby.

Considerable pains had been taken to make me comfortable.

The old sofa before mentioned was ousted in favour of a comfortable cot, with pillows and bed-clothing passably clean, and there was a cheerful fire burning in the grate.

About the entire chamber there was an air of tidiness as foreign to Penny's Fields as would have now appeared its ancient buttercups and daisies cropping out of the stagnant mire of its kennels.

I made these observations of the chamber's unwonted tidiness as I lay dreamy and languid, and but half awake, in a manner of speaking. It was some considerable time before I was sufficiently roused to identify myself as being the chief feature in the picture. I was in no pain, and experienced no other unpleasant sensation than that of thirst.

I suppose I made some slight sound with my dry lips, for immediately I was aware of somebody stirring in the room, and then a face was bending over me.

It was Lucy's face.

I recognised it at once, and then, like the sudden lifting of sluice-gates, a crowd of ugly recollections came back to me in a torrent—a tumultuous, roaring torrent, in which were all the ingredients of the terrible events recorded in the last chapter, but so jumbled and tangled together that no one feature appeared distinctly. My head was no longer easy, my eyes felt burning hot, and a cruel, throbbing pain beset my temples. I tried to sit up in the bed.

"Hush! you musn't get up. The doctor said that you must lie quiet still." And Luce gently laid my aching head back on the pillow.

"But I *must* get up," said I, pushing away her hands impatiently. "I can't lie here. I won't stay in this place; I'd sooner die."

"Oh, *do* be quiet, that's a good boy! do be quiet till she comes back. I'm only minding you for a little while, and she's sure to beat me for disturbing you."

And poor Luce wrung her thin hands together, and tears started to her eyes. I was at once subdued.

"I'll lie quiet," said I, "don't cry. I'm so muddled in my head that I hardly know what I'm doing. I know *you* though."

"And you don't like me," said Luce; "I don't know why you don't, I wish you did. Never mind, you are very kind to do as I ask you to."

She adjusted the coverlet I had disarranged in my struggles to rise, and then gave me a drink of barley-water conveniently contained in a teapot.

"What was it you said about the doctor?" I presently asked her.

"He says that you are to be kept quiet," Luce replied, "and that you must not be left for a moment. That's why I'm here."

Then came into my mind the remark Mr. Bender had made respecting my injury, "His thigh is broke, I think;" and then I was concious that my left leg was pressing the mattress like a weight of lead.

"My leg is broke, isn't it, Luce?" I asked of my little nurse.

"Not broke, only shot through," she replied, with a shudder; "it's an awful wound. Poor fellow! But there was more danger from the fever, the doctor said."

"The fever! What about the fever? Who's had it?"

"You have; you're hardly cured of it yet. Ah, you don't know how ill you have been!"

Decidedly I did not.

I had a mortal dread of "fever." When I lived in Rickett's Rents, "fever" sometimes raged there terribly hot, and when that was the case the number of funerals there was awful to think of.

I recollected, too, that sometimes there was almost a riot over a fever case, the people of the Rents being afraid of catching it, and the parish people insisting on carrying the patient to the hospital, and the patient's friends resisting the parish authorities all they knew.

I wondered why they hadn't packed me off to the hospital. I told Luce so.

"I don't know why they did not—at least, I don't know for certain, why," she replied, in a hesitating manner.

"It ain't that they are so fond of me that they couldn't part with me!" I bitterly remarked.

"I believe that it is that, in part," said she looking astonished. "Don't you know that it is?"

"I know that it isn't," I replied. "What makes you say that it is?"

"I didn't know," said Luce. I thought that being proud of you was the same thing as liking you. But, don't talk, dear. Shut your eyes, and try and go to sleep again."

Don't talk! After these last words of hers how could I help talking?

That one word, "proud," recalled to my mind with terrible distinctness the main features of the whole business. It was the word that Mr. Bender had used to express his admiration for me when he discovered that I had — unwittingly, as I solemnly declare — accomplished his wicked designs against the old diamond-polisher's property.

The bare thought of that awful mistake of mine caused my face to burn and my ears to tingle.

"Who says they are proud of me?" I hastily exclaimed.

"All of them," Luce replied in a whisper; "the two dreadful men who brought the doctor here to see you, Granny, the two boys, Jerry and Nat—all of them."

"Jerry and Nat! They know about it, then?"

"Not all; but they are proud of what they do know. I don't think they know all, because they are always asking questions of Granny about it, and she snaps 'em off short."

Then there was a pause, during which I pictured to myself the sort of little ruffian I was in the eyes of Jerry and Nat and their friends.

"'GO TO YOUR ROOM,' SAID SHE; 'I'LL SETTLE WITH YOU BY AND BYE.'"

No. 7.

"Do *you* know all about it, Luce?" I presently asked.

"Oh, I wish you wouldn't talk!" she exclaimed, in distress. "I'm telling you all this, and I should not. You'll tell her again, and then she'll hit me with her fists, and kick me."

"Tell her again! No, no: don't be afraid, Luce. But *do* you know all about it?"

"I—I'm afraid I do," she replied, shyly. "They *will* talk, you know, and they don't mind me listening. I can't help knowing all about it, Jack. I wish I could——"

"What do you wish? Don't mind what you say, Luce. I like to hear you talk; it does me good. What do you wish?"

"You won't be angry?"

"No, I won't be angry; why should I be? There, let me hold your hand in mine. Now tell me what it is you wish, Luce?"

"I will then; I wish, Jack," and she sunk her head down to my pillow, and whispered, timidly, "I wish that what you said when your fever was worst, and you did not know what you were talking about, were true. Oh, I do so wish it!"

"What did I say, Luce?"

"Oh, the strangest things; some of them couldn't come true—they were too dreadful."

"But what did I say that might come true, that you wish were true, tell me?"

"You said," continued Luce, lowering her head to mine still more, "you said, and repeated it over and over again, and cried it out so that everybody could hear you, that it was all a dreadful mistake; that you were only a helpless tool in the hands of those bad men, and that you hated them, and had tried to break away from them and could not."

"Well, go on, Luce," said I, finding that here she paused.

"And that you were a miserable boy, and wanted to be good! Yes, you said that," continued Luce, earnestly; "you said that more often than anything."

"Who heard me say it?"

"Granny, the old man, all of them," Luce replied.

"Did the two men—Bender and the other—did they hear me say it?"

"The man they call Bender did, I was in the room at the time."

"And what did he say? Did he seem surprised?"

"No, he wasn't surprised," answered Luce, quietly.

"Not surprised! What did he say then?"

Naturally I was somewhat curious to know what the burglar might think of my yearning after a better course of life—especially after what he chose to regard as such an unmistakable instance of my taste and ability for robbery and outrage.

"He laughed," said Luce, hesitatingly; "he laughed and turned to Granny; he said, 'Ain't it strange how much like dreaming being light-headed is? In one or the other, whatever you say or do, is sure to be according to the rule of contrary.'"

As Luce said these last words, she edged closer to my cot, and regarded me steadfastly and wistfully.

"Ah! but he was wrong!" I exclaimed returning her look.

"How wrong, Jack?" and she came yet a little closer to me.

"About what you say when you are light-headed being according to the rule of contrary: he is wrong for once, quite wrong."

And I spoke so heartily, and in so loud a tone, that my little nurse was alarmed, and clapped her hand over my mouth. But she seemed strangely pleased as well as frightened.

"Hush! dear," she exclaimed, her voice trembling as well as her hand. "Say it again, Jack, but not so loud, or they will hear you in the next room. Was he wrong, Jack, *was* he?"

"He never was further from right in all his life, Lucy."

"And you are a miserable boy, and you want to be good?"

"Miserable! I can never tell you how miserable I have been."

"Oh! I am so glad."

"I would rather be dead than go on as I've been going," said I, and I meant it. "I never wanted to do it; it was all a mistake from the first."

"Was it? What about the—the money in the purse they found in your pocket, was that a mistake?"

"Yes; I never put it there. I don't know who did."

"Ah! I think I do. I've heard them talking. Of course I couldn't be sure, but now I am quite sure."

It was Luce who now was rash. Had Granny at that moment come into the room, there would have been a pretty to do, for as she exclaimed that she was "quite sure," the strange little girl flung both her arms round my neck, and cried and sobbed so that any one listening outside the door might have heard her. I was not a little astonished at this sudden outburst of feeling.

"I did not think that you would be sorry, and cry about it," said I, "or I wouldn't have told you."

"Oh, it isn't that. It is because I am so glad that I cry," she replied, drying her eyes, and endeavouring to calm herself. "But I have been sorry, Jack; all along I have been sorry."

"All along; since when?"

"Since you first came here; since we were shut in the dark room together. I thought from your way of talking, that you was a different boy from those who came here, and that now I should have some one to speak to—it is so lonely when you have so much to suffer and no one to speak to, Jack—but after that it seemed that they had made you quite bad, and I thought that that was the reason why you turned away from me always and would hardly look at me."

"And so that *was* the reason, Luce. I was ashamed. I could not look at you or speak to you, because I *felt* bad. I felt that you were better than me—you who were a little girl and long used to this place, and I was ashamed. There, Luce, I wanted to tell you that a long while ago."

This confession of mine seemed to break down entirely the barrier that, since my memorable day in Penny's Fields, had been growing up and strengthening between us.

With a subdued exclamation of delight, poor Luce cuddled down to me, just as a loving little sister might, and took to crying again; and though scarcely knowing why, I cried too; and there was a pair of us.

It did me good to cry. My tears seemed as oil to the springs of my better nature, long neglected and lain to rust.

I don't know what the doctor would have thought had he looked in within ten minutes of our little explanation above recorded. The strictest quiet was what he had enjoined, and here we were engaged in confidential chat in the most eager manner.

There was so much to talk about, and, as far as I was concerned, at least, it was such a blessed privilege to talk freely and frankly after my honest speech had suffered so long an imprisonment.

To be sure, my confidant was a mere child, but a year or two older than myself; but that, possibly, was an advantage rather than otherwise, for I much doubt if I should ever have mustered sufficient courage to have revealed the narrative of my recent experience and adventure, stripped of the mask of pretence and make-believe they had worn, to an older person and one more worldly wise.

As the reader will readily understand, our conversation turned chiefly on the tremendous undertaking that had resulted in my being invalided at Granny Corston's house.

Hitherto she was but very imperfectly acquainted with the history of that precious business—her knowledge of it was gathered merely from the stray observations and ungarded remarks of Mr. Bender and his friend.

Both these gentlemen, Luce informed me, had been most assiduous in their attentions towards me since I was secretly conveyed into the house, now three days since.

Opening the door of the cupboard in a corner of my sick room, Luce disclosed for my inspection a generous assortment of good things, including mutton chops and jellies, and bottles of wine that Mr. Bender had day after day come laden with.

Likewise, she apprised me that Mr. Bender's praise of me was something extraordinary. Never in all his experience, he declared, had he ever met with such a "little brick" as I was.

Further, that it was his fixed determination to take me under his wing entirely as soon as I was able to get "to work again," it being his opinion that my talents were quite wasted over the paltry occupation I had been used to as Granny Corston's boy. He swore that never was such an amount of pluck exhibited by one so young, and Mr. Toby was quite ready to back him in his opinion.

From one and all of which evidences Mother Corston's unhappy young nursery drudge argued that her previous suspicions as to my declension from honest ways were correct, and that I well deserved all the blighting praise the two burglars bestowed on me.

But, when I came to enlighten her as to the true version of the affair, she was indeed amazed.

With her little wizen pale face, and her blue eyes wide open in awful wonder, she listened while I recounted what I had undergone since the evening when I was fetched away from Penny's Fields by Mr. Bender and his companion.

I told her of my preliminary trial-lessons in chimney-descending at the robbers' abode, and described to her those awful moments on the roof of the diamond polisher's house, when it was revealed to me that in his sight or out of it, it was the burglar's intention to hold fast to me, and not let me go.

I narrated to her my appalling encounter with the poor old cripple, from the time when my desperate courage failed me, and I sank, abject and quaking, with my face to his mattress, till when shot, and dizzy with pain and bewilderment, I obeyed Mr. Bender's imperative command, and permitted myself to be hauled up the chimney, while the poor old fellow so cruelly plundered was left cursing, and threatening, and imploring, and beating his naked fists against the bars of the iron grate.

"And you did not intend to rob him! You were so confused and flustered that you forgot all about the jewel-box in the bag!" Luce ejaculated, with raised hands.

"That was the worst of it," I replied. "I wouldn't care for my wound—for anything, if the poor old fellow had not after all been robbed. It does not help him my being sorry. I wish I could help him. I wish somebody would show me the way!"

"They were not his diamonds, then?"

"No, they were trusted to him to work on. Who knows what may happen? Suppose his master does not believe in his story of how he was robbed, and should put him in prison?"

"That would indeed be dreadful," said Luce; "but I don't think they would do that—at least, not yet."

"Why not?"

"They wouldn't put him in prison if he is ill, would they?"

"But he isn't ill. He is a cripple, but he is able to work."

"Ah! but you don't know all, Jack. He wasn't ill then, but he is now."

"Who told you? How do you know?" I eagerly inquired.

"Hush! I heard the two men telling Granny so. They had read it in the newspapers they said. When the man who works there came in the morning, he could not get in, and they broke open the door, and found the old man lying by the fire-place with hardly any life in him. He had a fit, I think they said."

"Suppose he was to die!" I exclaimed, as the terrible possibility flashed to my mind. "Did they say what a shocking thing it would be if he was to die, Luce?"

"No, they did not," she answered, with a shudder. "They said what a *good* thing it would be. It was the man named Toby said that 'I'd give the biggest spark of the lot to hear that the old beggar had kicked the bucket; there would be no chance of his recognizing the boy then.' Those were his words."

There was a dreary pause in our conversation after this. To be thought a robber was bad enough, but to have the sin of murder lying at my door! The bare idea was so overwhelming, that great beads of sweat gathered on my forehead as I lay and thought about it.

"When I get well enough I will find out where the diamond-polisher lives," said I. "I will, if I have to search all over London. I will find him out and tell him all about it."

"If he isn't dead by that time," said Luce. I wish something could be done at once. It may be too late by the time you are well."

"To be sure, it may be too late. Did the doctor say how long I should be ill, Luce?"

"A month at least, he said; perhaps two months. Poor Jack! it isn't you who could do anything at once."

"Who then?"

"I might, perhaps."

"You!"

"Yes. I'd do anything I could. I ain't afraid," Luce bravely replied; "they can't beat me more cruelly than they have. If you knew any one I could go to and tell them about it, I'd go. I would run away and never come back again if I knew where to run to. I'd——"

What more poor Luce would have said I don't know. At that very instant the door of the room was flung swiftly open, and Granny Corston, her eyes flashing with rage, came hobbling in.

Making at Luce, who, panic-stricken at the unexpected apparition, stood with her mouth ajar, and her thin hands clasped one in the other, the vindictive old hag caught at her long hair, and wound a bunch of it round her bony knuckles.

"You little viper!" she cried, giving the bony knuckles a wrench; "this is your obedience, is it? This is keeping quiet and not saying so much as a single word! Go on, you jade! If you knew where to run to you would be off. Where would you go? Out with it, come. About what would you tell if you could find any one to tell it to? No lies; tell me, quick!"

"I didn't—I couldn't—" poor Luce began, and could get no further.

"But I heard you, you hussy; I heard you say that you knew something that you would tell about. Out with it; what devilry were you hatching?"

And, as the cruel old woman spoke, she tightened her grasp on the poor little girl's hair, and gave her it a twist round till she shrieked in pain.

At least one thing appeared certain, Granny Corston had overheard only the fag end of our whispered conversation. It seemed pretty certain that she suspected no other than that Luce had been disclosing to me the sufferings she herself endured, and, acting upon this supposition, I cut in to Luce's relief.

"You know well enough without hurting her to tell you," I exclaimed. "She means that she would tell somebody, if she could, how you ill-use her. So you do ill-use her; it's shameful!"

"So she has been disturbing you with a snivelling story of what she has to put up with, has she?" exclaimed the hag, giving the girl's still imprisoned head a cruel shake. "And was that all she told you? Did she tell you that I keep her here in charity—that I feed her, and clothe her, and give her lodging, with no more profitable return than her whining and complaining? Did she—"

But at that moment there was a noise of feet tramping up the lower stairs, and, after pausing a moment to listen, the old woman hurried out of the room to listen on the landing who the new comer might be.

I took advantage of her momentary absence to impart to poor Luce a ray of comfort, out of a bright idea that had suddenly occurred to me. Like lightning, the most brilliant of ideas always come swiftest.

"Bear up, Luce, I've thought of a friend who will help us."

She cheered up wonderfully. "I'll go to him; can I find him? Where does he live?"

But there was no time to answer her; Mrs. Corston returned.

"Get to your own room, you ugly little cat," said she, taking Luce by the shoulders, "I'll settle with you by and bye; I shan't forget, you know that."

## CHAPTER XVI.

MR. BENDER HONOURS MY SICK CHAMBER WITH A VISIT—I GET A LINK OF THE BARGAIN BETWEEN HIM AND GRANNY CORSTON—GRANNY HAS REASONS FOR SUPPOSING THAT I TURN TRAITOR.

THE individual whose arrival had postponed the infliction of Granny Corston's vengeance on Luce, was no other than Mr. Bender himself.

"How is he to-day?" I heard him whisper, solicitously, as he neared the door.

"Oh, he's mending—he's ten pounds better than he was yesterday. I haven't left him a minute since you was here last," answered the wicked old story-teller.

"That's jolly! that's first-rate!" returned the burglar, heartily; and then he made his appearance, with his cap in his hand, and walking tip-toe.

I was so beset with terror of the man, that, had my hampered leg permitted, I should have turned my face to the wall; but, as it was, I was compelled to face him.

"Well, my little trump—my young fighting cock! how are you by this time?"

And approaching me, and finding nothing else to attach himself to, he took a bit of my hair between his finger and thumb, and shook it affectionately.

There was a marvellous difference in Mr. Bender's personal appearance since I last set eyes on him. Then, he was coarsely clad; now, he was a tremendous "swell." I hardly knew him.

His heavy, brutal mouth was partly hidden under a false moustache, and he wore kid gloves on his great, hairy hands. He no longer wore the heavy pilot jacket, but a dandified coat of velveteen, with mother-o'-pearl buttons, and a pair of tight-fitting trousers of black cloth, and a gorgeous waistcoat.

It gave me no satisfaction, however, to observe this change. Too well I knew what to attribute it to.

"I'm very well, thanky, sir," I answered, not knowing what to say.

"There he is ag'in!" exclaimed the robber, smiting the table with his big fist, in his admiration. Butcher me! if ever I met with such a kid afore. There he is a layin' on a sick bed, with one of his legs as good as broke, and as nigh to Davy Jones's locker as could be on'y the day afore yesterday, and the fust words he ses when he's asked the question is, 'Very well, thanky!' 'Struth! he's a wonder."

"You'd rather have had Tom, wouldn't you, Ben?" remarked the old woman with a sly chuckle.

"Tom!" repeated the burglar, with a contemptuous emphasis not at all flattering to the young gentleman in question; "Tom ain't fit to hold a dark lantern to him."

"Let you alone for knowing when you've got hold of the right article," returned Granny.

Not a word to the robber of Luce taking her place by my bedside as nurse—not a hint to him of the strange conversation between us, and which her sudden entrance interrupted.

It was evident that for some reaon, the crafty old woman desired that I should stand well in Mr. Bender's esteem. The reason presently appeared.

"Aye, aye, that's all very well," remarked the robber, with a slight relapse into his natural surliness, "I don't come to you for his character. Don't you try to make me believe to have found out qualities in him what I shall have to pay extra for. When he's well enough, I'll take him away, and stump up what we agreed on for him, and not another penny. D'ye understand?"

"All right, Bendy, all right," replied Granny, in a conciliatory tone. "Bless the man, musn't anybody admire him but yourself?"

"I *do* admire him !" returned Mr. Bender patting my head gently. "I never thought when I lost that dawg of mine, that tulip-eared bull-terrier— you remember him, Granny?—I never thought that I should ever be drawed towards anything agin; but I *am* drawed. It's human natur,' I suppose."

I saw plainly enough, now, what it was that induced Granny Corston to conceal my faults and failings from the burglar. It had been arranged between them that he in future was to be my master and that the sham blind beggar-woman was to receive a premium for the loss of my services.

This was jumping from the frying-pan into the fire with a vengeance!

It would never do, however, to make Mr. Bender aware of our decided objection to this arrangement at the present time.

To do so could have no other result than bring down on my head the spite both of the robber himself and of the old woman, who would be my "blood money"

out of pocket. So I lay with my eyes, shut, and made no remark whatever.

Mr. Bender was anxious to impress me with a sense of his good nature.

"Have you seen the whacking lot of good things I've brought for you—the wine and that !" he asked me.

"He hasn't seen anything yet," Granny answered for me; "he hasn't had his eyes open very long."

"Lor' bless you, there's any amount of it !" continued Mr. Bender, evidently glad of the opportunity for trumpeting his generosity. "There's grapes and there's oranges, and there's almonds and raisins! But they ain't good for you the doctor says. And then there's sherry wine and port wine! Pitch into 'em, young 'un— don't spare 'em! All I want you to do is to make haste and get strong on your pins ag'in !"

"I wish I was strong on 'em now, sir," I answered, fervently.

"That's the sort," said Mr. Bender, delighted. "We shall get on all right, no fear And, I say, Jack, look here— don't you go to think that I've forgot what I promised you. *You* don't forget it, I'll wager !"

I nodded my head.

"To be sure! Let a knowing young shaver like you alone for recollectin'! Let's see, how much was it to be? Was it a pound or thirty shillings ?" And he smiled good-humouredly.

"It was to be according to how well I pleased you, I think, sir."

"Right you are ag'in, my pippin! It *was* to be accordin' to how you pleased me, and you *have* pleased me! Now, I don't want to cocker you up, 'cos there's nothing wus for a young beginner; but, jest as a gentle hint of how well you pleased me, I shall make the twenty bob two sovereigns."

And, taking from his trousers pocket a full hand of the precious coins in question, he selected two therefrom, and gave them to me.

After another earnest exhortation to eat as much as ever I could, and pitch into the port and sherry wine, for there was plenty more where that came from, he bade me an affectionate farewell, though not before, in the fulness of his gratitude for my advance towards recovery, he had pressed on Granny's acceptance the handsome sum of ten shillings.

Soon as he had taken his departure, Mrs. Corston, adopting a wheedling tone, requested to be informed what it was that that ungrateful little vixen, Luce, had been talking about. She pretended to treat the matter with indifference, as though she was chiefly anxious lest she had been worrying my aching head with her idle conversation; but it was plain that her fears were rooted in ground of a very different nature.

"She's such an artful hussy, and has such a mealy-mouthed way of talking to you, that unless you are used to her—as I am, worse luck!—her lies sound so much like truth, that you are easily taken in by them."

"She didn't tell me any lies—I can answer for that," I remarked, evading the old woman's main question, for reasons that are obvious.

"Why can you answer?" asked Granny Corston, sharply.

"Because I've been witness to it lots of times. You *do* whack and knock her about, don't you?"

"But that wasn't all she told you. She said something about running away; she was whispering to you where she meant to run away to when I came in!"

"That she wasn't!" I replied, much relieved to be put in possession of such unmistakable a proof that the vindictive old hag was all abroad as to the real object of our discourse.

"Pooh! I know all about it. She told you, and, knowing what a staunch one you are, Jack, she made you promise that you would not tell. But you're too much of a man to be fooled by a chit such as she is. You're one of the real rowdy sort, you are, you know. Bold young Jack— hand and glove with Bender, the King of Cracksmen! Ha, ha! just fancy that whining, snivelling little wretch trying to come it over *you!* Tell me the joke, Jack; tell me where she is going when she runs away from here." Despite her affectation of treating the matter lightly, it was evident that the old woman was terribly anxious. But I could only repeat the answer I had already given her.

"She might run, and be hanged to her —she might rot under a hedge, for all I would care!" said the old woman fiercely. "Only—only, you see, Jack, I have promised—promised and sworn, and that's more—to take care of her, and I'm bound to. I'm under a bond, Jack; and if she ran away, and got into trouble, I should get into trouble too. You wouldn't help any one to get your kind old Granny into trouble? He's his Granny's own Jack. He's like the parrot—he won't talk till he gets something nice. Open your mouth, Jack, and I will drop this nice sugar-plum into it!"

Without explanation, these last remarks of the old woman would probably lead the reader to suspect that she was scarcely right in her head; but to me what she said was intelligible enough. She was willing to bribe me if I would tell her where it was that Luce proposed to run to. I was to open my mouth and tell her, and the "nice sugar-plum" I was to receive, as my reward, was the half-sovereign that Mr. Bender, a little while before, had presented her with.

"If you were to offer me all the money that's in your bag, I couldn't tell you what you ask," I replied. "I don't know; she did not tell me."

The old woman seemed at last convinced that I was telling the truth, but still her mind was uneasy. She crossed the room, and sat brooding by the fire for a few minutes. Then she came back to my bedside again.

"If she *had* told you, Jack, would you have told me?" she asked.

This was a poser; and none the less so because it was evident that a simple reply would not close the conversation.

"I would if I thought she was running into trouble," I replied.

"Why, what else could she run into—a child like her, without a friend in the world except myself!"

"If she has not another friend in the world she won't run away from you, that's very certain," said I.

"But she's such an obstinate little mule," continued Granny, coaxingly; "she may have got it into her head that she *has* a friend somewhere, d'ye see?"

I did not, and shook my head to that effect.

"I mean that she may have been listening wnen ——" and here the old woman paused.

"Who does she listen to?" I asked.

"Why, she listens when people are whispering, I believe. She is such a cunning little wretch, Jack, you never know when she is listening."

"But what could she hear?"

"She may have blundered on some name or some place mentioned, you know, and thought that it concerned her," replied Granny Corston, cautiously.

"So she may," said I.

"That's what I want to find out," returned Granny, biting her thin lips.

"Why?"

"Only for her sake—quite for her sake, as you must plainly see."

"If I wanted to know anything she could tell me I should ask her, if I were you," I innocently suggested.

"And what use would that be?" replied Granny, shrugging her shoulders impatiently.

"She would tell you, wouldn't she?"

"You don't know her. She has for me, already made up, at her tongue's tip, whatever I ask her. No, no, she wouldn't tell me, Jack, she wouldn't tell me; but I fancy I know who she would tell."

"Who?"

"You."

It was impossible to mistake the drift of the crafty old woman's speech now.

"Me! What makes you think so?"

"Oh, I've watched her ever since you've been here. She never looks at any one as she looks at you."

"She never did me any harm looking at me," I remarked, resolved to "stick up" for poor Luce as well as I was able.

"To be sure not. She can be soft and easy-going enough where she takes a fancy, the little fool. She did nothing but sob and cry all night when you were brought home with your leg hurt. I believe that you could wheedle anything out of her."

"But I never talk with her."

"That's your fault; she is willing enough to talk with you."

"But I never have the chance."

"I would make the chance. What is easier than for you to get her into conversation while you are lying here? She wouldn't want pumping even. The very first time she found an opportunity of speaking to you—this afternoon, I mean—she nearly blurted it out."

"Blurted what out?"

"Ah! that's what I want to know—what I'd pay handsome to discover. I'd give you more money than ever you had in your life, Jack, if you could find it out for me. You can if you like. For her sake, you understand, quite for her sake."

"I don't understand what you are talking about," said I. "How can I find out what you want, if you can't tell me what it is?"

"It's as plain as A B C," returned Granny; "I believe that she has been listening, and has misunderstood something that may get her into trouble. I want to know what that something is. I am sure I need say no more to a clever lad like you. What do you say?"

What could I say?

The old woman's proposition, and the terms of it, were of such an amazing character, that, for the moment, I could not perfectly comprehend them, let alone come to a decision.

Was I never to escape from the obstacles that so determinedly rose up, one after another, to hinder and baulk me?

No wonder that burglars, and robbers, and rogues in grain, made so much of me, when I appeared in their eyes a lad of such villanous sort! A contemptible little ruffian who could inveigle a poor little ill-used girl to make me her confidant, then betray her to, heaven only knew what, amount of cruelty, for the sake of what the old witch, her guardian, might choose to consider as "handsome pay." It was a great wonder that, in the extremity of my indignation, I did not express myself in terms that would have at once opened the old woman's eyes to the true state of the case.

What then might have happened I tremble even now to think of. Poor Luce certainly would have fared none the better for the exposure; while, as for me, without a friend in the world to inquire after me, and hidden away from everybody, in that den of infamy; crippled and quite at the mercy of my unscrupulous and furious enemies, the chances are that I should have been quietly murdered, my body, not improbably, finding a resting-place in the unhallowed earth of the cellar under the old house.

That such tragedies were not impossible in Penny's Fields, the demolition of that nest of vice and wickedness afterwards fully revealed.

But it fortunately happened that while Granny Corston was waiting an answer to her question, and I stood hesitating how to reply to it, a means of respite from the difficulty, if not of actual escape out of it, occurred to me.

If that other idea of mine—the one of which I had given Luce a hasty hint, might be wrought to a successful issue, it would send this precious scheme of the sham blind woman toppling over before it. Moreover, as I rapidly thought it over, it seemed to me that, after all, what at first appeared a difficulty might turn out an advantage.

"'WHAT'S ALL THE ROW ABOUT?' EXCLAIMED THE ROBBER."

It would be impossible for me to aid Granny in what she wished, unless I was permitted to converse privately with Luce.

This was exactly what I wanted, in furtherance of that little scheme of my own.

"Well, what do you say? You're a long time making up your mind," said Granny, a little impatiently.

"I'll do the best I can," I replied; "if she talks I shall listen; if she won't talk I can't make her."

"Aye, but she *will* talk, there's no fear of that."

"She will if you give her a chance; you drove her away when she was sitting with me just now."

"That was before the lucky idea struck me that she might serve my turn by talking to you. She shall have opportunity enough to talk if she's a mind to. I shall be going out this evening for three whole hours, and she shall come and sit with you."

And, delighted at her prospect of speedily discovering what troubled her so, and again promising me the handsome reward of ten shillings if I did her bidding to her satisfaction, the hideous old hag kissed me, and bade me try and doze while she prepared me some nice beef tea.

## CHAPTER XVII.

IN WHICH, AS CONSPIRATORS, LUCE AND MYSELF MAKE RAPID PROGRESS, AND SHE DEPARTS ON A VOYAGE OF DISCOVERY.

I HAVE no doubt that the cunning little arrangement that entered the wicked old woman's head served the good turn, amongst others, of saving Luce from the thrashing promised her, in atonement for the delinquency in which she was discovered.

At all events I heard no sound, either of flogging or crying, and when, in the early part of the evening, she was brought into my sick room, by Granny, there were no signs of recent weeping in her eyes, which were full of wonder at the sudden alteration in Granny Corston's temper.

As she afterwards informed me, it had been her sorrowful conviction that her rashness had spoilt her chances of talking with me, for good and all, and that any plan that might occur to either of us, for the undeceiving of the unfortunate diamond-polisher, must fall to the ground on that account.

What, then, was her amazement, when, not six hours afterwards, without any solicitation on her part, the fair opportunity she had forfeited was restored, may easily be imagined.

In order to avoid suspicion, however, Granny did not appear over eager to force Luce's company on me.

"If you would like to have her in here for an hour while I go as far as Temple

Bar, you may," said she. "It may help to pass the time away. Please yourself; if you would rather have her room than her company, say so."

As she spoke, however, she gave me a look, the meaning of which I fully understood.

Of course I replied that I should like Luce to sit with me; and enjoining her to take care how she behaved, on account of what she might expect if she did not, the old woman took her departure. We heard her descend the stairs, and shut the street door after her.

"What does it mean?" asked Luce, with her great eyes wide open.

"Oh, you must not ask questions of me, I replied, mischievously. "I'm your enemy."

"You?"

"So I am told."

"But who says so? Why are you my enemy? Have you been my enemy always?"

"Hush!" And I could hardly forbear laughing at the odd expression of wonder depicted on her countenance; "you musn't ask me. I'm a conspirator, Luce; at least, according to Granny's way of thinking, and I've got a job to do that will bring me in any amount of money."

"But what have I to do with it?" Luce asked, half smiling, and evidently suspecting that there was a joke at the bottom of my make-believe seriousness.

"You have all to do with it," I replied, "and what you've got to do is to sit down and tell me all about your intention to run away, and where you think of running to, and I am to hoard up all you say and report it to her."

"About running away! where could I run to?"

"Ah! that's best known to yourself," said I, laughing.

"But I know nobody—I've seen nobody but the people here, since I was brought here, when I was quite a little child." And the tears stood in her eyes.

"Never mind that now, Luce. Let us go on talking where we left off this morning, when she came in and interrupted us. But, first of all, tell me, can you read?"

Luce shook her head sadly.

"I think I could when I came here," said she; "but they won't let me, they keep me from it all they can, so that I have almost forgotten the way."

"And can't you write?"

"Oh, yes, I can write my name beautifully."

"You can write anything you mean, not only your name?"

"Yes, only my name," Luce replied, screwing up her lips mysteriously.

"I don't understand; why only your name?"

"They never let me practice anything else. I can write that quite well; I'll show you."

There was a pencil lying on the mantel-shelf, and a piece of white paper that had served as a wrapper for one of my medicine bottles; and, taking these materials, she wrote rapidly. Dunce as I was, I could easily make out what it was she had written—

"Lucy Heath."

"And so you mean to say that you can write that so nicely, and nothing else?" I asked, incredulously; "it's as easy to write one thing as another, isn't it?"

"I never have any occasion to write anything else, and that not often."

"How often?"

"Four times a year."

"Four times a year!"

"Well, oftener than that, perhaps; because, about a week before the time for writing *in earnest* comes round, they make me practice it. I've been practicing it all day yesterday, and this morning."

"But what do you mean by writing it in earnest?"

"I don't know, myself, what it means," replied Luce, innocently; "I only know that I have to do it. When the time comes there is a long account of writing and figures put before me, and I write my name at the bottom, and then the paper is sealed up, and put in the post."

"And you don't know what you sign your name to?"

"It is something very particular, I should think," replied Luce, reflectively, "because I recollect once, when my right hand was bad, through Granny striking it with the toasting-fork, the time was coming round, and I could not write, and you never saw the fuss that there was. Granny herself bathed it, and dressed it, and I carried it at rest, in a sling, one whole week, so that I might be able to hold a pen when the signing day came."

This strange revelation, however, although it bore so directly on the future of the poor little girl, whose acquaintance I had so strangely made, was of small interest to me at the time.

"It doesn't matter about your not being able to write," said I, "but I do wish that you were able to read."

"I wish I could, but what's the use?"

"Can't you read print in a newspaper?" I asked.

"I don't think I could," Luce hopelessly remarked. "Why?"

"Didn't you say that Mr. Bender said

that he had read the account of the old diamond-polisher being taken with a fit, in a newspaper?"

"Yes, he said so."

"Did he say what newspaper?"

"I don't recollect."

"That's a pity; but there, it doesn't matter, if you can't read, we must trust to my friend—he can read, I'll wager."

"What, to the man Bender, do you mean?" Luce asked in astonishment.

"No, no; he is no friend of mine; take my word for that."

"Who do you mean then?"

"Just peep outside, Luce, and see that no one is listening."

Luce did as requested, and reported the coast clear.

"Who is the good friend that can read, Jack?" Luce repeated.

"Not the burglar, but somebody who I hope will take him to task—the friend I mean is the person I hinted to you this morning."

"Yes—who is he?" Luce whispered eagerly.

"He isn't much to look at; I don't know much about him," said I; "and p'r'aps, after all, he won't be able to do much good; but we'd better try him than nobody."

"Is he rich?" Luce asked.

I could not help laughing. "He is a crossing-sweeper," I replied.

"A crossing-sweeper!"

"Hush! Yes; his name is Overshiner —Dan Overshiner; he told me so himself, and he sweeps a crossing this side of Waterloo Bridge."

And then, in order to impress my small confederate with a favourable view of what were our chances in the direction in question, I communicated to her the particulars of my meeting with the good-natured old sweeper.

"Yes, he would help us, I am sure that he would," Luce eagerly remarked, as I brought my narrative to a conclusion; no one but a kind-hearted man would have used a poor boy so well. Where did you say he was to be found, Jack? I'll go to him."

"Do you know Waterloo Bridge?" I asked her.

"I haven't been out of this street all the time I have been here," she replied, "but I would try and find the Bridge. P'r'aps you could tell me the way to go."

"That I can do; but the question is, is it worth the risk?" said I, my ardour cooling.

"What risk, Jack?"

"Why, you see, if you went away, and did not find him, you'd have to come back and give some account of yourself, and you know what would follow. No—I couldn't let you risk *that!*"

"But I shouldn't want to come back," said Luce, resolutely.

"What do you mean?"

"I've often thought of running away from this dreadful place, Jack; I know I shall do so some day. I've been making up my mind to for months and months, and I've been only——"

She paused, tears gathering in her eyes.

"Only what, Luce? Why haven't you run away before now?"

"I've been waiting for all the babies to be well. They never *are* well altogether. If they are quite well when they are brought here, they are sure to fall ill and pine, and they go on pining till they die."

And she crept closer to me, shuddering, as she uttered these last words in a low whisper.

"I grow so frightened sometimes when I lay and think about it," Luce continued, "that I am tempted to get up in the middle of the night and run away—anywhere!"

Here she paused, and then timidly went on.

"Jack, if this crossing-sweeper is such a good-hearted old fellow, he might——"

"Might what?" I asked, as Luce hesitated and regarded me wistfully.

"He might help me as well."

"I am sure that he would if he were able," I replied.

"Then I'll go," said she, decidedly.

"When?"

"Now—at once. Don't say anything more about risks, Jack. I'll go."

And she rose from her seat, looking as though quite prepared to start then and there.

"What shall I tell him if I find him?"

"We mustn't be in too great a hurry," I remarked. "We had better give ourselves all the chance we can."

"We shall never have a better chance than this," urged Luce, impatiently "Pray let me go."

"I don't want to hinder you, but it don't seem fair for you to run into danger on my account. What sort of weather is it?"

"It's setting in for wet, I think; the clouds look very heavy," said Luce, taking observations at the window.

"That's lucky."

"Is it? I'm glad of that. Why is it lucky, Jack?"

"Because he's more likely to be there in wet weather. It was a wet night when I first saw him. It would be better, I think, Luce, if it were dark when you went to see him."

"To be sure it would," she replied, readily; "if I started about now, it would be dark when I got there, wouldn't it? Is it far?"

"It is not very far."

"How long would it take to get there?"

"It would not take you more than half an hour, I should think."

"Why, I might, if I was lucky, go without being missed even," Luce remarked, musingly.

"What, to-night, do you mean? Did Granny say how long she would be gone?"

"She said an hour, but she is always later than she says. If I couldn't find the old crossing-sweeper, I might get back before she came home. See, it is beginning to rain now."

That was true.

Even as she spoke a few drops of rain came like tiny whispers of hope and encouragement, pattering against the window panes.

"But how are you to tell whether she has returned or no?" I asked.

Luce considered this formidable obstacle with puckered lips for several moments.

But she was not to be beaten.

"I could ask at the public-house at the corner of the Fields," said she; "Granny always calls there for a glass of rum before she comes home. The public-house people would be sure to tell me."

"And supposing that they told you that she *had* gone home. Then what would you do?"

"Oh, don't mind about that, Jack," she replied, desperately, "let us think about what will happen if we are lucky. See, it is raining faster. He is sure to be there. Pray let me go. What shall I tell him?"

Now the fact is, I had never thought about this, the most important feature of the whole business.

Hard driven for a friend, I had fixed on Mr. Overshiner; but on what unsubstantial grounds, the reader is already aware. It was one thing to discover the old sweeper at his crossing, and quite another to introduce to him by means of a messenger, such as Luce, the subject of my peril and anxiety, and that in such a way as not only to secure his sympathy, but his active interference.

I could not loose sight of the possibility that he might not remember my case at all.

"What shall I say to him?" repeated Luce, bustling about and pinning a ragged little woollen shawl over her thin shoulders in preparation for the venturesome journey before her.

"That's just what I'm puzzling my head about," I replied.

"Perhaps I had better first of all tell him your name and where you are?" Luce suggested.

"He dosen't know my name," I replied dismally.

"That's unfortunate; never mind, I'll describe you to him, he'll know then."

"I don't think he will," said I, my belief in the speculation rapidly sinking to freezing point, "it was quite dark when I met him. Ah, I'm afraid that we had better not try it."

But my little companion was more hopeful.

"Don't you fear, I'll make him remember you," she said. "I'll tell him about your changing his luck; about his tying up your cut knee. It can't be often that he has a boy's cut knee to tie up. Well, what shall I tell him?"

"But you can't go out in the rain like that; where's your bonnet?"

"I haven't got one; never had one," she replied, with a little impatience. "Be quick please, Jack, and say what I'm to tell him."

There was no use in making further objections with the business-like little woman.

"You know as well as I do what to tell him, Luce. Tell him everything as I've told it to you," I answered her.

"Very well. Now which is the way to go?"

I told her this, too, as she stood ready to start. "And look here, Luce," said I, the idea suddenly entering my head, "this money is of no use to me, take it with you and show it to him, it may make what you tell him easier to believe. Tell him it is the money Mr. Bender gave me."

And taking the burglar's two sovereigns from under my pillow, I wrapped them in a bit of paper, and gave the packet to her, and she carefully pinned it in a corner of her ragged frock.

Then hurrying over a kiss and a loving "good bye," lest I should see the tear that had started to her bright, hopeful eyes, she slipped out of the room and was gone.

---

## CHAPTER XVIII.

THE DESERTER IS MISSED, AND I AM IN IMMINENT DANGER OF BEING MURDERED AS HER AIDER AND ABETTER—HAPPY ARRIVAL OF THE "KING OF CRACKSMEN."

IT was little short of a miracle that the exciting events of the last few hours ensuing on my recent attack of fever and delirium did not throw me back into a worse condition.

That it ultimately affected my recovery I have little doubt, but at the same time the anxiety and the alternating flushes of hope and dread that beset me seemed to lend me strength and life renewed.

It was quite dusk when Luce took her departure, and my first fear was lest she should be stopped at the very commencement of her hazardous adventure.

The chances seemed woefully against her now that she was gone.

Granny might return before she was expected, and encounter the brave little messenger at the corner of the street.

Nat or Jerry Tyler might, according to their wont, be lurking in the neighbourhood, and their suspicions roused by her haste and her strange appearance, they might follow her!

These and a dozen other alarming suppositions haunted me, and for at least a quarter of an hour I lay in a sweat of terror, expecting each moment to hear something that would tell of the miscarriage of our desperate scheme.

I bitterly repented my selfishness in letting her go at all.

But the minutes flew by, until it became certain that at least she had got clear of the neighbourhood. Setting aside personal considerations, the weather favoured her, for the dusk soon became black darkness, and the rain was increasing.

To be sure it was very painful for me to conjure up before my mind's eye the picture of the kind-hearted little creature who, chiefly for my sake, was running such a tremendous risk, buffetting along the highway without so much as a covering for her head, and with her poor rags saturated and clinging about her; but it was at least some consolation to know that on such a night she would be less likely to attract observation.

In the front attic overhead, which was the nursery, there was an old-fashioned staircase clock that chimed the quarters as well as the hours.

Three quarters had now chimed since Luce had taken her departure.

According to our calculation, she would reach the crossing at Waterloo Bridge in half an hour.

If all then had gone well, by this time she had encountered old Dan Overshiner, and he knew all about the burglary at the diamond-polisher's, and my share in it.

What did he think of it?

What would he do about it?

It was not quite impossible that, as soon as Luce had revealed to him the strange story, he would drop his broom and accompany her back to Penny's Fields straightway.

If so, they would be here shortly—they would be back before old Granny was, and when she returned she would find the tough old crossing-sweeper waiting ready to tackle her.

Would he be a match for her?

Would he be a match for her and old Daddy as well, if she called him down to her assistance?

He might be, perhaps, if he brought his broom with him.

My anxiety grew so extreme that my temples throbbed with it.

Again the old clock in the attic tolled for a departed quarter of an hour.

If Luce had luck, she would be back with or without Mr. Overshiner, almost directly.

If Granny Corston found nothing to interfere with her original design, and kept her word, she too would be back, directly.

Which would win?

It was a match against time.

More important still, what would the winning be, and what the losing?

Once more the clock's chime made itself heard—Luce had been gone an hour and a quarter.

Even now she would be in time, if she returned immediately.

I strained my ears to catch the welcome sound of her coming in at the street door. I verily believe I should have detected the sound of her footsteps in the mud outside had they approached.

But they did not. The rain had driven everybody within doors, and not the least noise was to be heard out in the street or in the house but the head-racking, thud, thud, of old Daddy Corston's chair, as he sat rocking one of his babies to sleep.

Ding dong! ding dong! four times over, and then the clock struck nine.

Luce by this time had been away an hour and a half.

Then I heard the street door open, and a step in the passage, and for a moment my heart beat with joyful expectancy.

Only for a moment, alas!

It was a footstep, but not the light and hasty one of Luce's, that was heard in the passage.

Granny Corston had won the race.

I could hear the sound of the iron ring she wore on the boot of her short leg, clinking on the stairs as she ascended them.

Had Luce inquired at the public-house, no doubt the people there would have informed her that the old woman had been there for her customary glass at least. I could hear her hiccuping as she approached the door of the room where I was.

She softly opened it.

"Hallo! no light? What does this mean, you slut?"

It was evident from Granny's husky utterance that she was just a little tipsy.

Nor did this discovery tend to sooth my alarm. Bad enough, when sober, she was a perfect fiend when in liquor. I knew to whom her question applied, and was at least thankful that the "slut" was far out of her reach.

Not knowing what turn the old woman's rage might take, I deemed it prudent to feign sleep.

"What does this mean?" repeated Granny, in a loud whisper. "You little wretch, Luce, where are you?"

But no Luce answered. Approaching the bed, muttering under her breath, and treading very softly, the old woman groped for the chair in which she had left Luce sitting, evidently in hopes of finding her there still, and fast aleep; but, discovering the chair empty, her muttering gave way before an exclamation of undisguised rage and astonishment.

She hurried to the cupboard and speedily struck a lucifer-match and lit a candle. Then she came to my bedside and laid a hand on me.

"Jack! Jack!"

"What's the matter?" and I opened my eyes sleepily.

"Matter enough!" replied Granny Corston, her voice quivering with passion. "Where is she?"

"Where's who?"

"Why Luce, to be sure."

"How should I know where she is?"

"It is a lie!" exclaimed the old woman, fiercely, "you know and you won't tell me. But I'll find her, never fear, and when I do, let her look out."

With a vengeful glare in her beady eyes, the old woman stumped out of the room and up the stairs to the attic.

Presently down she came again, bringing that hideous old wretch, her husband, with her.

Such had been his hurry, that he had forgotten to lay the child down he had been rocking, and appeared with it still hugged to his hairy breast. Both of them looked frightened as well as amazed— Granny especially. She shut the door and came to my bedside, with her thin lips pursed determinedly.

"Look here," said she, "I want the truth, and I mean having it. Was you asleep when I came in, or only shamming?"

"I couldn't have been fast asleep; I heard you open the door," I replied, cautiously.

"When did Luce go out—how long since?"

"I can't tell you."

"Can't! you shall. You know what you promised me you would do when I was gone?"

" Yes."

" Did you do it ?"

" There was nothing to do."

" What do you mean ? She talked to you, didn't she ?"

" Of course she talked ; but she didn't say anything particular."

"Answer me, now !" and she bent over me threateningly. " How long has she been gone, and where has she gone to ?"

There was now no choice between betraying Luce and telling a lie.

" I know nothing about her going, or how long she has been gone. How should I, if I was aleep?"

And I really believe that the immediate danger might have blown over at this, had it not been for that prying old gentleman, Daddy Corston.

Granny had stood the candle on a table by the side of my cot, and, as illluck would have it, lying on this table was the identical scrap of white paper on which poor Luce had inscribed her name to show me how beautifully she could write.

The old man, as usual, was smoking a dirty little short pipe, or rather he had been smoking it, but in his alarm it had gone out. He wanted to light it again, and spying the scrap of paper, he took it up.

Then he made the discovery.

" Hullo ! why, what's this ? Old woman, look here !"

The old woman looked there as invited, and at the same moment uttered a cry of dismay and rage.

Snatching the bit of paper from his hand, her keen eyes instantly made out what was written thereon, and her face, flushed with drink, became in an instant ashy pale.

So you have been asleep all the while, have you ?" she exclaimed, turning to me, and speaking with a calmness that was more terrible than her most furious outburst. " You have been fast asleep all the time, and you know nothing !"

" I told you so, didn't I ?" I replied, feeling not a little uncomfortable at the unlucky turn affairs had taken.

"To be sure. You have been fast asleep, and know nothing about this, I suppose ?"

And she held up the fatal evidence of what had been the subject of my conversation with Miss Lucy Heath.

Now, one thing was certain ; the lie I had already told was broad enough to cover the affair of the paper—as far as *I* was concerned, at least. If I *had* been asleep all the time, I could no more have seen Luce write than I could have heard her talk ; and, furthermore, I am afraid that I can lay claim to no honest repugnance that stood in the way of my availing myself of the persistence in the falsehood.

But the fact is, my countenance betrayed me.

The discovery of the writing was of course so intimately associated in my mind with our secret conference, that its turning up so inopportunely was like a voice proclaiming against me. I could make no answer, but I could feel my face crimsoning under the old woman's vengeful gaze.

" Open your mouth, you viper, will you, and tell me what you know ? Once more, will you ?"

But I could not ; I could only lay helplessly staring at her, and her hideous old husband beside her.

Finding that I remained silent, in the white heat of her fury, Granny did a very brutal thing.

My bandaged leg prevented my moving in my bed, and I was ill and weak, and just recovering from a fever, and Granny, to induce me to open my mouth, struck me on that organ a blow with her bony knuckles, that set the blood trickling.

But I wasn't such a coward as to give in for such a trifle.

What was a blow on the mouth compared with what little Luce had found courage enough to face ;

"I've told you as much as I mean to," I replied, wiping my bleeding mouth with my shirt-sleeve, "if you hit me again I'll scream out murder."

"You'll scream out no more than is true, if you don't take care."

And Granny furiously leant over me with her clenched fists raised.

"I will know, I *must* know !" she exclaimed. "Put that brat down, old man, and lock the door."

Nothing loth to be at liberty to have a hand in any sort of diabolical mischief, the old man did as he was requested.

"Now tell me," cried Granny, "tell me where she has gone, and how long she has been gone ?"

"You'll get nothing more out of me," I replied, desperately.

"Tell me all that she told you—everything, or, as I stand here alive, I'll strangle you !"

And as she spoke, she unclenched her bony fists, and her hooked fingers hovered over me like the claws of a bird of prey.

To be sure I was very young, and on that account more easily imposed on ; but I knew something of the old hag's vindictive disposition, and the lengths she would go to serve her ends, and I sincerely believed that she meant what she said.

It was a shocking thing to lie there helpless and be strangled.

Luce had said that she would never return to the house if she found that the old woman had got home before her ; therefore, a full confession on my part could not affect her.

"I know where she has gone, but——"

And then I heard a hasty footstep ascending the stairs.

It must be my rescuer ; who else could it be ?

Instantly I altered my tune.

"I'm in here ! help ! Make haste, Mr. Overshiner, I'm in here !" I shouted, as loud as I was able.

The old woman's face seemed glowing in a white heat of rage. For a moment she stood as though irresolute, and then she plucked the pillow from under my head, and flung it on my face, as though bent on smothering my cries and me at the same time. But I struggled hard and pushed the pillow off.

The person ascending the stairs must have heard my cries, for the footsteps immediately became quicker, and the old woman and her husband looked aghast from one to the other.

When presently the handle was turned violently in the lock, the old man uttered an abject, whining cry, and Granny clasped her hands together in terror.

"Open the door ! What caper are you up to now ?"

Then their panic instantly subsided, while my hopes, raised for the moment to fever heat, sickened and died dismally.

It was not the voice of the friendly crossing-sweeper ; it was that of Mr. Bender, the burglar.

With an exclamation of relief, Granny

"IT WAS LUCE COME BACK AT LAST."

Corston hurried to the door, unlocked it, and flung it open.

"Oh, Lord! I'm so glad its you!" she cried. "He! he! I thought that the cat was out. Cheer up, old man; pull yourself together; it's nothing. You see who it is, don't you?"

Nor were these words of comfort and re-assurance altogether unnecessary.

In his fright the hideous-looking old fellow had not recognised the friendly voice, and had retreated to a corner, where, crouching behind a chair, he was quaking and whining to be "spared."

## CHAPTER XIX.

### IN WHICH, IN ALL PROBABILITY, I SHOULD HAVE BEEN MURDERED, BUT FOR GRANNY AND MR. BENDER COMING TO LOGGERHEADS.

"WOT'S the row about?" exclaimed the robber, halting at the threshold and regarding the scene before him in amazement.

Then, catching sight of my pale face all smeared with blood, his tone at once changed to one of indignation.

"Hullo! that's the way the wind blows, is it?" he cried, advancing with hasty strides to my bedside. "Somebody 'll have to settle for this. Why, dash my eyes and limbs, who's been hurting the lad? Speak out, you old witch, was it you?"

The person so uncivilly addressed replied by shaking her fist at me revengefully, and uttering an inarticulate sound of rage.

As for me, I had nothing to say. Evidently I had made a fine mess of it.

It was bad enough to have to contend against the old woman whom really I had not injured, but to be brought so suddenly face to face with one of the brace of ruffians whose ruin Luce and myself were deliberately plotting, was indeed leaping from the frying-pan into the fire. I lay bathed in a sweat of dismal apprehension, gazing helplessly from one to the other.

"Tell me, Jack," repeated the robber, "who is it that has been beating you? Wot have they been beating you for—you, the pluckiest and staunchiest little beggar to be found atween this and Whitechapel? It's cussed mean, that's what I call it."

"Aye, try *your* hand at making him speak, Benny dear," exclaimed the old hag, with a malicious chuckle, and still trembling with fury. "I've tried *mine*, as you can see."

"And what do you want him to talk about, eh?" asked the burglar, with a suspicious frown. "You've been trying to pump him, have you? Ha, ha! you find you had got hold of the wrong customer, eh, Jack?"

And then, turning to me with a triumphant chuckle, he continued—

"So they've been trying to sift you about wot was no business of theirs, and they beat you because you kept mum. Hag me, if your face was cleaner, I'd twist your old nose off your face!"

And the indignant robber flicked his broad finger and thumb so close to Granny's visage as to make her wink again.

"Aye, aye, but you'll sing another song presently, my brave boy," replied the old woman, with devilish pleasantry. "He won't peach—no, no, Jack's a staunch lad; he won't peach for nothing!"

"Wot d'ye mean by that?" the robber asked, looking at her curiously.

"He won't speak out till the time comes. He won't speak out to us or to you either; it isn't his game."

"Can't you out with what you mean without riddling, you old ape?" growled Mr. Bender. "Wot's he got to say that he won't speak out to me?"

"You had better ask him," grinned Granny, viciously.

"I ask him, or you, or anybody. Wot's he got to say that his master may not hear? His master wot means to take him in hand and make a man of him— wot thinks such a lot of him that he's come in a cab from Holborn this blessed time o' night to bring him a pot o' ointment wot he saw in a shop winder, and wot's warranted to cure bad legs of ever such a long standin'! Eh, wot do you mean by saying that he's got that to say that he won't tell me? You wants to pise, his mind agin me, that's wot it is!"

There never was a ruffian more unaccountable than Mr. Bender.

It was quite true he had come at that time of night to bring me a pot of the wonderful ointment in question. As he spoke, in proof of his assertion, he pro- duced it with a flourish from his coat-tail pocket.

It is not too much to say that this demonstration of his generosity towards me caused a spasm of something very like remorse.

At the same time, I could not forget that he himself had likened his regard for me to that which he had felt for a favourite bull-dog, once his property, and that his pride in me was founded on his false impression that I was a rascal extraordinarily cold-blooded and cruel for my age.

Further, that his whole and sole aim in getting me cured was only that I might again engage in such perilous, though, to him, profitable exploits, as that one in which I had earned such high distinction.

"I'll have him away from this," pursued Mr. Bender; "he ain't safe here. I'll have a cab to-morrow night and take him home, and my housekeeper shall nuss him."

"Aye, aye—you'll do this, and you'll do that! But first of all ask him to tell you who Mr. Overshyer is," remarked Granny Corston, maliciously.

"Who?"

"Overshyer," put in the old man (for so they had misunderstood the name I had called out). "Ha, ha! he mistook *you* for Mr. Overshyer, Ben. He heard you coming up the stairs just as he was drove in a corner, and was about to confess what a false-hearted young vagabond he was, and he altered his tune and squalled out for help and for Mr. Overshyer to come to him."

Mr. Bender's countenance was perplexed, and in the space of a few seconds underwent many curious changes.

"Yah!" he ejaculated at length, with much disgust, "you're a couple of old idiots ; its the wandering of his mind ; ain't he been so on and off for this three days ?"

"Yes, but there's *two* in it," said the old woman, with malicious deliberation.

"Two in it ?" and again the old suspicion returned to the robber's hard face.

"Lord knows how many may be in it by this time !" exclaimed the old man, giving way to his terror at the bare idea. "She's been away nigh upon two hours—long enough to go the round of all the police-stations in London !"

"She ! whom do you mean by she ?" exclaimed the burglar.

"Why the gal—our gal."

Mr. Bender had lowered himself on to the chair that poor Luce had sat on, but hearing these alarming words, he started up as though stung, while his face grew a shade paler, and his under jaw twitched strangely.

"Strike me a cripple !" he exclaimed, in a hoarse whisper. "I've come here to hear a summat. Shut that door, curse you, can't you? Now, wot about there being two in it ! wot about the police-stations ?"

"No, no, he's going too far, he always does, the drivelling old fool !" began Granny Corston, soothingly.

"Not a bit too far, not a bit !" continued the childish old ruffian, his fit of fright returning on him in full force. "We want to pisen his mind, eh ? We'd better pisen his body, too, the Judas—the blood-seller ! He'd hang us all, Ben ! Over-shyer is in the police ; I'd stake my life on it. Oh, Lord ! its a mercy we're not all murdered in our beds !"

The robber, by signs and gestures of menace, had in vain urged the old man to moderate his high-pitched shrieking voice, which had woke the baby he was by this time nursing again, and who added the music of its shrill little pipes to the discord.

"I shall do him a injury if he stays here another minute," growled Mr. Bender. "Take him away, and come back here, and let us have our little confab out. Stay though ; who's in the house ?"

"Nobody but ourselves and the kids in the —— "

"Bust the kids, they're nobody. No-•body in the house but ourselves, eh ?"

"Not a soul."

"Then we may as well slip the bolt of the street door."

And, so saying, he strode softly down the stairs to execute the little job himself, while Granny collared her idiotic spouse, and hauled him away to the nursery.

They—Mr. Bender and Granny that is —returned at the same moment.

The burglar was no longer a guilty man suffering under sudden panic, but a cool villain, with an appalling amount of cruel determination in his deep-set grey eyes.

He sat down on Luce's chair again, and taking from his pocket a pistol, placed it handily on the table.

"Don't be alarmed, Granny," he grinned, grimly, at the old woman's sudden exclamation of affright, "it isn't for you ; only when one hears so much talk about his friends in blue, one likes to make ready a warm welcome if they should happen to drop in on him. Now let's have this pretty story slick out. What's it all about ?"

His question was addressed to Granny Corston, but she had little to tell him.

Half dead with terror as I was, I had still sense enough to perceive that she scrupulously avoided all allusion to the secret that evidently existed concerning Luce.

She said nothing about the fag end of the conversation she had overheard between us, and which at first roused her suspicions that the little girl had made a discovery concerning her mysterious detention at the den in Penny's Fields, and that she had confided as much as she knew to me.

She gave Mr. Bender no hint of the private instructions she had given me to " pump " Luce, or of the alarming scrap of paper with " Lucy Heath " written on it and left behind by the fugitive.

She merely informed the burglar that she had " overheard us talking," and that Luce had run away in her absence, and what were her grounds for suspecting that I had sent her on a treacherous errand to a certain Mr. Overshyer as it seemed.

I thought that already I had seen Mr. Bender look his ugliest, but I was mistaken.

Never shall I forget his countenance as he turned to me.

" Who's Mr. Overshyer, Jack?" said he, calmly. " You may as well tell the truth, 'cos it's about ten to one that they are about the last words you ever will tell."

But though my life depended on it, I could not answer him. At last my overwhelming terror found relief in tears, and turning my face to the pillow, I could only cry and sob.

" You'll take no good by sulking, Jack," continued the burglar, with quiet determination. " When I ses a thing I sticks to it, even in common, and it tain't likely that I'll do otherwise if it's a matter of lagging (transportation) or scragging (hanging) p'r'aps. Come, out with it, afore you're sorry."

But I remained silent.

" I don't promise yer, mind, but there *may* be just a squeak for you if you make a clean breast of it. Don't you go to think cos I took a fancy to you and did all I could to nuss you up and get you well, that I'm soft-hearted—got a conscience, and that sort of rubbish. I ain't got no more conscience than a horse. I'd no more funk on killing anybody that piped on me, than I would on smashin' a gnat wot stung me. Same time, I tell yer there's just the shadder of a chance for yer if yer give a full account of everything."

" A full account of how you meant to betray him, he means," put in Granny, with sudden eagerness; " nothing else."

Mr. Bender's manner changed in a moment.

It was not so much the words as the tone in which the old woman uttered them, that was so remarkable.

" What did you say, old lady?" he asked, eyeing her keenly, as he bit his nether lip.

" You heard what I said, Benny dear," she returned, in a wheedling voice, which had on the robber about as much effect as though she had addressed herself to the table on which is arm rested. " You don't want to be bothered with a rigmarole of silly boy and gal talk; what you want to know is about his splitting on the diamond business."

But Mr. Bender shook his head and grinned in a manner that was anything but pleasant to behold.

" You're a rare old beauty, you are !" he exclaimed, in rising wrath, "but you must go to school agin before you are able to walk round me. Since you thought it worth your while to put your spoke in, let's know all about it. Now, what does 'tell him that, and nothing else' mean?"

"Nothing, Ben, 'pon my soul, nothing," replied Granny, earnestly, but at the same time changing colour guiltily.

"It's a lie!" exclaimed the burglar, furiously, "I'm being hedged in nicely amongst you. But I'll know all about it. What is it now that you want to keep back?"

And with his hand trembling with passion, he snatched up the pistol and cocked it with a click.

This was, indeed, a strange turning of the tables.

Had the malicious old woman designed serving me, which I need not remark was, of all things, the most remote from her intention, she could not have set about it in a manner more effectual.

To do Mr. Bender justice, I must say that I think I had inspired him with as much kindliness as it was in his nature to feel for man or beast; but, at the same time, there can be no doubt that an unfortunate turn in the tide of events had changed his love into bitterest hatred, and I believe he spoke no more than sober truth when he declared that he would no more "funk" over killing any one who "piped" on him, than he would on smashing a fly.

Taking this view of the matter, my escape was indeed miraculous. My escape so far, that is to say, for I was not yet sufficiently "out of the wood" to feel at liberty to congratulate myself.

On the contrary, as the reader will readily understand, between the two fires —the crafty, malicious old hag on the one side, and the brutal, unscrupulous man

on the other—I was pretty well consumed in mortal fright, and remained with no more ability to say a word than a waxen image.

Mr. Bender, however, suddenly roused me to consciousness. Finding Granny slow at answering his question, he turned to me.

"Jack," said he, in a kinder voice than before, "I begin to see through this business. *You* tell me—what is it that is to be kept back?"

Now, as the reader will readily understand, this was a ticklish question.

Well enough I knew to what Granny Corston alluded when she interfered to check my full confession of my conversation with Luce, although I was as much in the dark as Mr. Bender himself as to the motive for observing so much mystery in the matter.

It was concerning the written scrap of paper, that on which "Lucy Heath" was written, that I was to keep silence.

If I wished to serve the old woman that is to say. But I had no wish to serve her.

I hated her with all the wicked bitterness my heart contained; and with a reckless malice equal to her own, I at once perceived how I might further turn her discomfiture to my advantage.

"She does not wish me to say anything to you about the writing," I said.

"About the writing! Who's been writing? Who to?" and Mr. Bender's suspicious fury was stirred to its lowest depths.

"The writing on the——"

But Granny interrupted me.

"There's no writing at all, the wicked little liar," she exclaimed, making a furious lunge at me from the savage effects of which Mr. Bender's strong arm happily saved me. "Don't believe it, Ben."

"I must have some one else's word for it besides yours," said the burglar, with an ugly grin. "What was the writing, eh?"

"There is no writing. Kill him, the viper. Don't let him say another word. He'll only mislead you deeper and deeper till he manœuvres a rope round your neck. Do as you said you would, dear. Kill him. I'll never tell; I swear that I never will."

And strangely enough, and as though to verify Granny's accusation against me, that it was my design to trap the burglar into the hands of his enemies, at that moment there came a smart rapping at the outer door below, which, as the reader will recollect, Mr. Bender had securely fastened before the commencement of the angry controversy.

I made sure this time that it must be Mr. Overshiner who was knocking; but how could I hope that the poor old fellow would be able to assist me with the desperate burglar waiting for him with a loaded pistol?

"There, what did I tell you!" exclaimed Granny. "Do you hear 'em? they're after you already. It's his doings. I'll never tell if you'll do it, Ben, they shall cut me in pieces first."

But happily for me, and for her, too, probably, Mr. Bender's mind as regards murder had altogether altered.

"What! Kill the cub that the fox may escape!" he exclaimed, with an ugly laugh. "No, no, Granny, we'll leave killing till another day. But say your prayers, old woman. Say 'em, and go on saying 'em, *for I'm coming back.*"

And with these ominous words he replaced the pistol in his pocket and retreated rapidly from the room. In a moment, however, he was back again.

"Look here, old woman." said he, impressively, "that boy is *my* boy: mind how you handle him."

And after this friendly caution, he again disappeared, and his hasty strides were heard cautiously descending a flight of stairs that led to the back of the premises.

---

## CHAPTER XX.

IN WHICH DADDY CORSTON ADMINISTERS TO ME A COMPOSING DRAUGHT, FROM WHICH I AWAKE TO FIND MYSELF A PRISONER LEFT TO STARVE.—MY RESCUE IS DUE TO JERRY TYLER, WHO ACTS THE PART OF THE GOOD SAMARITAN.

IT was a great relief to me when, having paused at my bed-foot, eyeing me with the gaze of an infuriated cat, as though not at all decided as to what, under the circumstances, would be the best course to pursue, Granny Corston, without addressing a word to me, followed the example set by Mr. Bender, and quitted the room.

Though fully alive to their import, I

could get little comfort out of the burglar's parting injunctions to the old woman.

It was all very well to threaten vengeance and hint what would happen to her in the event of her harming me; that might have effect while he was by to protect me, but I knew enough of Granny's ungovernable and furious temper to make me quake for the consequences of his leaving me to her mercy.

Had I been able I would have got out of bed and crawled off anywhere away from her spite; but it was impossible. I essayed to rise, but the movement caused such acute pain to my hurt leg that, with a groan, I sank back again on the pillow.

I waited and waited, each moment expecting that the old woman would come back to me, and bearing in mind the advice Mr. Bender had given her, though it was uttered in derision. I thought that I might do worse than take it to myself. "Say your prayers, old woman," he had said, as an intimation that she had but a little time to live; and, according to my knowledge of Mrs. Corston's character, I probably had even less.

So I said *my* prayers, endeavouring to make up for my limited knowledge of pious petitions by earnest and reiterated implorings to God to protect me from the old woman's fury, or to take me to heaven in the event of her putting me out of the world.

And nobody came in to interrupt my praying, or to demonstrate what urgent need there was for it.

After Mr. Bender had gone the knocking at the street door was repeated; indeed, I had an idea that when Granny went away also it was to go down and see who it was seeking admission; but she went up to her attic instead, and, more inexplicably still, the knocking at the door came no more.

Hour after hour passed, still nobody came to me and I was terribly thirsty.

Had I dared I would have called out to any one within hearing to bring me a drink, but this seemed merely courting the peril I most dreaded.

By-and-bye I heard a footstep approaching my door, and the handle was turned in the lock. It was not Granny, however; it was Daddy, who carried a light in one hand and a basin of tea in the other.

Overjoyed to see no more formidable preparations for my assassination, I held out my hand gratefully for the comforting beverage.

Daddy spoke quite kindly.

"I thought it had better bring it, Jack," said he, with a grin, that showed his bare gums to their furthest extremity. "She ain't quite got over her tantrums yet, Jack. She'll be better in the morning."

Thanking him, I took the tea and drank it off at a draught.

I was too thirsty to take particular notice, but I thought it had a somewhat bitter taste; but that I attributed to its being stronger than Granny was accustomed to brew it.

"Is there anything else you want?" he inquired, the grin on his hideous face expanding, as though it were a capital joke to bring tea to an invalid."

"No, thanky. I think I shall do now," I replied.

"Oh yes, you'll do now, Jack. There ain't a doubt but that you'll do now," he remarked.

And in diabolical glee at the pretty trick he had played me, he made me a mock bow, and chuckling, carried off the candle, leaving me once more in the dark.

I speak about the "trick," but I had no suspicion of it at the time.

I only thought it strange that he should behave so, but it was by no means rare for him to indulge in apish antics when he was tipsy, and as likely as not he was so now. Indeed, I had no opportunity or inclination to think very much about it, I was too sleepy.

Troubled in mind, and weary in body, it seemed only to want that basin of tea to compose me to slumber, and desiring nothing so much, I made no effort to keep my heavy eyes open.

When I awoke it was broad daylight, and my head ached dreadfully.

That it was far beyond early morning I knew, for the sun was shining on the wall opposite the window, and I knew that that never was the case before noon.

This was puzzling.

My head felt so confused that it was several moments before I could call to mind when I was last awake.

It must have been more than twelve hours since, but I felt not in the least refreshed with my long spell of slumber; on the contrary, I was still languid and heavy, and loth to stir.

Presently my eyes wandered in the direction of the cupboard, in which all the good things Mr. Bender had procured for me, were stored; and, lo! the door was open, disclosing the shelves empty and bare.

This was strange. I was quite sure that last evening the wine bottles, and the grapes, and the jam and jelly pots were there.

Who had moved them while I was asleep? There was another cupboard in the room which was closed, and it was not impossible that Mr. Bender's presents had been moved thereto.

It was now many hours since I had eaten or drank anything, and I have no doubt that that fact helped considerably to spur my curiosity.

Without for a moment giving my injured leg a thought, I attempted to rise, and found that, excepting for a sharp twinge, I was able to do so with tolerable ease.

My long sleep at all events had done my leg good.

Indeed there was no great damage done to it; the pistol-ball had never entered the limb, but merely ploughed up the flesh on the outer side in an ugly way.

I managed to get out of bed, and shuffle along the floor to the closed cupboard.

I opened it, and it was empty as the other one.

I made a shift to reach the room door, to discover that it was locked and the key taken away.

What did it all mean?

I laid my ear to the door and listened, but beyond the leisurely ticking of the great clock upstairs, not a sound was to be heard—not even the wailing voice of an uncomfortable baby, and that was one evidence of the existence of animated nature seldom or never wanting up in the nursery.

Nothing but the ticking of the clock, which at that moment emitted four warning chimes, and then struck two.

I had been asleep fifteen hours then, and so soundly asleep that Granny or some one else had been able to remove everything from the cupboard without my being disturbed.

Now that I looked about me, I could see that the bolster had been removed bodily from under my head, while the pillow, bereft of its white outer covering, was flung into a distant corner.

Puzzle on puzzle! It was difficult enough for me to understand *how* this had been done without my knowledge, but a much tougher riddle to solve was *why?*

Presently a light broke in on the mystery of the displaced pillow and bolster at least.

Granny had been witness to my placing the two sovereigns the burglar had generously presented me with, under my head; it must have been in a vain search for this treasure that the avaricious old woman had so disarranged my bed-clothing.

It may have been some consolation that she had missed what she sought; but what did the fact of her hunting after it, together with the empty cupboard and the locked door, portend?

That I was abandoned and left alone!

So terrible was this suspicion, that, risking all consequences, I hammered at the door with my fists, and shouted my loudest, but with no other result than to hear the dreary, old, empty room echo back my cries mockingly.

Finding that it was hopeless to seek succour in this direction, I turned to the window, but barricading the lower half of it was a heavy wooden shutter, secured by a massive iron bar, and how could I, weak, and with but one leg to stand, reach up to unclasp it?

No; my suspicion grew more strongly confirmed each moment.

I was locked and barred in, and it was intended that I should remain so till I starved to death!

Here I was as securely a prisoner as though imprisoned in Newgate, and worse off, because there was at hand no gaoler who could open my door if he pleased.

Overcome by my never-ending misfortune, I climbed up on to my bed again, and there lay bewailing.

I might have so lain an hour or more, when I was roused by the sound of a footstep ascending the stairs. Whoever it was was welcome—Mr. Bender—even Granny Corston herself.

But better luck might be in store for me.

It might happen that Luce had been waiting to see Granny off, and that she had returned, bringing with her Mr. Overshiner.

I sat up on the bed and listened eagerly.

But alas! the footstep passed my door —went upwards to the front attic. Then, however, it was heard returning the way it had gone, and listening still, I heard a familiar voice muttering,

"Of all the rummiest goes this is the rummiest. All out, and the door not locked! The old 'un has took the kids out for a carriage hairing in the park, I shouldn't vonder."

It was the voice of Jerry Tyler.

Had he been my most loving and intimate friend I could not have greeted him more joyously.

"Jerry! Jerry! that you, Jerry?"

"Oh yes, it's Jerry," replied the young gentleman, halting at my door, and speaking in tones of withering sarcasm. "Wot's up, I wonder, when his rile 'ighness speaks so condescendingly to poor Jerry? Are you well enough to receive wisitors, my lord?"

"Oh, don't make a mock of me, Jerry!" I cried; "do come in, pray do."

Jerry tried the door.

"Can't be done, it's locked," said he "it's true I'm wore down to a shadder through grieving arter you, Bender's pet, but I'm no' as yet *quite* thin enough to creep through a key-hole. Ta, ta."

And as he spoke I could hear him turning away.

"Jerry, dear Jerry! don't go!" I screamed; "they've left me here to starve. Break open the door, pray do."

The tone in which I uttered this appeal touched Jerry's not naturally hard heart.

"Oh, if it comes to that, it's no trouble to burst a door open," said he, and next moment the lock yielded to the sudden pressure of his strong shoulders.

Now it must be pretty evident to the reader that, judging from the nature of Master Tyler's remarks, that his disposition was not perfectly friendly towards me.

Very likely he had heard something of my exploit with the renowned burglars, and of the high favour in which I stood with Mr. Bender, and was jealous. But, to do him justice, when the open door revealed me to him, the sneer on his expressive countenance vanished at once, to give place to pity.

"What, Jack!" (he had not seen me since my accident) "my eyes and limbs! you *have* altered! Poor cove! you *do* look a objik!"

And no doubt I did look particularly healthy and cheerful, with my thin face, and my cropped hair, and my leg bandaged!

I know I did not feel so, and Jerry's words of pity were enough to set me off crying again.

"Wot's the meanin' of it? Where have they all bolted to? How came you locked in?" were the eager questions that Master Tyler asked, one after the other.

"I don't know what it means, Jerry: I'm as much in the dark as you are," I replied.

"Oh, bust it, yer know, I can't bear animosity agin a cove wot's brought to this!" he exclaimed, turning back the cuffs of his coat.

"How can I help you, Jack? They've left you here to starve, have they? I'll jolly soon find you some grub."

And away he went upstairs again to the attic, and returned with the best he could find, some bread and butter, and a tea-pot with cold tea in it.

"Pitch into that," exclaimed Master Tyler, "and then tell us all about it."

But I could pitch into nothing but the cold tea; that, however, in my thirst, I drained to the last drop.

"It's one of the queerest rigs that ever I came acrost?" ejaculated Jerry, scratching his head as he cast his eyes round my disordered room. "I thought summat was up when I found the street door locked last night when I knocked at it."

"Oh, was it *you* who knocked at the door, Jerry?"

"Yes, I knocked twice, and then I was obliged to bolt."

"What for, Jerry?"

"Why, 'cos they was on my track as well as Nat's."

"Who was on your track?"

"Why, the perlice, on both our tracks," replied Jerry.

"And where is Nat?" I asked.

"Nat's nailed."

"What, took to prison?"

"I wish I was as sure of a dinner as Nat is of getting six months. That's what I came to tell Granny last night when I found the street door fast. Who made it fast, Jack?"

"Mr. Bender," I replied. "He made it fast because nobody should come in."

"How did he get out then? Who unbolted the door? Who locked you in here? *you* above anybody, who, only

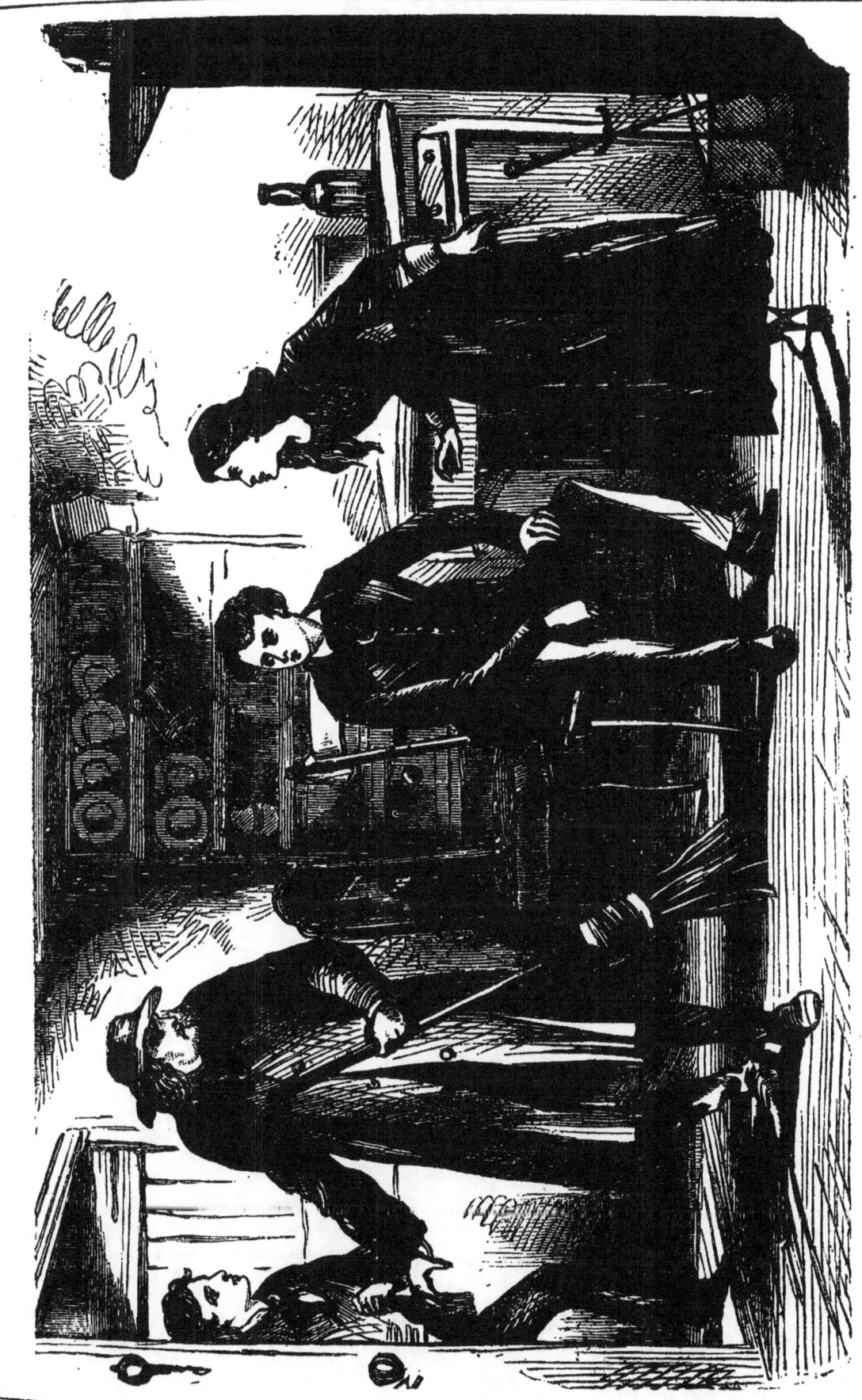

"I KNEW HIM AT ONCE AS HE STOOD ON THE THRESHOLD."

yesterday, was too precious to be looked at by a common cove like me, although he arst it as a favour. Bust me if it isn't like one of them domestic draymas wot they bring out at the Wic! When did Granny, and the old 'un and the kids go?"

"I don't know," I replied. "P'r'aps last night, p'r'aps not two hours ago. I have been asleep since about ten o'clock last night."

"No, they didn't go away this morning—leastways not since eight o'clock," remarked Jerry, his bewilderment evidently increasing.

"How do you know, Jerry?"

"Because I've been a doggin' on and off since then, hoping to ketch somebody belonging here I could 'give the office' to (give information) about Nat, rather than chance coming to the house. They must have gone away last night!"

"They'll come back again, of course, Jerry?" I observed.

"Blest if I know what to think on it," replied my young friend, stirring his hair into a still wilder state of confusion; "'course she means to come back some time, 'cos there's all the furniture. Hold 'ard! I'll jest run up agin and inwestigate the case a bit furder."

After an absence of about ten minutes, Jerry returned with a face even more perplexed than before.

"She's gone, Jack!" he exclaimed.

"And Daddy as well—all of 'em?"

"Daddy, and Luce, and the kids—all the precious shoot!"

"Gone, never to come back, do you mean, Jerry?"

"It seems so. All the drawers is empty wot the kid's clothes and the old woman's best gownd was kep' in. There's the tea-caddy wot the old woman kep' her tin in

turned upside down, with the lid open. She's took fright at something. Come, Jack, you know all about it; tell us wot it is that Granny has slip't at?"

There was no use in making any further concealment, at least, as far as my own secret was concerned.

I had fair reasons for supposing that Jerry was not devoted to Mr. Bender's interest. Whether or no, now that the people of the house had absconded, and Luce failed to return, Jerry was the only friend in the world I had; without him I might have lain and died.

I told Jerry all about it, from first to last.

Beginning at my acidental acquaintance with Mr. Overshiner, and carrying the narrative right through, including the burglarious descent of the chimney at the old diamond-polisher's, my miserable failure to make the frighted old cripple understand the true state of the case, my being shot, and my conveyance home in a state of insensibility.

I told Jerry everything, even the most important part of all—that which involved my league with Luce, and my entrusting her with the two sovereigns Mr. Bender had given me in order that Mr. Overshiner might be moved to regard the matter with proper seriousness.

Master Tyler listened to the narrative with the profoundest attention. As I proceeded, his eyes grew rounder, and his heavy under jaw gradually descended until his amazed mouth stood ajar an inch or more.

His first act on my completing my confession was to shut his mouth with a snap, and burst out into a fit of laughter so uncontrollable as to compel him to grasp the bed-post for support. Not unreasonably, I hope, I felt a little hurt.

" There is not much to laugh at, is there Jerry?" said I.

" I can't help it, Jack, 'pon my word I can't!" said he, laughing still louder; "it's all werry serious till you gets to the last part of it; and beggard· if that wouldn't make a horse laugh!"

" What last part?"

" Why your giving Luce the two pound. Ha! ha! that's about the richest thing I've heard for this month. *I* laugh; but you should have heard her!"

" Heard who?"

" Why, Luce, to be sure."

" Did *you* hear Luce laugh, Jerry?" I asked, a strange alarm seizing me.

" Course I did'nt; but I'll swear she did laugh," he replied. " Oh, lor! it's about the greenest thing you'll ever do in your life, that's *one* comfort; you'll never do a greener thing, Jack!"

" I don't know what you are talking about," said I; "isn't she big enough to take care of it?"

" Oh, hark at him!" exclaimed Jerry, breaking into a fresh fit of merriment; " she's big enough to take care of it! Rayther. Why you foolish young cuckoo, she's done you, clean as a whistle. She saw wot a soft cove you was, and she come it over you beautiful. Bust me if I can hardly believe it! She tells you she wants to be off, and you werry kindly put your hand under your pillow and purwide her with travelling expenses."

Jerry broke into another roar at my expense, but I didn't mind that.

*Now* I knew what he meant, and my mind was quite easy on that score.

" What makes you think that Luce would run away with the money, Jerry?" I asked him.

" Wot makes me think it! why, how could she help it?" he replied, his amazement at my question making him instantly serious. " *You* might be able to help it; arter wot you've jest now told me, and what I knew about you before, I shouldn't be astonished at anything *you* did; but it's different with us what's brought up in the ' Fields.' "

" But Luce wasn't brought up in the ' Fields,' leastways, she wasn't born here."

" Oh, she told you that, did she? Well, Luce ain't the wust amongst us, I will say that of her, but she could no more help bonin' that two pound than she could help having the hoopin' cough if it come in her way; its constitootional, as they say at the 'orspital. No, Johnny, my soft young friend, you've seen the last of your tin; now we'll talk about something else; wot do you mean to be up to? you can't stay here, with nobody to look arter you, don't yer know,"

" I *must* stay here, Jerry; I can't walk; you don't know how bad my leg is, Jerry."

" That's the werry reason why you can't stay here, young stoopid; you wants doc-·toring and nursing. Besides, from wot you've told me, if I was you, I should be inclined to make myself scarce out of Granny's way, as well as Bender's, soon as ever I could. He said that he was coming back, don't you know; and he isn't quite so fond of you as he used to be."

" That's true; but where could I go, Jerry, if I went away from here? Nobody would take me in."

" Ah! there, now, you see wot a young fool you was to part with all that money. But you ain't 'bliged to starve because you haven't got no money, don't yer know? the workus is bound to take you in. Say the word. I'll carry you there."

And truly, for the moment, Jerry's plan

seemed the most feasible that could be suggested.

But then I thought of Luce.

Spite of all that Jerry said, I was sure of her; and suppose she should come back presently with good news, and find that I was gone. This decided me at once.

"No, Jerry," said I; "it is very kind of you, but I can't go to the workhouse. I'd much rather stay here, just for a little while, anyhow, and chance it."

"Chance what?" exclaimed Jerry, gruffly.

"Everything. Never mind me, Jerry. I'll wait. I don't mind if you'll leave the front door on the latch."

There must have been something in my sorrowful tones that stirred that in the breast of the young thief that was unaccustomed to disturbance.

"Not likely," said he, coming to the bedside. "Come on, Jack, old fellow; you mightn't like the thoughts of it, but you'll be glad when you get there. Let's help you on with your togs, and I'll carry you to the workus as light as though you was a kitten."

And placing his strong arms round my waist, he hauled me up, never thinking of the pain he caused me.

"Don't, Jerry, don't!" I cried out. "Pray don't take me away from here. She's all I've got to hold on to, Jerry, and she's sure to come back. For God's sake, Jerry, don't carry me away!"

And with my arms about the neck of the bullet-headed young fellow, overcome by pain and apprehension, I fainted dead away.

*     *     *     *     *

When I came to myself, I was lying on the white bed, covered over with the bed-clothes, and Master Jerry Tyler was in the room, busy at the fire-place.

I did not know him at first.

He was divested of his long coat, and in his shirt-sleeves. His back was towards me, and I could hear by the scrooping sound that he was stirring with a spoon something in a saucepan.

The slight noise I made caused him to turn about.

"Hullo, my kiddy," he exclaimed, in a kinder voice than I thought him capable of, "you've come to, then?"

"What's been the matter, Jerry? What are you doing?"

"Lay quiet, young 'un," he replied, "it'll be ready in a minute."

"What will?"

"Your supper. I'm making you some gruel."

"You're a good fellow, Jerry," said I, with tears in my eyes.

"You wait till you gets it before you give me a character," he replied, with a grin, stirring away all the time; "there's another beggar; ah! that's smashed yer! D'ye mind lumps in it, Jack? I don't think there's many werry big 'uns left in it by this time."

I did'nt care a bit for the gruel, but I wouldn't have told Jerry so for a trifle; and as for lumps, I believe I gave him to understand I rather preferred them than otherwise.

Presently he turned the gruel into a yellow quart jug without a handle, for want of something handier.

It certainly *was* "lumpy," but I contrived to swallow a good drop of it, evidently to the great satisfaction of Jerry, who sat by.

"That was very good, Jerry," said I, as I handed him back the jug.

"P'r'aps I shall do better next time," said he, puffing with a mysterious air at his stumpy black pipe. "I mean to have a go in at making mutton broth by-and-bye."

"Who for, Jerry?"

"Oh, you'll see; but there, it ain't no secret; you shan't go to the workus, Jack. I'm a going to stay here and look arter you."

And, strange as it may appear to the reader, having made this generous avowal, Jerry blushed crimson to the roots of his stubby hair, and cast down his eyes, as though detected in something he felt heartily ashamed of.

"Oh, Jerry!"

"It'll be out-and-out conwenience for me, don't yer see?" he interrupted, hastily. "I shall be lonely in the lodgings wot I halve with Nat, now he's put away, and it'll be getting my hand in the cooking line; one don't know wot he might want one of these days, don't you know? It'll be quite a little holiday for me."

"But you can't be always here, Jerry; you'll have to ——"

"Now, that'll do. Never mind wot I shall have to do. I'm goin' to have a holiday, I tell you—*altogether* a holiday. I've made a promise to do it."

He blurted out these last words as though he had no intention of doing so, and looked so foolish immediately afterwards, that I could not forbear asking him—

"Who did you promise, Jerry? What made you?"

You would have thought that Jerry was right down savage at the question, from his manner of turning round on me.

"How could I help promisin'," said he, "with you a looking so awful bad, and a chucking your arms round my neck, and crying 'For God's sake?' How *could* I help promisin' when I thought you was dead, and I was all of a shake so I couldn't unhook your hands from me? Don't you go a arskin *who* I promised—don't you say another blessed word about it. I'm goin' to have a holiday, I tell you."

I was so amazed at Jerry's strange remarks, that, had I been inclined just then to say "another word about it," I don't think that I should have been able.

Evidently he had somehow sustained a very severe fright, for, even while he briefly hinted at the cause of it, his lips trembled, and something curiously like tears stood in his eyes. In *his* eyes! The devil-may-care, brazen-faced Jerry Tyler! I lay still fully half-an-hour thinking about it.

Meanwhile, with his brow puckered in determination, and his shirt-sleeves rolled back, Jerry was not idle.

Softly stepping up and down stairs, he fetched out of Granny Corston's room such articles of domestic utility as it afforded, and that might be useful to him as cook and housekeeper.

He brought down crockeryware and saucepans, and a kettle, and made several journeys, conveying coals in a washing-bason, so that our store of fuel might be durable.

Lastly, he brought down a mattress and a rug, and rolled them up tidily, and stowed them in a corner ready, for use.

And so, duly installed as my nurse and companion, Jerry Tyler kept his "promise" with amazing fidelity through four days.

Somehow he found money to supply our needs, to say nothing of many luxuries he insisted on providing for me, and though some of the latter would hardly have been sanctioned by an experienced attendant on a sick person, they were one and all flavoured, as it were, with the spirit of Jerry's self-sacrifice and generosity, and the enjoyment derived from them on that account compensated, I dare say, for what they lacked in other respects.

I didn't know where he got money from: I never pressed him particularly, being afraid of eliciting the truth; but once, when I hinted on the subject, he assured me that "it was all right, he was borrowing."

Meanwhile, neither Luce, nor Mr. Bender, nor Granny Corston returned.

I grew the more anxious because, as Jerry on the fourth day informed me, his holiday "according to promise" depended for its duration entirely on my state of health.

"Don't hurry yourself on my account, Jack," said he, "but as soon as you're on your pins again I must get to work."

I knew what that meant.

Jerry would go back to his old wretched business, and I should have to turn out of the old house and shift for myself, losing my chance of ever again seeing Luce.

Under such conditions, I am afraid that I was not sufficiently grateful for my rapid recovery. I might almost as "well be without a leg to stand on," as to gain a footing in the world again only to be bowled over by the first strong temptation that crossed my path.

Wearily as the hours dragged along, me all the time listening and longing for Luce, they would doubtless have appeared much longer had not Jerry been able to read, and endowed with an affection for literature of a romantic turn.

There was a "lending library" somewhere near Penny's Fields, and at the rate of a penny a volume, Jerry must have expended considerably more than a shilling there, within the brief space of four days.

He was a terribly extravagant reader. Descriptions of the picturesque he would pass by invariably with a snort of derision, while anything in the shape of a display of the "tender passion" excited his ire to that degree, that every offending page he flouted over was in danger of being torn from its binding.

What Jerry liked was mystery and bloodshed.

Within the first two days, his demands for books with "summat haunted in 'em," had quite exhausted the small shopkeeper's stock.

Jerry was not at all particular what it was that was "haunted"—a mill, a mansion, or a forest, so that there was a "spectre" in the business—the fiercer and more unaccountably cruel, the better he was satisfied.

He used to kindly read aloud, as he sat by the fire of evenings, and I have heard the fire-irons jingle together, as his shaking knees smote the fender.

"There now, that's what I call a clippin' story!" Jerry would exclaim, as he closed the volume, and wiped the perspiration from his forehead.

On the fourth evening of our companionship, having devoured everything else in his peculiar line of reading, he returned again to a story that had pleased him more than all—"The Mottled Myth of the Moated Grange"—the "Mottled Myth" turning out to be a tabby cat, accidentally bricked up in a chimney, along with its mistress, whom a sanguinary-minded nephew had murdered.

There was a little love-making in the tale, but that altogether Jerry generously overlooked in his admiration for the intensity of its tragical features.

The murdered countess, who was quite a young creature, was dotingly in love with a young gentleman who occupied the attic floor of a cottage adjoining the Moated Grange, and beguiled the tedium of his illness (he was consumptive) by playing the flute out-o'-window, having been privately informed of the countess's love for music.

Fearful lest his aunt should marry the consumptive stranger, her nephew, as before stated, murders her, and bricks up her body in the chimney, and, without knowing, her favourite cat also.

Immediately afterwards the Grange is haunted.

Mysterious and unearthly sounds are heard in all parts of the mansion, and of nights on the roof, and a ghostly figure is dimly perceived crawling on all fours over the tiles, but nobody, not even the love-sick young gentleman, who still continues to play mournful tunes on his flute, suspects that the strange apparition has anything to do with the countess's disappearance.

At last, one stormy midnight, the love-sick young gentleman hears a scratching at his garret window-pane, and, opening it to discover the cause, there stands the " Mottled Mystery," bearing in its gaunt jaws a long tress of the murdered countess's auburn hair, and so the crime is brought to light, and the murderer punished as he deserves.

The good reader is doubtless wondering what there was in such a rubbishing romance so to impress its main incidents on my memory ; he will cease to wonder presently.

It was rather late—past ten o'clock indeed—but, having got what he called " into the marrer " of the story, Jerry was loth to quit it, and sat reading away, with the candle on the mantel-shelf and his feet on the fender.

I was well enough to sit up now, and I was seated close by Jerry's side, listening with all my might for the horrors that I knew must come, as soon as he turned the next leaf.

"'Ah ! he sighed,'"read Jerry ; "'alas ! it is in vain. I play but to the idle winds' —and with that he closed his winder, and returned his moosical insterment to a drawer. But hardly had he done so, and, with a dismal mone, flung hisself on his couch, when a strange, unearthly scratching sound, was heard outside and ——"

And at that moment Jerry started to his feet with a cry of terror, and the romance slipped from his hand and rolled under the grate.

The catch of our door-lock was turned, and a strange little figure stood dimly revealed in the doorway.

It was Luce come back at last !

## CHAPTER XXI.

### IN WHICH JERRY IS VERY MUCH ASTONISHED.

AT the conclusion of the foregoing chapter I say "it was Luce," as though there could be no doubt of it, and that I recognised her instantly.

That, however, was hardly the case, I am sorry to tell.

It was Luce, but she was wonderfully altered.

She had always been pale and thin, but never as now.

Owing to our candle being conveniently placed on the shelf, the door end of the room was thrown into deep gloom, and in it Luce's white face looked like a light almost.

She stood there without moving, being, I dare say, little less amazed than we were, to see me in such strange company.

I knew her at a second glance, however, and hastily hobbled across the room, crying out her name; on which she came forward as eagerly and flung her arms round my neck, and at once fell a sobbing and crying in a way that instantly convinced Jerry that it could be no supernatural visitation.

He picked up the "Mottled Myth" from where the cinders were falling on it, and dusted it, and snuffed the candle with his fingers, and turned about with it in his hand to behold the interesting spectacle.

"I knew that you would come back!" I exclaimed, hugging her in my arms, and feeling now more than ever how much I wanted her. "Jerry, didn't I say she was sure to come back!"

"Certainly you did. I thought she would come back some time or another," Jerry replied, with a sneer, that I understood well enough.

"I might have been back long ago, but I was afraid," said Luce, shivering in her rags.

"But did you see him? Did you find him where I said you would?" I asked, eagerly.

"Oh! no, no; I was unlucky all the time," she replied. "O! Jack, I might as well never have gone."

"Ezackly!" grinned Master Tyler.

"You did not find him?" said I, with my heart sinking dismally. "What made you so long gone, Luce?"

"I have been waiting, and waiting, all day, and till late at night, and he has never been there once," said poor Luce, not heeding Jerry's interruption. "I came back here last night, and the night before, thinking to take the worst Granny could do to me, rather than lay out in the dark and the cold. Last night I pulled the string of the door, and came right into the passage; but I daren't come no further. I shouldn't have dared now, but I felt that I should die if I held out any longer."

She laid her little, cold face on my shoulder as she spoke, and my heart was so full that I could not say a word.

Master Tyler, however, was not so deeply affected.

He laughed.

"Wot was it you was afraid of dying of, Luce?" he asked.

"Oh! I was so cold, so miserable and hungry!" she sobbed.

Master Tyler's laugh became a roar now.

"Get out you artful little wretch!" he exclaimed. "Don't you be gammoned, Jack. Wot do you mean about miserable and hungry? Wasn't ten bob a day enough to keep you going?"

Luce looked up wonderingly and innocently.

"Does *he* know?" she whispered to me.

"Yes, he knows," I replied, feeling that nothing would have given me so much satisfaction as to have been able to have punched Jerry's head for his brutal insolence; "he knows all about it, and has been very kind to me. Why can't you be just a little kind to *her*, Jerry?"

"Bah! you young greenhorn! d'ye think I want to have a hand in murderin' of her?" he replied, still laughing. "Don't you hear what she says? *Your* kindness has nearly been the death of her. Now, look ye here, Luce," he continued, suddenly looking serious and knowing, "you can't humbug me, don't yer know, if you can him. Wot have you done with that two pound?"

"What, the two sovereigns Jack gave me to mind?" she asked.

"Precisely," replied Master Tyler, with a sneer; "they're the werry identical two pound I *do* mean."

"Here it is," Luce replied quietly, and out of the folds of her poor old tattered frock she produced a bit of dirty paper, and opening it, revealed two bright sovereigns!

Somehow, this was no more than I expected, but the effect on Jerry was curious to behold.

Never, even during his reading of the most thrilling passages of the "Mottled Myth," had I seen his countenance exhibit so rapid a series of emotional changes.

He opened his eyes wide, and screwed up his mouth.

He opened his mouth, and winked incredulously with both his eyes.

He essayed to whistle, but his amazed jaws fell helplessly ajar before he could accomplish it.

He scratched his head with as much ferocity as though it were his most deadly enemy, and, finally, he set down the candlestick and sank down on to a chair, exclaiming—

"Thunder me blue! if it don't lick cock-fighting!"

And having so emphatically expressed himself, he was powerless to say another word, but sat eyeing Luce with all his might and main.

"Where is Granny?" Luce asked, in a frightened whisper; "is she out?"

"You needn't be afraid of her; she has gone away altogether. Come and sit by the fire, and I'll tell you all about it."

And I began the curious story, but had not proceeded far with it, when Jerry abruptly broke out again—

"Do you mean to say that you've been going about miserable, and cold, and hungry, and had them two sovereigns all the time?"

"I had them to give to some one. They wasn't mine," Luce simply replied.

"And you laid out in the cold, didn't you say?"

"Yes."

After a pause, Jerry remarked, in a voice that was somewhat husky,

"But how did you get your grub? Since you would not break into the two sovereigns, how did you get it? Of course you didn't—"

It was strange that Jerry should hesitate to utter a word that was so familiar to him, but he *looked* what he meant, and Luce replied—

"No, Jerry, I did not steal it. I'd sooner have died."

"Then you begged it ?"

"What else could I do ?" Luce replied, her face flushing crimson. I did not do it till I was too weak to ask almost. P'r'aps that is why I got so little give me !"

Jerry regarded her with his eyes full of amazement as she made this simple answer. She spoke so quietly and uncomplainingly; all her sorrow, indeed, seemed to be on my account, because she had failed in her errand.

"Beggar me if I knows wot you are made of !" he exclaimed, incredulously. I knows one thing; you open a cove's eyes to the sort of stuff *he's* made of. Thundering bad stuff, there's no mistake about that."

"You must be hungry now, Luce," I remarked.

"I've had nothing to-day but a ha'porth of bread I bought this morning, but I'm not very hungry. I'm so glad to find you better," she answered.

"Had nothing but a a'porth of bread all the blessed day, and had them two sovereigns on her all the time !" exclaimed Jerry Tyler.

And to my unutterable amazement, the conscience-stricken young thief there and then bent his face against the mantel-piece and fell a blubbering, his chest heaving, and his quick, heavy tears, pattering down on to the fender.

"Don't cry, Jerry," said Luce, laying her hand on his arm.

"Ow ! Who can help it ?" exclaimed Jerry, his grief becoming uncontrollable. "A little bit of a scrimp of a gal like you a doin' all this, and me, a great, hulkin' willin', big enough a'most to carry a hundred of bricks, would rather go a nailin' than be without his bacca even !"

And the unlucky youth, his better nature probed to the quick, wriggled in the agonies of remorse.

Luce tried to comfort him.

"It wasn't so bad to bear as you might think, Jerry," said she, her hand sliding down his arm to his hand, which she timidly pressed; "it wasn't as though I was alone quite."

"Oh ! you wasn't alone quite; I thought you said you was," said Jerry, a little of the old hardness returning to his face.

"You are never alone when you say your prayers, Jerry. That's the time to say your prayers, when you are most in want."

"Ah ?" said Jerry, shortly, and as though he would rather change the subject of conversation.

"It is quite true, Jerry : I've found it so, so I know it is wonderful. You'd never believe it without trying it. God can warm you without clothes, and take away your hunger without food."

Knowing what Jerry was, I was half sorry to hear Luce talk so.

I knew the time when three words of this sort of discourse, directed at the young reprobate, were enough to set him cursing and swearing in sheer mockery and derision.

Now, however, although with a sort of surliness, he snatched his hand out of Luce's, and folding his arms, rested his forehead on them, he made no further movement of opposition.

I thought it prudent to sign to Luce to say no more to him, and Jerry remained with his face concealed, the restless tapping of his foot betraying the uneasiness of his mind.

Presently he suddenly roused, and with a strange laugh exclaimed—

"Ah! it's all werry well for them as knows how to do it; it's different with a cove like me. Why, if I was once to begin saying my prayers for what *I* want, jiggered if I should know where to leave off,—I want such a jolly lot. But what's the use of talking when I don't know the language even?"

And without another word he looked for his cap, and found it, and hurried out of the room.

We thought to be sure that he had gone off for the night at least.

Bearing in mind what Luce had said about the small quantity of food she had partaken of lately, I made as much haste as my limping leg would permit, to set before her the remnants of our humble dinner, which she devoured with great eagerness, despite Jerry's faulty cookery.

Over the meal, and after it, we found so much to talk about that more than an hour passed.

She told me that since the hour she went away in search of Mr. Overshiner, except during such hours as it was quite improbable that he would be at his post, she had kept constant watch for him, and all in vain. The strangest part of it was, that not finding him there the first night, she had ventured to inquire of the apple-stall woman at the street corner, and was by her told that the old crossing-sweeper was at work the day before, as usual, but she had not seen him since.

This was perplexing, and added not a little to our disappointment.

It proved one thing, however: Luce had made no mistake as to the whereabouts of Mr. Overshiner's crossing.

While we were despondingly discussing what we should do, some one was heard ascending the stairs, and Jerry Tyler once more made his appearance.

## CHAPTER XXII.

IN WHICH JERRY TYLER CONFESSES TO HAVING MADE A SECOND PROMISE—HE DISCOVERS THAT LUCE IS A "HERO-INE," AND SHOWS HIMSELF IN A FAIRER LIGHT THAN THE READER HAS YET SEEN HIM.

THERE was a sheepishness about the young fellow's looks and movements, plain to be discerned through his transparent attempt at jauntiness. He closed the door, and advancing to the fire-place, placed himself between Luce and myself, with his coat-tails under his arm, and his back to the fire, and for fully a minute said not a word.

"Look here, you young 'uns!" he remarked presently, puffing hard at his everlasting short pipe, "I'm a goin' to make a fool of myself. 'Fact; I've done it already. Now the cat's out!"

And Jerry was suddenly seized with a fit of coughing, as though some of his smoke had "gone the wrong way," so that he was compelled to use his pocket-handkerchief with great vigour.

"How do your mean, made a fool of yourself, Jerry?"

"Well, p'r'aps *you* won't call it so," he replied, scratching his head doubtfully, "and it's only to be hoped that it won't turn out so. Whether it does or no, I'm in for it."

"In for what, Jerry?" I asked, anxiously. He spoke so seriously, I began to feel alarmed. "Is it my fault?"

"Not this time; leastways, not entirely," Master Tyler replied, with an odd contortion of countenance; it's *you* who's got to answer for it, young person."

And as he spoke he turned to Luce.

"Me, Jerry?"

"Yes, you; you seven wonders of the world all knocked into one," Jerry answered, his blunt, common-place face, lighting with enthusiasm. "I don't know whether I shouldn't feel 'shamed to knock under to a bit of a thing like you; but somehow I don't."

Jerry took a few hurried whiffs at his pipe.

"Lord! there's nothing for you both to look so funky about," said he presently, with a somewhat thick utterance. "I've been and made another promise; that's all about it."

"Made another promise, Jerry?"

"Ah! sort of renewed the pledge, as the pawnbroker ses!" he replied, with a grin, which, however, he instantly suppressed. "Rare thing to joke about, ain't it?" he continued, sneering seriously at his levity. You look stunned, both of you. Nat'rally you are!"

"I don't know what he means. Do you, Jack?" Luce asked.

"Oh, yes, *he* knows; he was im*pli*-cated in t'other affair," remarked Jerry. "It's a rum business for me to be going in for, isn't it?"

I had an inkling now of what the bashful young fellow was talking about, as possibly the reader has; if he has not, permit me to jog his memory, as to a certain observation Jerry had used, respecting a "promise" he had made that time when I fainted and lay apparently dead in his arms.

How he kept that "promise" has already appeared.

"Yes," continued Jerry Tyler, "I haven't had much practice, d'ye see, so p'r'aps I may break down at my second attempt. There's a kind of difference in the way it was made. Fust one was jerked out of me in a fright: this 'ere last one was more deliberate."

Luce and I looked at each other, but we said nothing.

"Only fancy me," Jerry broke out again in a minute or so; "only fancy me a walking about the dark walks in St. James's Park, a putting questions and answers to myself, and trying to screw up my courage to make a promise so uncommonly out of my line. I'm blistered! wot 'ud Nat say if he on'y knowed it?"

It almost seemed that this last was an aspect of the question that had never appeared to Master Tyler before.

For several seconds he said not another word; but that he was suffering from some mental disturbance was evident from his winking and blinking, and head-shaking, and the frequent unintelligible sounds he gave utterance to.

"Well, there, it's done, and it can't be undone!" he exclaimed, aloud. "I was too long over tryin' to do it, to back out of it all in a minute. Awful trouble it was," he continued, with a sheepish sidelong glance at little Luce; "couldn't get it out—not real and hearty, don't you know—till I got back here agin. Fact; it was down stairs in the passidge that the promise was made, just afore I come up, just now. Now you know all about it."

And, as though he had delivered his mind of a considerable load and felt all the easier for it, Jerry refilled his pipe cheerfully, and drawing a chair towards the fire, composed himself for a comfortable smoke.

"I'm all ready to listen when you're ready to begin," he remarked presently, finding that we did not break the silence.

"Begin what, Jerry?"

"Why, the history of this ere gunpowder plot of yours. I'm a new pardner in the firm, don't yer see," and then, interrupting himself, he continued, with a sheepish attempt at laughing, and making light of the matter—

"Oh, I beg your pardon, Jack, Luce, and Co.; p'r'aps you don't care about taking another pardner into the concern?"

"If you can help us, Jerry, we shall be very glad," I remarked.

"Werry good; that settles it. Fire away, and let the new pardner into all the secrets and pertick'lers."

Although, as before mentioned, Jerry kept up a pretence of the jocularity that was natural to him, it was quite evident to us that he was perfectly in earnest.

That it was quite possible for him to keep a "promise" when he chose to make one, even though it involved an inconvenient departure from those habits and customs that had become his second nature, I had abundant proof during the last few days.

Besides, how would treachery avail him?

Supposing even that he knew where Mr. Bender was, what reward could he hope to obtain by conveying to him anything that I could confide to him?

Presuming that Jerry knew where Granny Corston had fled to, of what worth would be Jerry's treachery to her? To be sure he could inform her that Luce had returned, and so help her, if she was so desirous, to get Luce back into her clutches again. But that he might do without putting himself to the trouble of acting the hypocrite.

"Fire away," repeated Jerry; "don't be afeared. I'm staunch, so help——no, I won't swear to it; p'r'aps you'll be more likely to trust me if I don't. Set it down along o' the promise which I daren't break. There now, p'r'aps you're satisfied?"

We were. I looked at Luce, and she returned the glance, and that was sufficient.

Late as it was (nearly twelve o'clock by this time) as we sat over the fire we confided to our new "pardner" what our scheme was, and what at present had come of it.

I don't think that it was our intention to make special allusion to the mystery concerning Luce. The fact is, we attached no importance to it.

Master Tyler, however, with his natural shrewdness and more mature experience, looked at the affair from a different point of view. Soon as mention was made of the written name on the scrap of paper, and the amazement and consternation its business had occasioned Granny Corston and her hideous old husband, the interest he had manifested during the previous part of the narrative increased ten-fold.

"Hold hard!" said he, "go back to the beginning of that there part—start afresh from where you showed him how beautifully you could write your name!"

Luce did as requested, wondering at the eagerness of her listener.

"Ah! and so that's all, eh!" he exclaimed; trying in vain to puff life into his pipe that had died out grey and cold, so absorbing had been the attention he had bestowed on Luce's story.

"That's all. It isn't much, is it, Jerry?"

"Not much!" and Jerry's eyes opened to their widest. "Isn't it enough? My eyes! Little did I think, when I made my promise, that I was a goin' to be inter-dooced to adwentures and reweal-ations of this ere sort!"

And Jerry regarded us, and especially Luce, with strange wonder.

"What is there so strange about it, Jerry?"

"Oh, nothing!" replied Master Tyler, in mild sarcasm, "nothing, you precious pair of innocents. Only this much; the 'Mottled Myth,' which, as you knows, Jack, is the stunningist story I ever come nigh, isn't a patch on this ere romance of yourn; that's all."

"But I told you a good deal about it before," I remarked.

"Wot, about the diamond business? Pooh! that's a werry tidy story; but where is it when you claps it alongside the t'other?"

"What other?" we asked, regarding him in astonishment.

"Wot other? why, the other that sent Granny packing. The other wot'll get in the papers, and be hollered out by the coves wot serves the omlibuses with 'Standards' and 'Telegrafts.' ''Ere you are, sir!—Second edition of the "Inweigled Airess!" 'Ere you are, sir! full particklers of the kidnappin' of a forrin' young princess!'"

And, in his excitement, Jerry skipped across and across the room, calling out the startling news, and doing a brisk trade in imaginary "Standards" and "Telegraphs" with omnibus riders.

"Don't you know what you are?" he abruptly demanded, stopping short in his pacing and facing Luce.

"What am I, Jerry?"

"You're a hero-ine," he replied, regarding her enthusiastically. "Ah! you are, and no mistake. You are as out-and-out a hero-ine as ever was put in a story book!"

And having delivered himself of this prophetic opinion, Jerry Tyler sank on to a chair, and regarded Luce in silent admiration for the space of fully two minutes. Presently he desisted from this occupation, and turning to the fire, rested his chin on his hand, and went off into a brown study of some considerable duration. Finally, he took from his pocket a stump of black-lead pencil and a bit of paper.

"Overshiner — corner of Waterloo Bridge, I think you said?" he remarked, as he wrote it down.

"That's it, Jerry. What are you going to do?"

"Well, its like this, you see," said our new partner, nibbling the pencil stump thoughtfully; we can't do anything by ourselves. Somebody 'll have to go to the perlice, and, if it makes no difference, I'd rather be excused. Familiarity breeds contempt, as the copy-books tells us," continued Jerry, whose waggery would crop up at times in spite of him; "and at present I'm not on wisiting terms with the perlice. More are you, Jack. More are you, Luce, though you are a hero-ine. The circumstance of you're living with Granny Corston would get you a month if you was a angel."

"But I never did anything to make me afraid of the police; it isn't my fault that I am living here," urged Luce.

"It makes no sorter difference," replied Jerry, with a shrug of his shoulders; "the perlice knows best about that; if you don't believe it, ask 'em. No; we mustn't go to the perlice about the diamond business, anyhow. It wouldn't pay 'em to believe that we was doing the right thing."

"Wouldn't pay 'em, Jerry?"

"They'd be just a hundred pounds out of pocket," said Master Tyler, mysteriously.

"How?"

Jerry hesitated for a moment. At last said he—

"I don't see why I shouldn't tell you; you didn't mind trusting me."

And as he spoke, he withdrew from his pocket a greasy-looking piece of paper folded into a little square, and opening it, he placed it in my hand.

"There," said he, "that's wot I mean."

But I was almost as much in the dark as ever. The paper was printed all over in large letters, but on the top were some of larger size than the rest, and I could make out one, and two noughts, and R-E-W-A-R-D.

I handed it to Luce, but she could do no more with it than I could.

"It is something about '£100,' I can see that," said she.

"And R-E-W-A-R-D, spells reward, doesn't it, Jerry?" said I.

"That's it. That's the fust line of it," Jerry replied, smiling piteously at our ignorance. "'One hundred pounds reward!'"

"What a lot of money! What's it offered as a reward for, Jerry?"

"For you," Jerry replied, coolly.

"For me!"

"To be sure; you're one of the 'gressors, ain't you?"

"What's a 'gressor, Jerry?"

"Ah, now, see what it is to be a scholard!" he replied, with mock gravity, as he pulled up the dirty tips of his shirt-collar. "See what a awful thing it is to be hignorant? Here's the laws of your country makin' 'fectshonate enquiries after you, and going to the expense of printing jolly big bills for you, and you all the time knowing nothing about it. Here, I'll read it to you."

And spreading the placard on the table, to my astonishment he read as follows:—

"'Whereas, on the night of the 12th of September, the premises of Mr. Peter Bastable, diamond-polisher and setter, of Church Lane, Chelsea, were burglariously entered by the chimney, and jewels of great value stolen; the said Mr. Peter Bastable being at the same time murderously assaulted.

"'The actual robbery was committed by a boy, apparently of about twelve years of age, of sturdy build and with lightish hair.

"'From the circumstance of a rope ladder being left behind, it is assumed that the thieves so gained access to the roof of the house, and that the boy was assisted in his descent and ascent of the chimney by means of cords.

"'The stolen jewels were secured in a black japanned box, and, besides those below enumerated, included an antique cross, composed of diamonds of large size, with an emerald centre. The cross is engraved on the back, "Through Life and Beyond, L. H."

"'A reward of One hundred pounds will be paid to any person who shall give such information as shall lead to the detection of the aggressors, or any one of them, and the recovery of the property. And a further reward of Fifty pounds will be paid by the owner of the cross above-mentioned, on its restoration.'"

And then followed a long list of diamonds and emeralds, and rubies, representing in value quite a small fortune.

But there was something that amazed me more than the amount of wealth, in stealing which I had been made the unlucky instrument.

If I understood the contents of the bill aright the reward was to be given to " any person" who could give information.

"There, my waluable young friend!" Jerry remarked, good-humouredly, as he re-folded the placard and put it in his pocket. "Fancy you being worth all that money, and being 'bliged to eat dry toast for breakfast! It's werry hard, isn't it?"

"But does it really mean that the reward —a hundred pounds—will be paid to *any one*?"

"That's wot it says, anyhow."

"But I mean to any one who——"

"Tom, Bill, or Harry—they won't be particklar, I'll wager!"

"Yes; Tom, Bill, or Harry—or Jerry!" said I, feeling a lump rising in my throat.

"Or Jerry!" he responded, affecting a short laugh. "Little they'd care so as

they got their three thousand pounds worth for a hundred.

"And you've known this all along?"

But Jerry shook his head emphatically.

"There you're wrong," said he, "and lucky p'r'aps, I did't. I didn't know it till yesterday morning when I went to see if my old chum, Quilter Wilkins, would lend me another half-crown till things mended; it was then that I see it sticking agin the wall, and tore it down."

"You went to borrow money, and all the time you might——"

"What?" Jerry interrupted, abruptly.

"You might have—— Oh, Jerry *you* might have had that hundred pounds! You know you might!

"Course I might, if I'd a know'd it soon enough. But don't I tell yer it wasn't till yesterday mornin' that I know'd it? That was after the promise, a precious long while, don't you know? There, that'll do, I ain't done nothin' wot I deserves stranglin' for, I hope! Besides, this ain't in order, don't you know? The hero-ine in the Wic piece don't hug and kiss the 'umble characters!"

The latter part of Master Jerry's sentence, although unintelligible to the reader, may be easily explained.

For the moment, nay, for several moments, I was so overwhelmed by the revelation of Jerry's noble behaviour, that I could do nothing but sit on my chair, and behold him in speechless wonder. It was Luce, who was "out of order," according to the enactments observed at Her Majesty's Royal Victoria Theatre. Thankful to the bottom of her kind little heart for the service Jerry had rendered me, she fell on his neck, and cried, and kissed his unhandsome face till it positively blushed, all the time that he was struggling to free himself, and declaring that there was no "call" for anything of the kind.

"Besides," said he, "I tell you if I hadn't have made the promise, the money would have hardly been worth the tryin' after. Ten to one, if I had gone and said 'Come with me and I'll show you where the boy is who got down the chimbly,' they would have got me to show 'em, and then collared me as one of the gang. You don't know 'em as well as I do, so you had better say no more about it."

"Well, but what is to be done, Jerry?"

"On'y one thing. It's no use us making a move, we must get some 'spectable party to do it. Crossin'-sweepers don't reckon fust class in general, but this one

seems to be rayther an uncommon sort, judging from your account of him."

"I am sure that he is, Jerry; if we could only find him we should be all right, I am certain."

"Oh, as to finding him, I'll manage that, if he is to be found," Jerry replied, confidently. "We can do nothing to-night, however, and to-morrow will be a long day, I reckon, so suppose we adjourn."

Luce's room upstairs remained just as when she last slept in it, and thither she retired; and, shortly afterwards, after making fast the door below, Jerry betook himself to his mattress in the corner, declining to say another word concerning his projects, on the ground that it was "illigetimit" to discuss it unless all three partners were present.

## CHAPTER XXIII.

OUR NEW PARTNER SETS OUT TO FIND MR. OVERSHINER, AND IS SUCCESSFUL.—
ACTIVE MEASURES ARE DECIDED ON.

HE was up and away next morning without waiting for breakfast even. Indeed, I did not wake until I heard him softly unlocking our bed-room door.

"Don't wait for me, Jack," said he. "Keep the coffee hot. I'll be back with some news in three hours, without fail."

He returned even in less time than that he mentioned. It was barely nine o'clock, and we had not yet concluded breakfast, when a knock came at the street door (we had withdrawn the convenient string for obvious reasons), and Luce, descend-

ing to see who was there, I heard a strange as well as a familiar footstep.

The stranger was Mr. Overshiner! I knew him at once as he stood hesitating on the threshhold.

He still wore the tarpaulin cape and cap, but his face, so jolly, and rosy, and shiny with rain, when last I beheld it, was pale and wan.

"There now, old gentleman," remarked Master Tyler, who was behind the old crossing-sweeper and peering over his shoulder, "p'r'aps you can believe your own .eyes. That's the young cove—the little boy, I mean—wot you tied up the knee of, and that's the young gal wot waited about for you like I told you."

"I've been ill; laid up with rheumatics since Sunday, that's why I haven't been at the crossing," exclaimed the kind old fellow, glancing keenly around the room, and venturing to enter it a little further.

"You remember me, sir?" I remarked.

"Now I do," he replied, promptly. "I know your voice again, but you are strangely altered, if I rightly remember you. You are thinner and taller by a long way."

"He's been fine-drawed through a chimbly, didn't I tell you?" remarked the incorrigible Jerry, in high spirits that his efforts as a partner had been so promptly successful.

"You told me so many things, my lad," returned old Dan, regarding Jerry with a comical mixture of suspicion and admiration, "that really my head is all topsy-turvy thinking about 'em. Many terrible things. I'd rather forgive you for lying than believe that half you told me was true. It would be too dreadful."

"Well, I don't ask you to believe me," remarked Master Tyler. "I didn't from the first. Wot I said was, 'come and see for yourself;' and wot you said was, 'but suppose it is all true, why does he send for me?' and wot I answered was, 'while we are jawing here you might trot to where he is, and ask him all about it. He's got no other friend in the world, he says, and he knows that you are a kind-hearted old buffer as won't deny him.' Wasn't that your messidge, Jack!" continued Jerry, addressing me.

"I don't think I said buffer, did I, Jerry?"

"Well, it was some other affectionate word, if it wasn't that," he replied, all the while busying himself in making ready a cup of hot coffee for the "old buffer's" entertainment.

"Thank God, I'm not the man to keep back from helping man, woman, or child, as far as I am able," remarked the old crossing-sweeper, cheerily. "I should never again expect to be helped myself if I did. How far I may be able to help you in this strange business, I can't say till I know more about it."

So, as he sat there, with his tarpaulin cap on his knees, and his weather-beaten old face puckered in amazement, we told him the story, keeping back nothing. We told him of Jerry's generosity in resisting the temptation of touching the hundred pounds that was offered for my apprehension as an accomplice in the burglary, and we showed him the printed placard in proof. Likewise, we informed him how that Luce had carried about with her through four days the two sovereigns with which Mr. Bender had rewarded me, so that she might show them to him as some sort of guarantee of the truth of what she had to tell him, and how that, pinched and hungry as she had been through all that long time, it had never come into her head to spend a penny of the money; which last mentioned item of information so affected the old man that his eyes twinkled with tears, and drawing Luce close to his side, he said—

"That's *your* place, my poor little one, till some one shows a better right to you. Lor! I should make my fortune at the crossin' in a year if I only had such a fountain of luck as you to fall back on."

"Well, wot's to be done, guv'ner?" Jerry asked.

"Why, nothing that I see that might not have been done without me," replied Dan Overshiner, stroking his chin reflectively; "it is a case for the police, decidedly."

"Wot, go to 'em straight and tell 'em all about it?"

"I don't see that you can do better."

"Thanky. I sees how I can do much better," returned Jerry, in great disgust. "I'd rather go quite another road, if you've no objection."

"Then I'll go," said the old man, quietly.

"And d'ye know wot'll happen then?" asked Jerry, with the air of a person in a position to speak authoritatively on the matter.

"They'll take up the matter without doubt."

"E'zactly! They're good at taking up," returned Master Tyler, with a sneer; "but fust of all, you know, they'll take Jack up; that you may lay your life on."

"What! put me in prison after all?" I exclaimed, in alarm.

"After all what? After it appearing that you are one of the 'gressors wot's mentioned under the reward; that you are the interèstin' young cove with lightish hair wot got down the chimbly and nailed the swag!" replied Jerry Tyler, speaking sarcastically and more savagely than I had heard him for several days. "Yes, Jack, my boy, I'm afraid that even all them favourable facts won't save you from the wrong side of the iron grating."

The old crossing-sweeper evidently felt the force of Jerry's argument.

"But what else can be done?" said he.

Jerry scratched his head as though a key to the dilemma might be found lurking in his stubbly hair.

"If we on'y had a little money, now," said he, presently.

"What for?" asked Mr. Overshiner.

"Enough to pay for a cab to Chelsea."

"What would you do at Chelsea?"

"Look here, mister," said Jerry, impressively, "I ain't to be reckoned on at all. I couldn't do anything at Chelsea, or anywheres else in public about this bisness. I've got private reasons for courtin' seclooshun, as they say. But wot I was thinking of was, that you might go to Chelsea and put out a feeler like. You might take Jack with you if it came to that," continued Jerry, improving on his original idea.

"That might be done. That shall be done," said Mr. Overshiner, starting up at once and putting his cap on. "It ain't far to Chelsea, we can walk there."

"Too far for a chap wot's on'y got one leg, mister," remarked Jerry, nodding towards me.

"Ah, I forgot that, poor little boy. I've only got twopence halfpenny in the world."

"There's that two pounds, you know," said Jerry, doubtfully.

"What, isn't that spent yet?" exclaimed the old man, briskly. "Then we'll spend it now; it couldn't be laid out better. Go and fetch a cab at once, my lad."

"Don't I tell you I musn't be seen in it at all," said Jerry, angrily; "besides, whoever see any carriages, 'cept the fever wehicle, in Penny's Fields? You'd have a mob round it in almost a jiffy. No, it must be managed better than that."

And Jerry, whose faculty of invention was at full stretch, paced the room reflectively.

"You must wait till dusk, I suppose,"

said he, presently, "and then you must slip off quietly. You never can tell who's on the watch in these parts. D'ye think you might manage to limp along as far as Tuthill Street, Jack, if the old gentleman lent you a hand?"

I tested my ability on the spot, with Mr. Overshiner's permission, and found that it might be managed as Jerry suggested.

It wanted yet several hours of dusk, and the old crossing-sweeper would, I believe, have returned to his work by Waterloo Bridge, only that he seemed so determined not to lose sight of Luce. Indeed, as the evening came on, to our great astonishment, he insisted on my little companion accompanying us to Chelsea.

"She's safe enough here," said Jerry. "I'll look after her."

"Maybe, my good lad, but d'ye see she can't be *too* safe," returned the old man.

And so it came about, that, kindly assisted, indeed, half carried by Mr. Overshiner as far as Tuthill Street (luckily without exciting the curiosity of any of the inhabitants), we hailed a cab, and keeping Luce with us, bade the driver take us with all speed to the corner of Church Lane, Chelsea.

We could give no more exact direction, for, as the reader is already aware, I knew no more of whereabouts the old diamond-setter lived than the police placard told us, and it did not at all chime with the secrecy of our errand to acquaint the cabman with the name of the individual residing in Church Lane we were about to visit.

It was quite dark by the time we arrived at the end of our journey and were set down.

At the corner of Church Lane there was a little shop where fruit and cakes were sold, and here Mr. Overshiner made a small purchase in our behalf, while he went forward to reconnoitre.

In less than ten minutes he was back again, but with a countenance painfully perplexed.

"I've found the house," he whispered, when we had got outside the shop; "I couldn't well miss it, for there is a name-plate on the door; but I don't know whether we ought to go there just now."

"Why not?" I asked.

"The blinds are all drawn, and there is a carriage at the door. It is a doctor's carriage, I think."

"Perhaps he is very ill; we had better make haste," suggested Luce.

"Aye, to be sure, there's something in that; only I thought that since our business is of so uncommon a sort, it would have been better if we had been able to transact it as quietly as possible. Better a little too early than altogether too late, however."

It was evident that Mr. Overshiner had got it into his head that the drawn blinds and the doctor's carriage were unfavourable signs of the crippled diamond-polisher's condition of health.

"I'll knock at the door," whispered the old man, as we approached the house, "while you stand back a little. You are none so handsomely dressed, Jack, and the little girl having no bonnet, the servant who opens the door may take us for beggars, and close it again before I can say a word."

So Luce and I stood aside while Mr. Overshiner knocked a modest knock at the door.

It was opened instantly.

Judge, however, of my amazement and horror, for I was close enough to observe, when I perceived that it was not a servant who opened the door, but a policeman!

Instinctively I made a step towards running off at a smart pace, but my wounded leg brought me instantly to a standstill.

"Well, what do you *want?*" I heard the policeman harshly ask.

"We—we've come on business," Mr. Overshiner stammered, quite put out of his reckoning by the unexpected apparition.

"We! Who are **we?**" demanded the officer.

Mr. Overshiner indicated me and Luce standing in affright not ten paces off.

"Myself and these children."

"Well, what is your business—cadging? If so, you've come to the wrong shop, old man."

"No; we've come to see Mr. Bastable on an affair that is highly important to him."

"Well, call again to-morrow; he's busy."

"We have something to tell him about the stolen diamonds!" exclaimed Mr. Overshiner, desperately, as the policeman was about to close the door.

Very much swifter than it was closed, it was opened again however.

"About the burglary! You and which children? These two?"

And in a twinkling he darted out and secured Luce and me, and in less than five seconds he had us safe within the house; that house I had entered once before in so strange a fashion—and turning the key in the lock, placed the former in his pocket.

"If you are speaking the truth, you are the most welcome visitors that have showed a head here these six days," said the policeman.

## CHAPTER XXIV.

### WHICH IS SOMEWHAT MELO-DRAMATIC.

LEAVING us for a few moments, the officer hurried up-stairs; presently he reappeared and beckoned us up. On the top floor we found a door open, and entered, the policeman bringing up the rear.

He, however, was brought to a standstill just at the threshold, and for the simple reason that I blocked the way.

It was the same room! There was the work-bench by the side of the bedstead, there was the chimney up which I had made such a terrible exit, there was the grate against which the frantic old cripple had beat his fists so despairingly!

A vivid remembrance of the whole terrible scene flashed back to my remembrance, and I verily believe I should have sank down had not the policeman seized me roughly by the shoulder and held me up. He hurt my leg so that I could not refrain from uttering a cry of pain.

JACK'S SWEETHEART, LUCY.

"Gently!" exclaimed Mr. Overshiner. "He's lame; don't hurt him. He is barely recovered from a cruel wound made by a pistol-bullet, gentlemen."

And as he spoke he bowed humbly towards the occupants of the chamber who were at the further end of it.

There were two persons. One was the old diamond-setter himself, in bed and looking ill and ghastly, with his features bleached and pinched, and his eyes dull and sunken, and with a white woollen night-cap on.

The other person sat by the bedside.

He was a tall, elderly gentleman, handsomely dressed, and with a kind, sad face. There was a lamp on the table, by the invalid, but shaded, so that it might not be hurtful to the sick man's eyes; consequently, that end of the chamber where we were was enveloped in gloom.

Before Mr. Overshiner spoke, the invalid was lying with his head on the pillow, screening his weak eyes with one hand as he gazed in our direction the better to make out who we were. No sooner, however, had my old friend made his little explanation, than he started up in his bed, with a suddenness that caused the gentleman sitting with him to utter a cry of alarm.

"A pistol-bullet!" he exclaimed, with painful eagerness. "Lame of a wound so caused! Let me see him—bring him closer—closer!"

And collaring me, in the true professional style, the police-officer led me to the bedside.

It was quite as well that I was in such safe hands.

Much as I had altered, he knew me again instantly; when last we met he was half crazed with fright, and his view of my face was certainly of no longer than ten seconds duration, and that by uncertain moonlight; but his terror had fixed my image too distinctly on his mind's eye for him to forget so soon.

Springing from the bed, he made a grasp at my throat with both his long, lean hands.

"My jewels!" he screamed; "my diamonds and emeralds! Where are they? Tell me, or I'll strangle you!"

And no doubt his will was good to do it, but, just in the nick of time, the police-officer plucked me out of his clutches.

"Calm yourself, my poor friend," remarked the elderly gentleman, "your affliction makes you unjust. What can a harmless little lad such as this know about your stolen jewels?"

"Ask him what he knows," gasped the invalid, sinking back on his bed, well-nigh breathless with his late violent exertion. "He is the house-breaker—the thief, I tell you!"

Hearing this, the gentleman regarded me with increasing amazement, while the police-officer's hand sought the pocket in which he usually carried a pair of hand-cuffs.

"Surely you are mistaken!" exclaimed the gentleman, incredulously.

"No, no, no! I know him I tell you. If it were seventy years ago, instead of a few days, I could not forget his hateful face. It was he who awoke me in the night, with my jewel box in a bag about his throat! It was he who would have stabbed as well as robbed me had I not been too quick for him. Oh, I know him!"

Now, as the reader is aware, beyond the poor old fellow's imagination, there was no foundation for the latter part of his accusation. To be sure, during our struggle, when he opened the cupboard door, I saw, and made a grasp towards, a knife there lying, but it was to cut the cords by which Mr. Bender held me, and not against him that I wished to use it. Falling on my knees, I cried—

"No, no! indeed you are mistaken, sir—"

"I thought no other," remarked the strange gentleman.

"You are mistaken, sir; I never meant to hurt you, but you would not listen to me. It is quite true that I carried off the jewel box—"

Now it was the strange gentleman's time to be amazed.

"What! quite true!" he interrupted, "*you* carried off the jewels?"

"If you will permit me, sir," chimed in Mr. Overshiner, in a respectful voice, "perhaps I can explain the matter more clearly than the lad may be able to do."

"*You!* are you one of the gang, then? Of course you must be, or how should you know about the burglary?"

And the police-officer pounced on Mr. Overshiner's collar with a sure grip.

But the old fellow was strangely patient under the indignity.

"Sir," said he, in his mild, kind voice, and turning his honest face towards the strange gentleman, "do I look like a thief?"

A dozen witnesses called to speak as to Mr. Overshiner's character could not have been more convincing than was his tone and manner.

"Let him sit down, officer," said the strange gentleman, "and we will hear what he has to say."

What my old friend had to say I need not here repeat. It was no more nor less than the story of my acquaintance with Granny Corston, and my exploit with Mr. Bender, and all that had happened to me since.

It should be observed that in the course of the narration, Luce was alluded to but incidentally, as "a little girl living in the house." Indeed, she could scarcely be said at present to have been a feature of the bed-room scene. She stood by the wall, by the door, and no one noticed her.

It was curious to witness the effect on his audience of the story Mr. Overshiner had to relate.

At its commencement the cripple in his bed was evidently disposed to treat the revelation as some paltry fiction got up that he might be further imposed on, and he grew more and more interested as the narration proceeded; and, at its conclusion, was listening eagerly.

As for the strange gentleman, he was the picture of wrapt attention from begining to end.

As Mr. Overshiner concluded, the latter turned quickly to me.

"And this house at Camberwell, my lad," said he, "where is it to be found?"

"That is more than I can say," I replied.

"You neither know the house nor the name of the road or street it stands in?"

"I only know that we went through Camberwell Gate, and paid the toll, and that, almost immediately afterwards, we turned to the left."

"And stopped at once?"

"Oh, no, we went in and out of many streets after that."

"Precious little to be made out of *that*," grumbled the police-officer, who, with a note-book and pencil in his hand, was fishing for a "clue." "Was it a little house, or a big house?"

"A small house; one of a long row."

"Do you think you would know it if you saw it again?"

"I am afraid not, unless——"

And here I paused, an odd recollection occurring to me.

"Unless what?"

"Unless I could see the chimney-pots of the house from the road."

"What about the chimney-pots?"

"There is one of them in the row on Mr. Bender's house that has a cowl on the top of it, and the rim of the cowl has been mended with bright new tin. I saw that when I was on the roof."

"D'ye recollect the shape of the cowl?" inquired the officer, using his pencil, and with a pleasant twinkle in his shrewd eyes.

"It was a dumpy thing, a sort of hood. I remember at the time fancying that it looked like a great garden snail."

The officer glanced at me intelligently. "You couldn't have described it better," said he. "I know the sort of cowl you mean, exactly. We shall make something out of the information, I hope, sir!" said he, addressing himself to the strange gentleman.

"I sincerely trust so!" the latter returned; and then turning to me, he continued—

"You saw the contents of the japanned box, my lad?"

"No, sir. I never saw the box, or its contents, after it was taken from me by the burglars."

"Nor heard them speak of what the box contained? You did not hear them mention anything about a diamond cross?"

"No, sir."

"Alas! my dear sir, I am afraid your chance of recovering that treasure is very slight," dolefully remarked the old cripple in the bed. "They were rare stones; diamonds, that told of their value with a thousand sparkles!"

"They might have been of the dullest paste, and yet have been as precious to me," remarked the strange gentleman, mournfully. "Brutal and hardened as these robbers may be, I doubt if they would keep my treasure from me, if they but knew how, and for what, I so dearly prize it."

"If you'll pardon my saying as much, my dear sir, I don't think you quite know the disposition of that sort of men," politely remarked the police-officer. "They'd steal their mother's coffin-plate, and sell it for old metal, if they were hard up for a quartern of gin."

But I very much doubt if the strange gentleman heard a word of the officer's sagacious remark.

He was otherwise engaged.

I have said that, hitherto, little Luce, having no concern in the burglarious business we were discussing, stood back, and alone, quite lost in the gloom that pervaded every other part of the chamber, excepting that were the sick man lay.

Presently, however, this position of affairs was marvellously altered.

From the first time of the strange gentleman speaking, I, who happened to be then looking in Luce's direction, observed a strange alteration in her demeanour.

Dimly as I could make out her face, I could perceive that it had quite lost its downcast, bashful expression; and that, with her head erect, and eyes wide open, she was gazing with wondering painful earnestness towards the group about the cripple's bed.

I remarked this, but it did not strike me as being very extraordinary. She had shown so much affection for me, that I thought that this was but a continuation of it, and that she was only anxious on my account.

But her emotion had a deeper source, a source wonderful, and little short of miraculous.

Again the strange gentleman spoke, and attracted by the slightest sound proceeding from where the little girl was standing, I looked there again, and saw that she had taken a step forward, and that her hands that had hitherto hung by her sides, were now clasped, while the same inexpressible look filled her great blue eyes.

"Did they but know how much, and for whose dear sake I so highly prize it!" ejaculated the strange gentleman, and clasped his hands before his eyes as though to conceal the sudden emotion that overwhelmed him.

When, lo! the marvellous impulse that had so moved Luce, quickened, and with hasty, noiseless steps, she left her dark corner and advanced to the centre of the room, and there she stood, white as a marble statue, and with her eyes open and fixed, as one who walks in her sleep.

Excepting the strange gentleman, we all observed the unaccountable movement, and wondered what it might mean.

Mr. Policeman observed it, and like the matter-of-fact man he was, at once proceeded to set his curiosity at rest.

"Hullo!" said he, "must you put a spoke in, too? Well, what have you to say?"

But Luce had nothing to say. She had speech, ears, eyes, but only for one person, and that one was the strange gentleman who sat with his head bowed and his face resting on his clasped hands.

Hearing the observation the police-officer had made, however, he now looked up suddenly.

He looked up, and his great dark eyes, wet with tears, grew larger still in stupefied amazement as they encountered the spell-bound eyes of the ragged, bare-headed little girl who stood in the middle of the room.

His chest heaved, and his lips worked convulsively, as though struggling to speak and unable to do so. At last, throwing up his arms, he cried, in a strange, unnatural voice,

"*Through life and beyond!* Oh, God! is this life? or is it a mocking vision?"

And then, with a still louder cry, he fell face foremost, to the ground.

Nor did he fall alone. As he raised his arms and stumbled forward, Luce, in her beggar's dress—Luce, the nursery drudge and cruelly-used little victim at Granny Corston's den in Penny's Fields—awoke suddenly, as one wakes from a frightful dream, and exclaiming, "Papa! papa!" flung herself on the prostrate man, her long, tangled locks of auburn mingling with his black, glossy hair.

## CHAPTER XXV.

IN WHICH THE VEIL OF MYSTERY THAT HAS HITHERTO ENVELOPED LUCE IS LIFTED.

I FIND myself now arrived at a stage of my story from which, had I been trained as a "sensational" writer, I might see my way to the manufacture of any number of very pretty pages.

"Through life and beyond!" was the thrilling ejaculation of the wonder-stricken man, as he beheld the fantastic little apparition that appeared before him.

"Through life and beyond!" as the police placard declared, was the legend inscribed on the back of the diamond cross that had been stolen with the other jewels from the cripple's keeping.

Either this was a singular coincidence, or there existed explainable circumstances, linking Luce both to the legend and the exclamation. Truth is stranger than fiction. There *did* exist such circumstances.

How, for the present, the police-officer (who, by-the-bye, was only present at the diamond-setter's abode at the poor old fellow's earnest request, since he was too ill to be removed therefrom) was prevailed on to take no movement in the matter on the strength of the evidence recently brought to light ; how that a doctor was sent for, and the insensible man restored to consciousness, are matters the dry details of which would possess no interest for the reader.

Suffice it, he was so restored, and this was the extraordinary explanation he had to give—the ragged, bare-headed Luce nestling closely to him the while.

He was a younger branch of a rich and influential family, and it was his fate, as it has been that of thousands before him, to fall in love with a lady who was suffering under that most repulsive of afflictions—poverty.

In all else she was rich. In accomplishments, in beauty, in amiability; but through their golden-rimmed spectacles the young gentleman's relatives could see none of these, or if they could see them they were pleased to regard them only as so many lures the wicked witch had set in motion to entrap their infatuated young gentleman, and they gnashed their teeth of pride and " caste" against her with the greater fury.

But he being a brave young gentleman, with a will of his own, set their implorings, and warnings, and threatenings even, at defiance, and married her.

He made no secret of the alliance, and for a time his grand relatives found sufficient vent for their vials of wrath in shutting their doors against him and treating him as a stranger.

But this was only for a little while. By-and-bye the poor lady gave birth to a daughter. Then their alarm took a fresh turn.

The awkward fact was, that just about this time there died a certain individual in whom the chief members of the Heath family took a lively interest.

Considering that for very many years the person in question had been just about as cross and "cantankerous" towards her relatives as it is possible to imagine, the said interest was unaccountable to all who did not know the key to the mystery.

Miss Lucy Heath, a maiden lady of advanced years, held the balance of the family estate in her fair fingers, and, not unnaturally, the more the said fingers became shaken with the palsy of old age, the more affectionate and solicitous were her relations to guide and direct them.

When the old maiden lady gave up the ghost, and her will was read, there was a pretty commotion.

The chief expectants were four nephews, of whom the gentleman who had so rashly married was the youngest. Quite unknown to the rest, the queer-tempered maiden lady had always looked kindly on the youngest nephew, and secretly congratulated him on his marriage.

The diamond cross, an ancient family relic, was her marriage gift.

The legend on the back of the cross, foreshadowed her benevolent intentions.

These were briefly the terms of the will, the reading of which created such a panic amongst the dry-eyed "mourners" assembled to hear it.

"To that one of my four nephews, Ralph, Ezra, Robert, and Peregrine Heath, who shall first marry, and produce a legitimate daughter, and christen her Lucy Heath, I give and bequeath half my personal estate, and to the said Lucy Heath, provided she live to the age of seven years, I bequeath the remaining half. In the event of the said child's demise before the age of seven, what would have been her share of my estate shall be equally divided between my three other nephews."

Of the four nephews, only one, Robert, was already married.

The others were not of the marrying sort.

With a comparatively rich and easy-going father, their monetary wants were tolerably well supplied; and, if it happened that at an unlucky venture at gambling or horse-racing they were unable to pay up for a time, they were never known to pine in shame or remorse.

"It will be all right when Aunt Luce dies," said they. How much they were out in their calculation the reader has already seen.

Ezra was the eldest—the deepest in debt, and consequently the most furious when he heard that a Lucy Heath was born.

The fact is, that seeing no other way out of his difficulties, as a last desperate resort he had married in hopes of carrying off the prize.

When he found himself jilted, and in addition burdened with a wife, the best of whom that could be said was that she was as unscrupulous as he was himself, his condition of mind may be easily guessed.

He, however, was the only one of the three who chose to conceal his sentiments on the subject. He affected to be quite reconciled with his lot, and speedily manoeuvred, so that himself and his wife were on terms of intimacy with his more fortunate brother.

Assisted by his brother's bounty, Ezra Heath and his wife lived in ease in a sweet little house deep down in the country; and little Luce's health being indifferent, it was proposed by Mrs. Ezra that she should go and reside with them for a few months.

Suspecting nothing wrong, Robert was

gratified with his brother's kindness, and the child was taken away.

It was never afterwards seen by its parent.

Ezra's house was not a great way from the sea, and little Luce's playground of an afternoon was the beach. She was a bold child of her age, and divesting her little feet of her shoes and socks, would go out knee high to meet the tide, prattling, and laughing, and plashing the water.

Writing to her parents, Ezra mentioned how the little one occasionally amused herself, and Robert wrote back, begging his brother and sister-in-law to see that such frolic was unattended with danger.

Almost immediately there came a letter with a black seal.

The letter was hastily written, and with every evidence of the most poignant grief.

What the fond father so anxiously had intimated *might* happen, *had* happened. On the previous afternoon, dear little Lucy's shoes and socks were discovered on the beach, but the child had disappeared!

Every search had been made, both along the craggy and hilly coast, and by the boatmen with their drags. But, alas! to no purpose. With quenchless grief and dismay, Ezra Heath was compelled to the conclusion that the rash little darling had been over bold, and, advancing too far into the water, a wave had carried her away, and out to sea.

At this time Lucy Heath was five years old.

Fast as special train could carry them, Robert Heath and his wife hastened to Cragsbourne, but only to have their worst fears confirmed. Fishermen, villagers, one and all agreed that the disappearance of the little girl was accounted for in the manner Ezra Heath had described. They came back to London, and mourned her dead.

Three months afterwards, prompted by Ezra, one of the brothers reminded the disconsolate father of the terms of the aunt's will, and each received his part of little Lucy's fortune, which amounted in all to twenty thousand pounds.

Lucy's mother never recovered from the shock the child's untimely death had caused her. Within three years, she pined away and died, leaving her husband lonely and disconsolate, indeed. As she died, she pressed her bridal gift, the diamond cross, to her lips, and with a faint smile murmuring, "'Through life and beyond,' darling," gave it into his hands.

No wonder, then, that he so highly prized the precious relic—that he should cherish it, and love to see it shining in all its hopeful radiance.

It was in order that the gems might be displayed in their fullest glory that it had been entrusted to the most celebrated diamond-setter of the day, old Bastable, of Chelsea.

How it was stolen the reader already knows.

As far as Luce was concerned, she could throw but little light on the mystery.

The long course of privation and ill-usage she had undergone in the hands of Granny Corston, had tended little to the development of her faculties, and she had no recollection at all of living by the sea.

As need not be stated, she was perfectly oblivious of ever having been washed off the beach.

What she did recollect, in a vague, disjointed way, was that a long while ago, a beggar woman came to her, and while a tall, dark man stood by and threatened her if she made any noise, stripped off her pretty clothes, and made her put on rags that the beggar woman took out of her basket.

Likewise, that the beggar woman had a pair of shears, and cut off her long curls, and the tall, dark man laughed, and took the curls up, and threw them in the fire. As well as this, she remembered that she and the beggar woman travelled a long way along the road, sometimes sleeping in barns or under a stack of hay, until they came to London.

Whether or no the beggar woman and Granny Corston were identical, she could not say. She had an idea that she was ill as soon as she got to Penny's Fields, but of this she was not sure.

If anything, however, was wanted as crowning proof that poor Luce was indeed the bereaved gentleman's long-lost daughter, it was furnished in the little girl's own handwriting.

Young as she was, when she was kidnapped away, she had received some education, and had already began to write curiously well for a child.

Dearly treasured in his pocket-book, her father still preserved the last tiny letter she had written to "Dearest papa and mama," from Cragsbourne, and her signature thereto being compared with that which she now wrote, presented a likeness that was unmistakable.

As the reader will readily imagine, the wonderful and unexpected restoration of my faithful little companion to the arms of her father, for the time quite put the business that had taken me and Mr. Overshiner to Chelsea, in the shade. As for Luce, not a word could I get to say

to her; indeed, so complete had been the shock the amazing discovery had occasioned her, that, by the advice of the physician who had been called in to attend on her father, she was conveyed to another room, and there put to bed, a nurse attending her.

When the commotion had somewhat subsided, however, it was my turn to appear on the stage, as it were, again.

Acting on the suggestion of the police-officer in possession, the inspector from the nearest station was sent for, and he took down in writing all that I had to tell.

Likewise, he noted down at length a description of Granny Corston.

"You need not print bills for her apprehension," said Mr. Heath; "such a course may frighten the wicked old wretch away, and of all things I wish her secured, not to punish her, but that she may be compelled to confess all that she knows of this diabolical business. I will pay down a reward of a hundred pounds to any person who will arrest her, or cause her to be arrested."

"Thank you, sir," said the inspector, touching his hat, with a confidence that boded ill for Granny Corston's lengthened enjoyment of liberty.

"And instead of fifty I will give a reward of five hundred pounds for the recovery, uninjured, of the diamond cross," continued the generous gentleman.

The inspector touched his cap again, but not so briskly.

"You think its restoration is hopeless?" exclaimed Mr. Heath, with a sigh.

"I can't say, sir. In the first place, it of course depends on its existence after the lapse of a week."

"And in the next place?"

"Well, you see, sir, so very much depends on the exact truth of the information we have got, and further——"

"Yes, what further?" interrupted Mr. Heath, with a little impatience.

"To give us a good chance of success, we should have the fullest assistance from those best able to give it."

And as he deliberately said this, he eyed me keenly.

"I will do my best, sir; I will do anything," I remarked, interpreting his look.

"Well, if I was in your position, young gentleman, I think that *I* should," replied the keen-eyed inspector, with a meaning shrug of his shoulders. "You had best come along with me; and you, too, old gentleman," he continued, addressing Mr. Overshiner, "and I will take care of you both till the morning."

This was alarming.

After all, then, I was to taste of that durance of which Jerry Tyler had so graphically hinted, and with Mr. Overshiner, too, who had done no manner of harm.

Luckily, however, we had a friend in Luce's father.

"That would be but a poor instalment of what we owe these poor fellows for the good they have brought us," said he smilingly. "I think we may take their word that they will be forthwith coming in the morning. Or, perhaps," said he, turning to the invalid, "now that you are convinced of their friendly intent, you would not object to their staying here for to-night?"

Mr. Bastable had no objection; he only stipulated that we should share the room where slept the police-officer on guard; but it mattered little to us where we slept.

## CHAPTER XXVI.

### UNEXPECTED APPEARANCE OF MASTER JEREMIAH TYLER—HE IMPARTS USEFUL INFORMATION—HE SUSPECTS ME OF TREACHERY!

WE slept in the front parlour, and as the mattress on which we reposed was close by that which accommodated the police-officer, we had no opportunity for comparing notes.

With his mind at peace, Mr. Overshiner was soon asleep; but I was so excited by the disturbing events of the last few hours, that I lay awake, hour after hour, and even when I closed my eyes for a few minutes the least noise caused me to wake with a start.

It must have been between six and seven o'clock in the morning when I was startled by a sound with which I was perfectly familiar.

"Whew-whit."

It was a shrill whistle—Jerry Tyler's whistle.

"Whew-whit."

This time it seemed so close that I started up in bed. And as though a string connected him with me, the vigilant police-officer at the same moment sat bolt upright too.

"Whew-whit," whistled Jerry, for the third time, and the sound could scarcely have been plainer had he applied his lips to the key-hole.

I was altogether amazed, and could only rub my eyes and look about me, wondering what it could mean.

"Who's that?" the policeman asked, stepping stealthily out of bed and slipping his legs into his trousers.

"It's—it's Jerry Tyler, I think, sir," I replied, in confusion.

"And who's Jerry Tyler?" he demanded suspiciously. "Is this a plant; did you expect him?"

"No, sir."

"He knows where to find you, it seems."

"Yes, sir, he—he knew where we were coming."

"And you don't know what brings him whistling here at this time in the morning?"

"I do not, indeed; I know no more than you do."

At this time Mr. Overshiner awoke, and was about to inquire what was the matter, when the police-officer signed to him to be silent.

"This is a business that me and this young fellow can settle without your interference," he whispered. "Hush! Whoever it is, he is close under the window now. I can hear him. You recollect what you promised last night to the inspector?"

"What, sir?"

"That you would do anything to help us."

"And so I will," I replied, heartily.

"Very well, then. Now's your chance. The one who is whistling is your friend, you say?"

"Oh, yes, I know him very well. He——"

"Hush! Does _he_ know anything about this diamond business?"

"Yes, all about it."

"And he comes here at this unseasonable hour, and unexpected by you? If it's true, as you say, he has come to bring you information that won't keep, eh?"

"I don't know what brings him here," I replied, and, as the reader knows, this was quite true.

"That's what we've got to find out," said the intelligent policeman.

He said no more, but softly as possible took down the iron bar that secured the window-shutter.

Then he crouched close under the window, and signed to Mr. Overshiner to do the same.

"Now, open the window softly," he whispered to me.

"And what then, sir?"

"Call to him quietly, and let him tell you all that he has come to tell. Let him tell you all freely, mind, without the least hint from you that there is any one in the room here beside yourself to listen. You understand?"

It was impossible to misunderstand. Yet, what was I to do? No doubt the police-officer was quite right in his surmise that Jerry had come to tell me news that would not keep.

But what was the nature of the said news?

Perhaps it was of a sort that, imparted in the hearing of a third person, might involve the half-reformed young thief in serious difficulty.

Should I chance everything and do as the police-officer bade? Yes, I would. It might be rather hard on poor Jerry, but how could I help loving faithful little Luce better than I loved him?

I could not reach as high as the window.

"Stand on me, and let me hold your feet," suggested the sagacious officer, "then you will be sure of not falling out."

So, as he reclined along the ground, I mounted up on to his chest, and softly, and by degrees, opened the window.

Jerry was now on the opposite side of the way, but he made me out at once, and, with wondering eyes, stepped rapidly over the road.

"'Struth, Jack!" was his first observation, "you *here!*"

"Hush! Yes, Jerry. Why not?"

"Why not! Why Daniel in the den, o' lions is nothing to it. How come you to be lodged here? Where's Luce? Where's old Birchbroom?"

"What brings you here, Jerry?" I inquired, evading his questions.

"Blessed if I know; inkstink—I s'pose it couldn't be nothing else. All I know is that I wanted to find you, and that now I have found you."

"What did you want to find me for, Jerry?" I whispered, for he was now quite close.

"To warn you."

Here the police-officer gave me a significant shake by the legs.

"To warn me of what, Jerry?"

"Leastways, when I say warn you, p'r'aps it's more to do with Luce. Granny's come home."

("Steady, now!") the police-officer exclaimed, in the softest of whispers.

"When did she come home, Jerry?"

"You hadn't been gone an hour last night when I met her, just as I was coming out."

"Did she ask about me, Jerry?"

"She asked about everybody, but she was most partickler in askin' about Luce.

She's dead set on gettin' Luce back agin."

"What did you tell her?"

"Well, I told her about a peck and a 'arf of lies, as nigh as they could be measured," grinned my young friend.

"You didn't tell her where we had all gone to?"

"No fear. I said that you was off, I didn't know where. At the same time, I threw out a hint that I thought I knew where to drop on Luce."

"You did!" I replied, in tones of regret. "That was wrong, Jerry. What did you tell her that for?"

"'Cos I'm out of work, and wanted a job!" and Jerry winked the most artful of winks.

"What had what you told her to do with getting a job?"

"I wanted the job of ferretting Luce out; don't you twig?"

"No, I don't. You don't mean to say that you mean to turn round on us, Jerry?"

"Was there ever sich a prewokin young greenhorn! He will no more take a 'int than he'll take a ankersher! Didn't we want to know where Granny had gone to live?"

("Good!") whispered the officer, giving me a nudge.

"To be sure we did."

"Well, don't you see, she hain't come back to the Fields to stay; she only come back to find out how matters was going on. She told me that. 'Well,' said I, 'I rather think that I know where to pitch on her'—Luce, don't you know—'I'll make inquiries.'

"'I'll give you ten shillings if you will hunt her out for me, Jerry,' said she, in a mighty fluster.

"'But,' said I, 'actin' the artful, don't you know, 's'pose I find her, and don't know where to find you?'

"'I'll tell you what, Jerry,' ses she 'you was alwis a favorite of mine, Jerry, and I can trust yer; I'm living with the old man and two kids at 84, Keate Street, Spitalfields.'"

I could feel a sudden disturbance of my animated platform, and immediately afterwards the sound of a pencil on paper. My friend was writing down the address. He was growing excited.

("What about the warning?") he whispered up to me, meaning that I should lead Jerry back to the starting point of his communications.

But, unhappily, he whispered too loud, and Jerry had sharp ears.

"Who's that?" he eagerly exclaimed, starting back from the window. "Who whispered?"

I could feel that I turned guiltily red, and my eyes fell before his.

"It is all right, Jerry," I stammered,— "I—I—"

But at this moment the police-officer slipped from under me, and made to open the window wider, that he might spring out and secure the startled informer. He had on neither his glazed hat nor his blue coat, but Jerry scented his breed instantly.

I shall never forget the look of reproach he cast on me.

"What! turned sneak on me! *You!* Send I may live! I'd as soon a thought of the stars fallin'!"

And, turning about, he darted off at a speed that convinced the officer, who was looking out at the window, how hopeless it would be to attempt to pursue him.

Besides, he had obtained what he chiefly wanted.

This was Granny Corston's present address.

It was necessary to make a move at once, however. It was only reasonable to assume that Master Jerry Tyler, in his mortification at what he now regarded as an attempt on my part to "sell" him, might be tempted to take his revenge on us by putting Granny Corston on her guard.

In less than an hour the inspector and Mr. Heath, and the crippled old diamond-setter, were closeted together, discussing this new turn in the tide of affairs.

Shortly afterwards, two experienced detectives set out for Keate Street, Spitalfields.

---

## CHAPTER XXVII.

### I AM PLEDGED TO AN ENTERPRIZE BRISTLING WITH DANGER.

MATTERS appeared to be progressing towards a triumphant end, but I was in the last degree miserable.

What appeared to be the grand joke of the business in the eyes of the police authorities, was the very thing that made me feel almost ready to run away and have no more to do with it.

I allude, of course, to the dismay and sudden flight of poor Jerry Tyler.

What could he think of me by this time?

Why, only that I was a contemptible, mean, little hypocrite, who had availed myself, while I was helpless, of his generous, self-sacrifice, to turn round on him as soon as I found new friends, and mock him and "sell" him.

Mr. Overshiner's concern was even deeper than mine.

"He'll slide all back again, that's the great fear !" said he. "I do believe that he had set his feet determinedly in a better path, and now he will probably be altogether disgusted, and grow more reckless than ever."

Soon after the men had departed in search of Granny Corston, the police inspector sent for me. He was alone, and I made bold to speak to him on the subject, but he wouldn't listen.

"That's an affair may be seen to by and bye," said he. "We have more important work before us at present. I say *we*, Master Jack, for if you would prove yourself what you would have us believe, you must take your share in it."

"I am quite willing, sir," I replied.

"Aye, aye, that is easily said," he continued, shaking his head, "but, perhaps, it may be harder work than you think for. At the same time, my lad, as I need not tell you, it will be no small matter to save yourself from being shut up in prison for a couple of years or so."

I tearfully nodded my assent to this.

"Especially," continued the cunning official, who all the time was looking much more closely after his own interest than mine, "especially as, if you show yourself made of the true stuff, there is a gentle-man willing to take you by the hand, and make a man of you."

"You mean Luce's father, sir?" I asked him, anxiously.

"If you guess again, you'll be wrong," he replied.

"Could I see Luce, sir, just for five minutes ?"

"Do what? Why, what the dickens are you thinking about ?" he returned, apparently much shocked. "What can a little ragamuffin such as you are—a young fellow with a charge of burglary hanging over his head, have to say to a young lady ?"

I felt my lips tingle.

"Did *she* say that ?" I asked.

"Not she," replied the inspector, shrewdly seeing his advantage, "that is what *I* say. No, no ; as far as I can make out, she will be very glad to see you—when you've done the best you can towards setting right the ugly business you had a hand in."

"Tell me how I can do it," I exclaimed, desperately. "I will do anything."

"Well, I've been thinking it over," said the inspector, reflectively, "and there seems to be *one* way in which you can help us a great deal. If you had pluck enough, that is."

"Count on that," said I.

"You say, ' count on that,' but see how precious soon you will alter your tune when I tell you what the plan is !" and he grinned in an aggravating way.

"I am past being afraid ; tell me what it is."

"That's soon done. D'ye think you could walk a bit if we got you a crutch ?"

"I could walk a short distance—a mile, I dare say."

"Far enough to find the house where

this Bender lives, if we rode as far as Camberwell Gate?"

"I'd try."

"D'ye think that having found the house you'd likewise find pluck enough to get inside and make friends with Bender?"

He looked hard at me as he made this astounding suggestion, and I felt my heart beating at full gallop; but I tried to steady my voice, as I replied—

"If I thought there was a chance of doing it, and it would do any good, I would try."

"Why, as for the chance, there's nothing to speak of against it," remarked the inspector, affecting to shrug his shoulders, and make light of the matter. "It is quite certain that he more than half believes that you were innocent of plotting against him. It is the old Granny he thinks is to blame; he as good as said so on the night of the row, didn't he?"

"That's true, sir."

"Well, then, since he half thinks that you are on his side, it's just about certain, if you went to him innocent like, and as though you had no doubt that he would take you—as he promised to, you must recollect—that he would be quite convinced that what Granny Corston told him was only a trumped-up story."

Although I couldn't shut my eyes to the danger of the plan the inspector proposed, there certainly did seem a chance of its accomplishment.

"And if I get in all right, what then, sir?" I asked.

"Oh, it would be as easy as A B C after that. You know what we want—in the first place, the jewels, especially the cross you heard them talking about last night," he continued, lowering his voice, and looking towards the door. "In the

second place, we want to nab Bender and Toby with as little trouble as possible."

"But I don't see how that you could nab them any easier for me being in the house."

"That we will talk about presently; let us settle one thing at a time. Are you willing to do your best?"

I reflected for a few moments.

Truly it would be a grand stroke of business to redeem myself from the danger by which I was surrounded, and that I should do so, provided I were instrumental in rescuing what Luce's father held so precious, I felt certain.

Besides, as far as I could gather from the inspector's mysterious remarks, Luce herself expected that I should be the means of restoring the treasure. This resolved me.

"Yes," said I, "I'll make the attempt."

"Then, the sooner we set about it the better," said the inspector, starting up with alacrity. "But look here, my lad, this is a matter *quite* between ourselves. You understand? If the plan miscarries, you won't say a word about it to any one?"

"Yes, sir—I understand."

I did not ask him if Mr. Overshiner was included in the prohibition. Anyhow, when I returned, as he bade me, to the room where I had left my old friend, I told him all about it.

He didn't at all like Mr. Inspector's scheme, but seeing that I was inclined to face it out without flinching, he did not say anything to daunt me.

"Anyhow, I'm glad that you told me, Jack," said he, squeezing my hand affectionately. "I shan't be far away from you all the time, you may rely on that."

In a short time the inspector returned

with a neat little crutch that suited me as though it had been made to my measure.

"The trap's at the door, and we'll start as soon as you like," said he, addressing me; and then, turning to Mr. Overshiner, he continued, "as for you, old gentleman, the inquiries we have made satisfies us that your story is something like correct. You may go. If we want you, we'll send for you. And here's a sovereign for your trouble so far."

The old man took the money, and bade me good-bye, at the same time giving me a look I well understood.

The "trap" the inspector had alluded to as standing at the door was a common covered carrier's-cart, with tail-board behind; and with a brown smock and a "billy-cock" cap on, the inspector himself might have been the commonest carrier that ever drove a nag.

Within the cart I found two other persons; one, from his costume, a sweep, and the other a fish-hawker. There were the fish-scales shining on his dirty jacket-sleeves and his fish-basket, to prove it.

I was not a little astonished presently to discover that they were both disguised policemen.

By the time we jogged through Camberwell-gate, twelve o'clock was striking. Then we took a turning to the left, and drew up at a public-house where there was a stable-yard, and there the carrier's-cart was put up.

For the time I lost sight of the fish-hawker and the sweep; but when, after drinking a pint of beer at the bar, Mr. Inspector came out of the public-house with me, there I saw them, one on either side of the street, sauntering along, as though never in their lives had they met each other before.

"Now, Jack," exclaimed the make-believe carrier, "keep your eyes open, and put your best leg foremost."

And so I did. But, despite the great assistance the crutch was to me, my other leg lagged painfully behind.

Up one street and down another; it was tedious work. After an hour and a half we were no nearer to what we sought than at starting.

Presently, however, our friend the sweep, who somehow contrived to be always in the same street with us, turned suddenly about and sauntered leisurely towards us. He did not pause when he reached us, but, as we walked on, whispered rapidly,

"Nine doors from the bottom, on t'other side."

"Right!" responded Mr. Inspector, in a satisfied tone.

It was a long distance to the end of the street, and about midway there was another street. Into this we turned.

"You heard what he said?" said the inspector.

"Yes, I heard."

"How do you feel?"

"Don't let us stay talking about it," said I, for I felt terribly nervous; "let us go at once."

"Come now, that's plucky! You bear in mind all that I told you coming along?"

"Yes."

"Then be off, and good luck to you. Don't give way to funking, whatever happens. Recollect that we are always within earshot."

Summoning up all the courage within me, I turned my halting steps towards the last house in the street but nine, while the inspector strolled away.

As I neared the street's end, feeling

every step I took more and more lonely, I made out a figure that was no stranger to me.

It was Mr. Overshiner.

He had a new birch-broom in his hands, and was most industriously sweeping a crossing from one side of the road to the other.

I did not feel half so down-hearted now.

Approaching number nine (I knew the door again), I raised the knocker, and knocked softly.

The woman I had seen there before opened it.

"Is Mr. Bender at home, ma'am?" I asked.

For a moment she started, and looked embarrassed.

"Yes—no. That is, I——"

"Who's that, Bet?" I heard a familiar voice from the back parlour exclaim.

"Come inside," said the woman hastily; "come in quick, don't stand there."

I obeyed her, and stepped into the passage. Next moment a door opened, and I was face to face with Mr. Bender.

---

## CHAPTER XXVIII.

IN WHICH I DO A THING THAT HAS AN UGLY SAVOUR ABOUT IT, UNTIL THE READER REFLECTS ON ALL THE FACTS OF THE CASE, WHEN I AM SURE HE WILL "HONOURABLY ACQUIT" ME.

I COULD not have looked very formidable, leaning on my crutch, and shaking and pale, but had I been a stout six-foot man, armed with authority for the burly burglar's arrest, he could hardly have worn a more terrified aspect as he stood in the doorway staring down on me.

"Why, what the blazes do you want here?" he exclaimed, as soon as he could speak. "Who sent you here? What do you want?"

Bearing in mind the lesson Mr. Inspector had taught me, I replied very humbly, that I had come to Mr. Bender, simply because I had nowhere else to go; that Granny Corston had deserted the house, and that I should have starved had it not been for Jerry Tyler, and that now Jerry was gone too. At the same time I reminded Mr. Bender of his expressed desire to have me at his house.

While Mr. Bender listened, his countenance underwent many changes; but it was anything but serene when I had had my say.

"Aye, aye; that's all very prettily said," remarked he, taking me by the shoulder and marching me into the back parlour; "but answer this fust of all—how did you find me out?"

And he fixed his sharp eyes full on mine.

But I was able to tell him exactly the truth, and I was thankful to hear him laugh.

"Hang me, if there ever was such a kid!" he exclaimed. "So it was the mended chimbly-pot, was it?" But instantly his brow lowered again.

"Now, look here, Jack," said he, "it don't seem likely that you would come a thrusting your head into my jaws if you was afraid I should bite it off. But there was something about that little business that night at Granny's that I can't yet make out, and I must be able to make it out, mind yer, before I can look on yer like I used. Wot about the writin' on the paper, and Luce, the gal, going off and not coming back?"

But I had my story ready again, thanks to Mr. Inspector, and since it was mainly true, I was able to tell it with less difficulty. I told him all about Luce having to sign the quarterly papers, and her suspicions that Granny had no right with her, and her determination to run away. That part of the story I told him that was not true, was that Mr. Overshiner was her friend and not mine.

The woman was present, and heard all that I said.

"There you are, my dear!" she exclaimed; "what did I tell you? I knew that it was all that old hag's malice!"

"'Pon my soul, I begin to think that you were right, Bet," laughed Mr. Bender, evidently much relieved.

"To be sure I am," Bet replied. What made her run away? She did'nt run on *your* account, that's certain. It was because she was afraid of being hunted out by the gal's friends!"

This sagacious explanation of the mystery completely routed Mr. Bender's vanishing suspicions.

"Give us your paw, young shaver! he exclaimed; "and I'm jolly glad to find that I was not out in my calkerlations on yer. I'll make a man of you yet, if you

on'y behave as you ought. Let him have some dinner, Bet, I lay my life he's hungry; and then he'll lay down a bit and have a rest. Thunderin' tired he looks, hoppin' all the way from Westminster here."

And, strange as it may appear to the honest reader, to hear Mr. Bender speak in this kindly way, made me feel mean and ashamed. However, I speedily fortified myself with the reflection that he had not scrupled to risk my life to serve his own ends, and probably would do so again if he ever found the chance.

It was but little dinner that I could take, and was glad to be alone in the same bed-room that I had before occupied to lie down. The great danger, at least, was over.

What I had now to do was to keep my ears open for intelligence as to the stolen jewels.

It was evening before I was called downstairs, and there, at the tea-table, sat Mr. Toby, as well as Mr. and Mrs. Bender. And Toby, who had heard of my arrival, and the strange incidents connected with it, grinned, as he shook hands with me, and said he was "werry glad that I had made what he had said about me come true." To which I modestly replied, "that I was very glad too."

They talked in the freest manner of "business," before me. From their conversation, I speedily discerned that "the sparks" were still the prime theme of discussion.

I could hear that a certain "Tilly," or Matilda, a person in Mr. Toby's confidence, had been successful in disposing of five of the said "sparks" that very day.

Mr. Toby verified his statement by

handing over several sovereigns to his partner.

"She couldn't do anything with the emeralds, cos old Isaacs had gone down to Portsmouth on business," Toby said.

"All right," said Mr. Bender, taking the little packet Toby gave him; "take 'em upstairs and put 'em with the rest, Bet."

And Bet took them. And I heard her go upstairs into the room overheard, which was Mr. Bender's bed-room.

"Did you lock the drawer?" Mr. Bender asked, when she came down again.

"To be sure I did," said she, and showed him the key.

What they talked of after this I scarcely know. In a moment I had made a discovery that might not have transpired in the course of days.

I knew where the bulk of the stolen property was deposited.

Foremost of the instructions that Mr. Inspector had given me was this.

"Keep your eyes and ears open, and try and find out where the bulk of the 'swag' is, or where it has been taken to. You may bolt as soon as you like after that. You'll find a friend in the street, whether it is day or night."

But it was very easy to say "bolt as soon as you like." I should like to have "bolted" now; but how could I? The door of Mr. Bender's abode was kept constantly locked and bolted for obvious reasons.

Early in the evening the three—Bender and the woman, and Toby—proceeded to "make themselves comfortable" over strong grog, and they handed me a glass several times, and I pretended to drink, though without swallowing a sip.

I was too deeply engaged, thinking and listening.

"You don't drink, Bet," observed Mr. Bender. "Come, give your mind to it."

"She's in the dumps, 'cos of the approaching separation!" laughed Toby.

"Pooh! wot's six weeks?" said Mr. Bender, lightly. "I shall be back, and turned every spark into blunt before Christmas. It couldn't be done here not before half-a-dozen Christmases. We've found that out."

"You'll do as you like, I suppose!" observed the woman, dolefully, shaking her head, as she drained her glass of its full contents.

Where was the burglar going to? I listened in vain—no more was said on the subject.

One thing was quite certain, however—Mr. Bender meditated going away with the stolen jewels, which he found a difficulty in disposing of in London.

When would he start? That very night, perhaps. It was impossible to say.

"You can go to bed as soon as you like, Jack," said Mr. Bender. "You are noddin' now, I can see."

"Thank you, sir, I'll go now, then," I replied.

And full of the idea that *something* must be done at once, I took a candle and limped upstairs.

"You can find your way without bein' shown, said the woman; and, as I left the parlour, the three prepared a comfortable game of "single dummy" whist.

As before mentioned, the room I was to occupy was on the same floor as Mr. Bender's bed-chamber. Mine was the back room.

As I reached the landing, I gently tried the front room door.

It was unlocked!

I had got it into my head that *some-*

*thing* was to be done, but beyond that I seemed to be led by instinct rather than reason. I felt as though I really *had* been drinking of the liquor I only made a pretence at.

I went into my own room and took off my jacket and my shoes.

Then I stepped out on to the landing, and listened most attentively.

From the deadened sound of talking and laughing it was certain that the parlour door was shut, and the players intent on their game.

I took my candle, and, noiseless as a cat, entered Mr. Bender's bed-room, in one corner of which stood a chest of drawers. I tried them, one after the other; they were all fast locked!

To be sure, after what the woman had said, I might have expected this; still I thought that there might be a chance.

It was quite an accident that led to my next important movement.

As I was at a standstill, and wondering what I could do, I thought I heard the door below open. To have been discovered in that room, I knew would be death, and nothing short of it.

I stept to the door in my fright, and softly closed it and locked it.

Mr. Bender was curiously careful in the matter of bolts and locks. Attached to his bed-room door, top and bottom, were a pair of bolts, very stout and heavy. With as little noise as I had used in locking the door, I shot these bolts to the full extent of their sockets.

Not without an accident, alas!

To reach the top bolt I had to mount on a chair, and in scrambling down again my lame leg failed me, and down I came, chair and all, with a terrible clatter!

I was in for it now with a vengeance!

Before I could gain my legs I heard a sudden commotion below, and then a hasty clattering up the stairs.

Mr. Bender's was the first voice I heard.

"By Heaven, it's the boy!" he exclaimed, as he found my room in darkness and empty. "He heard us say where the box was! But he's played his last trick! Come out, you young——!"

But at this point Mr. Bender, with his hand on the handle of the front room lock, suddenly paused. Then he broke out again with the fury of an enraged bull-dog.

"H—l and fury, he's done us arter all! He's bolted in top and bottom!"

And at the same moment there came a tremendous noise at the door, telling that Mr. Bender had thrust his heavy shoulders against it.

But fortunately it was just against such attacks as these that the burglar had so carefully fortified his premises. The bolts held fast.

There was only one course to pursue.

I hastened to the window, and, being unable to raise it, I seized one of Mr. Bender's boots, standing handy, and with the heel of it demolished several panes of glass, at the same time screaming "Police! police!" at the top of my voice.

It was awful to hear the horrid imprecations and battering at the door then.

"Rot him, I'll stop his mouth if I swing for it," I heard the roaring voice of Mr. Bender exclaim.

Although my head was out at a hole I had broke in the window, I could hear him run down stairs. In another moment he was out at the street door, and with something shining in his hand and pointing at me.

Then a figure rushed from the shadow of the wall, and with some tremendous weapon struck Mr. Bender full across the face, felling him to the stones, while his murderous pistol exploded harmlessly in the air.

My preserver was old Dan Overshiner. Faithfully on the watch, he appeared on the scene in the nick of time. It was the new birch-broom in his sinewy old fists that had laid the burglar low.

Now the danger was over. Before Mr. Bender could regain his legs Mr. Inspector and half-a-dozen police-officers were about him, some securing him, while the rest rushed up the stairs, arresting Bet and Mr. Toby just as they were making up their minds that they had best make the best use of their legs.

That was the signal for my unbolting the door. But Mr. Inspector at present was too eager, in a professional sense, to give a thought to my welfare.

"What about the goods?" said he; "where are they?"

"I am not quite sure. In one of those drawers, I think."

In almost less time than it takes to tell every lock was burst, and presently the precious japanned box was revealed. In a desperate hurry Mr. Inspector tore it open.

"By jove, it's here!" he exclaimed, with a radiant countenance, as he closed the box with a snap and tucked it into the breast of his coat.

"What's there, sir? the cross?" I asked.

"Hush!" he replied, with a frown, but at the same time he nodded, assuring me that my surmise was correct.

---

## CHAPTER THE LAST.

IT is all over, ladies and gentlemen. My story is told. "But, with land Wrecks and Rescues, as with those that happen at sea, it is no more than proper to relate how fared the survivors when, at length, they reached a friendly haven. Besides, I should hope that, to some extent, the sympathies of my good-natured readers are enlisted in behalf of my little fellow voyager, Luce.

First, however, as to the "villains" of the piece. Brief and eloquent are the terms in which the Newgate records relate the fate of Messrs. Bender, Toby and Co. The principals of that precious firm are now serving the fag end of their twenty years of transportation, while the "Co.," which was female, found safe asylum for half that term at Portland.

Mother Corston was luckier. On condition that she honestly revealed all that she knew of Luce's abduction, she was allowed to go unprosecuted, and it cannot be denied that she observed her part of the contract in the handsomest manner.

Within forty-eight hours of her capture by the detectives, who went to Keate Street in search of her, Ezra Heath was in custody, and waiting examination before a magistrate. But the sudden and heinous exposure was too much even for a coward such as he was. His own silk brace served in place of the hangman's rope, and he was found dead and cold, suspended from the bars of his cell.

It need not be remarked, that the old hag's occupation as a "baby farmer" was at an end. The consequence was, that she found it necessary to exert herself more actively in her other nefarious pursuits, and, the eye of the police being on her, she was finally sent for a long period to practice industry at Coldbath Fields.

Let us see! Is there a ruffian left to deal with?

Yes—no! Jerry shall *not* be classed with the ruffians.

Far be it from me to speak harshly of poor Jerry on account of what he was when I first knew him. Goodness only knows what I should have done in my extremity, had it not been for him!

And to think that, after all, I should be so nearly the cause of his plunging neck and crop into those evil courses, from which his two promises had done so much towards weaning him!

But, kind Providence be thanked, it was not to be. At the present writing, "Tyler, shoemaker," may be seen inscribed over one of the neatest little shops in Camden Town. The boots I have now on are a pair of Jerry's best make.

"Which speaks well for you!" I think I hear the reader exclaim. "*You* can't have come out of the fight so badly off, since you can afford to wear boots of the best make!"

Again I invoke that same kind Providence alluded to in Master Jerry Tyler's case, in thankfulness, while I declare that I have come excellently well out of the fight.

Miss Lucy Heath—Heaven bless her! —so wonderfully rescued from the jaws of vice and death, has ever proved my constant friend. How much of her father's bounty towards me is due to her I may never know. But here I am, at the age of twenty-three, healthy and prosperous, and with as much learning as the best of masters could cram into my thick head.

And there, too, in his easy-chair, on the other side of the fire, as I write these last lines, calmly perusing his Sunday newspaper, with his silver-rimmed spectacles on, sits old Father Overshiner! That is better than all, for he is a dear old fellow, and I verily believe implanted in me all the goodness I have. He lives with me constantly, and, please God shall continue to do so while I am able to find him a meal and a bed to rest his white old head.

And now, dear reader, with your permission, I will let the curtain drop.

**THE END.**

*Vincent Brooks, Day & Son, Gate Street, London,* w.c.